SALVATION
OF A SAINT

ALSO BY KEIGO HIGASHINO

Malice

The Detective Galileo Novels

The Devotion of Suspect X
Salvation of a Saint
A Midsummer's Equation (forthcoming)

SALVATION OF A SAINT

Keigo Higashino

TRANSLATED BY ALEXANDER O. SMITH
WITH ELYE ALEXANDER

MINOTAUR BOOKS
NEW YORK

SALVATION OF A SAINT. Copyright © 2008 by Keigo Higashino. Translation copyright © 2012 by Alexander O. Smith. All rights reserved. Printed in the United States of America. For information, address St. Martin's Press, 175 Fifth Avenue, New York, NY 10010.

www.minotaurbooks.com

The Library of Congress has cataloged the hardcover edition as follows:

Higashino, Keigo, 1958–
   [Seijo no Kyūsai. English]
   Salvation of a saint / Keigo Higashino ; translated by Alexander O. Smith ; with Elye Alexander. — First edition.
       p. cm.
   ISBN 978-0-312-60068-6 (hardcover)
   ISBN 978-1-250-01586-0 (e-book)
   1. Physics teachers—Fiction. 2. Police—Japan—Tokyo—Fiction. 3. Murder—Investigation—Fiction. 4. Mystery fiction. I. Smith, Alexander O. II. Alexander, Elye J. III. Title.
   PL852.I3625S4513 2012
   895.6'35—dc23

                                                                    2012035862

ISBN 978-1-250-03627-8 (trade paperback)

Minotaur books may be purchased for educational, business, or promotional use. For information on bulk purchases, please contact Macmillan Corporate and Premium Sales Department at 1-800-221-7945, extension 5442, or write specialmarkets@macmillan.com.

First published in Japanese under the title Seijo no Kyūsai by Bungeishunju Ltd.; English translation rights arranged with Bungeishunju Ltd. through Japan Foreign-Rights Centre/Anna Stein

First Minotaur Books Paperback Edition: September 2014

D 10 9 8 7 6 5 4 3 2

ONE

The pansies in the planter had flowered—a few small, bright blooms. The dry soil didn't seem to have dimmed the color of the petals. *Not particularly showy flowers, but they're tough,* Ayane thought, gazing out onto the veranda through the sliding glass door. *I'll have to water them when I get a chance.*

"Have you heard a single word I've said?" Yoshitaka asked.

She turned around and smiled faintly. "Yes, everything. How could I not?"

"You might try answering more quickly, then." Yoshitaka, lounging on the sofa, uncrossed and recrossed his long legs. In his frequent workouts, he took pains not to put on too much lower-body muscle—nothing that would prevent him from wearing the slim-cut dress pants he preferred.

"I suppose my mind must've wandered."

"Oh? That's not like you." Her husband raised a single sculpted eyebrow.

"What you said was surprising, you know."

"I find that hard to believe. You should be familiar with my life plan by now."

"Familiar . . . Maybe so."

"What are you trying to say?" Yoshitaka leaned back and stretched his arms out along the sofa top, ostentatious in his lack of concern. Ayane wondered if he was acting or if he truly was that nonchalant.

She took a breath and stared at his handsome features.

"Is it such a big deal to you?" she asked.

"Is what a big deal?"

"Having children."

Yoshitaka gave a derisive, wry little smile; he glanced away, then looked back at her. "You haven't been listening to me at all, have you?"

"I *have* been listening," she said with a glare she hoped he'd notice. "That's why I'm asking."

The smile faded from his lips. He nodded slowly. "It *is* a big deal. A very big deal. Essential, even. If we can't have children, there's no point to us being married. Romantic love between a man and a woman always fades with time. People live together in order to build a family. A man and woman get married and become husband and wife. Then they have children and become father and mother. Only then do they become life partners in the true sense of the word. You don't agree?"

"I just don't think that's all marriage is."

Yoshitaka shook his head. "I do. I believe it quite strongly and have no intention of changing my mind. Which is to say, I've no intention of continuing on like this if we can't have children."

Ayane pressed her fingers to her temples. She had a headache. She hadn't seen this one coming. "Let me get this straight," she said. "You don't need a woman who can't bear your children. So you'll throw me out and switch to someone who can? That's what you're telling me?"

"No need to put it so harshly."

"But that's what you're saying!"

Yoshitaka straightened. He hesitated, frowning slightly, before nodding again. "I suppose that from your perspective it would look that way, yes. You have to understand, I take my life plan very seriously. More seriously than anything else."

Ayane's lips curled upward, though smiling was the furthest thing from her mind. "You like telling people that, don't you? How you take your life plan so seriously. It was one of the first things you said when we met."

"What are you so upset about, Ayane? You have everything you ever wanted. If there's something I've forgotten, just ask. I intend to do everything I can for you. So let's just stop all this fussing, and start thinking about the future. Unless you see some other way forward?"

Ayane turned to face the wall. Her eyes fell on a meter-wide tapestry hanging there. It had taken her three months to make it; she remembered the material, special ordered direct from a manufacturer in England.

She didn't need Yoshitaka to tell her how important children were. She had wanted them herself, desperately. How many times had she dreamed of sitting in a rocking chair, stitching a patchwork quilt, watching her belly grow larger with each passing day? But God, in his mischief, had made that impossible. So she had given up—it wasn't like she'd had a choice—and resigned herself to living without. She had thought her husband would be okay with that.

"I know it might seem silly to you, but can I ask one question?"

"Yes?"

Ayane faced him again, taking a deep breath. "What about your love for me? Whatever happened to that?"

Yoshitaka flinched, then gradually his smile returned. "My love for you hasn't changed a bit," he said. "I can assure you of that. I *do* still love you."

That was a complete lie, as far as Ayane was concerned. But she smiled and said that was good. She wasn't sure how else to respond.

"Let's go." Yoshitaka stood and headed for the door.

Ayane glanced at her dresser, thinking about the white powder hidden in a sealed plastic bag in the bottommost drawer on the right.

Guess I'll be using that soon, she thought, the last glimmer of hope fading beneath the shadow inside her.

As she followed him out the door, she stared at Yoshitaka's back, thinking, *I love you more than anything else in this world. That's why your words were like a knife stabbing me in the heart.*

That's why you have to die, too.

TWO

Hiromi Wakayama began to suspect something when she saw the Mashibas coming down the stairs. Their smiles were clearly forced—Ayane's in particular.

"Sorry to keep you waiting," Yoshitaka said as he reached the bottom of the stairs. A touch too curtly, he asked her if she'd heard anything from the Ikais.

"Yukiko left a message just now saying they'd be here in about five minutes," Hiromi told him.

"Guess I'll get the champagne ready, then."

"No, let me," Ayane said hurriedly. "Hiromi, would you mind getting the glasses?"

"Not at all."

"I'll set the table, then," Yoshitaka said.

Hiromi watched Ayane disappear into the kitchen before she walked over to the tall cupboard against the dining room wall. The cupboard was an antique that had cost somewhere in the neighborhood of three million yen, or so she had heard. The glasses inside were all suitably expensive.

Carefully, she took out five champagne flutes: two Baccarat and three Venetian-style. It was customary in the Mashiba household to offer the guests Venetian-style glasses.

Yoshitaka was busily setting out placemats for five at the eight-person dining table. He was an old hand at dinner parties, and Hiromi had gradually picked up the routine.

She arranged the champagne flutes at each place. She heard the sound of running water from the kitchen. She stepped closer to Yoshitaka.

"Did you say something to her?" Hiromi whispered.

"Nothing in particular," he answered without looking up.

"You did talk, though?"

He glanced in her direction for the first time. "About what?"

"About what!?" she was going to say when the doorbell chimed.

"They're here," Yoshitaka called into the kitchen.

"Sorry, I've got my hands full. Can you get it?" came Ayane's reply.

"Absolutely," Yoshitaka said, walking over to the intercom on the wall.

Ten minutes later the hosts and their guests were sitting at the dining room table. Everyone was smiling, though to Hiromi it looked forced—as if they were all taking great pains not to disturb the casual mood. She wondered how people learned this kind of artifice. Surely the skill wasn't inborn; Hiromi knew it had taken Ayane at least a year to blend into this particular scene.

"Your cooking is always just exquisite, Ayane," Yukiko Ikai exclaimed between mouthfuls of whitefish. "You don't often see a marinade getting the attention it deserves." It was typically Yukiko's role to praise each dish during dinner.

"Of course you're impressed!" her husband Tatsuhiko said from the seat beside her. "You always just get those mail-order instant sauce packets."

"I make it myself sometimes."

"Aojiso sauce, maybe. That minty stuff."

"So? It's good!"

"I rather like aojiso myself," Ayane put in.

"See? And it's good for you, too." Yukiko smiled.

"Please, don't encourage her, Ayane," Tatsuhiko grumbled. "You'll have her smearing that sauce on my steak next."

"Why, that sounds delicious!" Yukiko said. "I'll have to try it next time."

Everyone laughed except for Tatsuhiko.

Tatsuhiko Ikai was a lawyer. He was the legal advisor for several companies, including Yoshitaka Mashiba's. He was also significantly involved in the management of it. The two men had been friends since college.

Tatsuhiko retrieved a bottle from the wine refrigerator and offered to pour Hiromi a glass.

"Oh, I'm fine, thanks," she said, placing her hand over the rim.

"You sure? I thought you liked white, Hiromi."

"Oh, I do, but I've had enough. Thanks."

Tatsuhiko shrugged and poured some for Yoshitaka instead.

"Are you not feeling well?" Ayane asked.

"No, I'm fine, really. I've just been out drinking a lot lately and I don't want to overdo it."

"Ah, to be young and going out to parties all the time!"

Tatsuhiko filled Ayane's glass before glancing at his wife and bringing the bottle to his own glass. "Yukiko's off alcohol for a while, so I'm usually drinking alone."

"Right, right, of course," Yoshitaka said, his fork stopping in midair. "I suppose you have to abstain, don't you?"

"Unless she wants to drink for two!" Tatsuhiko said, sloshing his wine a little. "Whatever she eats shows up in the milk, after all."

"How long before you can drink again?" Yoshitaka asked her.

"About a year, the doctor says."

"A year and a half, I'd say," her husband said. "Two years wouldn't hurt. And if you're going to go that far, you might as well quit altogether."

"So I get to take care of the baby and not have a sip for years? Not going to happen. Unless you're planning on taking care of our little prince? Then I might reconsider."

"Fine, fine," her husband said. "But wait a year, at least. And then take it easy, hmm?"

Yukiko glared at him but her smile quickly returned. She gave the impression that this sort of marital exchange was a pleasant little ceremony that she actually enjoyed.

Yukiko Ikai had given birth two months ago. It was their first child, and one for which they had waited a very long time. Tatsuhiko was already forty-two, and Yukiko was thirty-five. They fondly described their pregnancy as sliding into home base at the end of the ninth inning.

The gathering tonight was something of an after-the-fact baby shower. It had been Yoshitaka's idea, and Ayane had made all the arrangements.

"So the kid's with your parents tonight?" Yoshitaka asked.

Tatsuhiko nodded. "Yep. They told us we could stay out as late as we wanted. Said they were actually looking forward to taking care of a baby again. Sometimes it's convenient to have your parents living nearby."

"Though, to be honest, I'm a little worried," Yukiko admitted. "Your mother takes a little *too* much care of him sometimes, if you know what I mean. My friend says you should let them cry a little bit before you go pick them up."

Hiromi stood up from her seat, noticing that Yukiko's glass was empty. "I'll go get you some water."

"There's a bottle of mineral water in the fridge, just bring the whole thing," Ayane told her.

Hiromi went into the kitchen and opened the refrigerator. The fridge was enormous, with double doors that opened in the middle. The inside of one door was lined with bottles of mineral water. Hiromi plucked one out and returned to the table. As her eyes met Ayane's, Ayane's lips moved, forming the words "Thank you."

"It must really change your life, having a child," Yoshitaka was saying.

"Certainly your home life revolves around the kid," Tatsuhiko replied.

"I should imagine. But doesn't it affect your work, too? They say having children increases your sense of responsibility. So, how about it? Do you find yourself going that extra mile now that you're a daddy?"

"As a matter of fact I do."

Ayane took the bottle of water from Hiromi and poured a glass for everyone, a smile on her lips.

"Speaking of which, isn't it your turn next?" Tatsuhiko said, his glance shifting between Yoshitaka and Ayane. "You've been married for how long, a whole year now? Aren't you tired of the newlywed couple thing yet?"

"Honey!" Yukiko swatted her husband's arm. "That's none of our business."

"Fine, fine," Tatsuhiko said with a forced chuckle. "To each their own, I suppose." He downed the rest of his wine, his eyes turning to Hiromi. "What about you, Hiromi? Don't worry," he held up a hand, "I'm not going to ask a single woman anything improper. I was just wondering how things are at the school. Everything going well?"

"So far so good. There's still lots to learn, though."

"Well, you have the best teacher," Yukiko said. She turned to Ayane. "So are you just leaving everything to Hiromi these days?"

Ayane nodded. "I'm afraid I've already taught her everything I know."

"Well, that's impressive," Yukiko said, smiling at Hiromi.

Hiromi's expression warmed and she cast her eyes downward. She was sure that neither of the Ikais cared much about what she did. They were just trying to find some way to include her, the younger fifth wheel at a table with two couples, in the conversation.

"Which reminds me," Ayane said, standing, "I have a present for you two." She fetched a large paper bag from behind the sofa and brought it back to the table. When she revealed its contents, Yukiko gave an exaggerated yelp of surprise, covering her mouth with her hands. It was an elaborate patchwork bedcover, intricately quilted. It was much smaller than the usual size.

"I thought you could use it for the baby's bed," Ayane said. "And when he gets too big for it, you can hang it on the wall as a tapestry."

"Oh, it's marvelous!" Yukiko said, an ecstatic smile on her face. "Thank you so much, Ayane." She clutched the edge of the quilt in one hand, feeling the fabric. "I'm sure he'll love it. Thank you!"

"That's quite the gift. Don't those take a long time to make?" Tatsuhiko asked, turning his eyes toward Hiromi for confirmation.

"How long *did* that one take, half a year, maybe?" Hiromi asked Ayane. She was only vaguely familiar with the process for making this particular style of quilt.

Ayane furrowed her brows. "I don't exactly remember—" she said, then turned her attention to Yukiko "—but I'm glad you like it!"

"Oh, I love it!" Yukiko said. "But I don't know if I should accept it. Honey, do you know how expensive these are? A genuine Ayane Mita bedcover goes for a million yen at the gallery in Ginza."

"Whoa," Tatsuhiko exclaimed, his eyes going a little wide with genuine surprise that something made out of little bits of cloth sewn together could cost so much.

"Frankly, I'd never seen her invest so much passion into one of her quilts before," Yoshitaka told them. "Even on my days off she'd be sitting there on that sofa, working her needles. All day long, sometimes. It was an impressive display of dedication."

"I'm just glad I finished it in time," Ayane said quietly.

After dinner the party relocated to the living room, where the men announced they would move on to whiskey. Yukiko wondered aloud if she could have some coffee, so Hiromi headed back into the kitchen.

"Oh, I'll make the coffee," Ayane said. "Why don't you get

some glasses and water for the whiskey? There's some ice in the freezer." Ayane went to the sink and filled the kettle.

By the time Hiromi returned to the living room with a full tray, the conversation had turned to gardening. The Mashibas' garden had numerous small outdoor lights placed at clever angles; even at night the various shrubs and potted plants were attractively displayed.

"It must be tough taking care of so many flowers," Tatsuhiko said.

"I'm a little fuzzy on the details," Yoshitaka replied, "but Ayane does seem to tend to them pretty regularly. There's a few up on the second floor balcony, too. She waters those every day. I couldn't be bothered myself, but she doesn't seem to mind. She really does love her flowers."

Hiromi got the impression that Yoshitaka wasn't particularly engaged in the topic of growing things; she was aware of his general disinterest in the natural world.

Ayane brought coffee for three back from the kitchen. Remembering the whiskey, Hiromi hastily began pouring water into two glasses.

It was already past eleven when the Ikais started making rumblings about going home.

"Well, that was a feast. And quite a present, too!" Tatsuhiko said, standing. "You should come over to our place next time—of course, it's a complete mess with the baby and all."

"I'll get around to cleaning soon enough," Yukiko said, jabbing her husband in the ribs before giving Ayane a smile. "You'll have to come see our little prince. Though he looks a bit more like a fat cherub right now."

Ayane assured her she'd love to come visit.

It was getting close to the time when Hiromi needed to be heading home, too, so she decided she would leave with the Ikais. Tatsuhiko offered to have their taxi drop her off at her apartment.

"Oh, Hiromi, I'll be out tomorrow," Ayane called out as the younger woman was slipping on her shoes in the entranceway.

"That's right, it's a three-day weekend, isn't it? Are you going away?" Yukiko asked.

"Not really, just to my parents' place."

"That's up in Sapporo?"

Ayane nodded, smiling. "Yes, my father isn't doing so well, so I thought I would keep my mother company. It's nothing serious, mind you."

"Well, that's too bad. And here you are giving us a baby shower!" Tatsuhiko looked sheepish.

Ayane shook her head. "No, please, don't worry. Like I said, it's nothing serious." Turning her attention back to Hiromi, she said, "If anything comes up, you have my cell number."

"When are you coming back?"

"Well . . ." Ayane made a little frown. "I suppose I'll have to give you a call when I know for sure. I won't be away that long."

"Right, okay." Hiromi glanced toward Yoshitaka, but he was staring off into the distance.

Finally taking their leave, the three of them walked down a side road from the Mashibas' house to the main street, where Tatsuhiko hailed a cab. As Hiromi would be dropped off first, she got in last.

"I hope we didn't talk too much about children," Yukiko said as the taxi pulled out.

"So? It *was* a baby shower," Tatsuhiko said from the front seat.

"I was just thinking that we should have been a little more considerate of their situation. They're trying to have children, aren't they?"

"Yoshitaka said something along those lines a while back . . ."

"What if they *can't* have children? You haven't heard anything, have you, Hiromi?"

"No, nothing. Sorry."

"Oh," Yukiko muttered, sounding disappointed.

Hiromi wondered if they had offered her a ride home in hopes of prying information out of her.

The next morning, Hiromi left her apartment at nine o'clock, as usual, to head over to Anne's House in Daikanyama. They'd converted an apartment into a classroom where they taught patchwork quilting. The school was Ayane's brainchild, and thirty or so students came to learn techniques directly from Ayane Mita herself.

As she walked out of her building Hiromi was surprised to find Ayane standing there, a suitcase by her side. Ayane smiled when she saw her.

"Ayane! Is something the matter?"

"No, I just wanted to give you something before I left." Ayane reached into her jacket pocket and pulled out a key.

"What's that for?"

"It's a key to our house. Like I said, I'm not exactly sure when I'll be able to return home . . . I was hoping I could give you this just in case anything came up."

"Well, I guess so."

"Would it be a problem?"

"No, it's not that. But this is a spare, isn't it? You have your own copy?"

"Oh, I don't need one. I can just call you on my way home, and if you can't make it, my husband will meet me."

"If you're sure . . ."

"Thanks." Ayane took Hiromi's hand and placed the key in it, closing her fingers until she was holding it tight.

"So long," Ayane said, and she walked off, pulling her suitcase behind her.

"Wait," Hiromi said, thinking. Then, more loudly: "Ayane?"

Ayane stopped and looked around. "Yes?"

"Oh . . . nothing . . . just, have a safe trip."

"Thanks." Ayane gave a little wave and resumed walking.

The quilting classes ran until late in the evening, and Hiromi hardly had a moment to herself. By the time she was seeing the last students off, her neck and shoulders were as stiff as wood. She had just finished cleaning up the classroom when her cell phone rang. She took a look at the display and swallowed. It was Yoshitaka.

"Classes all done for the day?" he asked as soon as she lifted the phone to her ear.

"Just now, yes."

"Great. I'm out with some clients now, but I'll be home as soon as I'm done. You should come over."

He spoke so casually that Hiromi wasn't sure how to respond.

"Unless you have other plans?"

"No, not at all . . . you're sure it's okay?"

"Of course it's okay. Suffice it to say, she won't be coming back for a while."

Hiromi stared at her handbag. The key Ayane had given her that morning was tucked inside the inner pocket.

"And there's something I wanted to talk to you about," Yoshitaka added.

"What?"

"I'll tell you when I see you. I'll be home at nine. Just give me a call before you come." He hung up before she could reply.

Hiromi ate by herself at a pasta place, then gave Yoshitaka a call. He was home, and there was excitement in his voice when he told her to come over quickly.

In the taxi on the way to the Mashibas', Hiromi languished in a bit of self-loathing. It irked her that Yoshitaka didn't seem to have a shred of guilt about what was going on. Yet, at the same time, she had to admit her own happiness.

Yoshitaka greeted her at the front door, smiling. He didn't hurry to get her inside. His every movement was calm and assured. In the living room, she smelled coffee brewing.

"It's been months since I made my own coffee," Yoshitaka said, coming up from the kitchen with a cup in each hand, neither of them on a saucer. "Hope I didn't mess up." He handed her one of the cups.

"I don't think I've ever seen you set foot in the kitchen."

"Maybe not! I haven't done much of anything since I got married."

"She's a very devoted woman," Hiromi murmured. She sipped her coffee. It was dark and rather bitter.

The corners of Yoshitaka's mouth curled downward. "I put in too much coffee."

"Want me to make some more?"

"No, don't bother with it now. You can make the next pot. And I didn't ask you here to chat about coffee." He set his cup down on the marble tabletop. "I talked to her yesterday."

"I thought you might've."

"I didn't tell her it was you. She thinks it's someone she doesn't know. If she believes me at all, that is."

Hiromi thought back to that morning, to Ayane's face when she handed her the key. She hadn't seen any scheme behind that smile.

"What did she say?"

"She accepted it."

"Really?"

"Yes, really. I told you she would."

Hiromi shook her head. "Maybe it's not my place to say this, but I can't understand how she could just *accept* it."

"Because those were the rules. Rules *I* made, but still . . . At any rate, you've got nothing to worry about. It's all settled."

"So we're good, then?"

"Better than good," Yoshitaka said, putting an arm around Hiromi's shoulder and drawing her close. Hiromi let herself fall into his embrace. She felt his lips by her ear. "You should stay the night."

"In the bedroom?"

Yoshitaka's mouth curled into a little smile. "We have a guest room. It's got a double bed."

Hiromi nodded, still feeling a strange mix of bewilderment, relief, and lingering unease.

The next morning, Hiromi was in the kitchen about to make coffee when Yoshitaka walked in and asked her to show him how.

"I only know what Ayane taught me."

"Good enough. Show me," Yoshitaka said, crossing his arms.

Hiromi placed a paper filter in the dripper and poured in coffee grounds with a measuring spoon. Yoshitaka leaned closer to check the amount.

"First you put in a little hot water. Just a little. Then you wait for the grounds to sort of swell." She poured a little boiling water from the kettle into the dripper, waited about twenty seconds, then began to pour again. "You pour it in a circle. The coffee rises up a touch as you pour, and you want it to stay at about the same level. Then, as you're pouring, you watch the lines on the serving pot and take the dripper off the moment you have enough for two. Leave it on and it'll get weak."

"Surprisingly complicated."

"Didn't you used to make coffee for yourself?"

"With a coffeemaker, yeah. Ayane threw it out when we got married. She said coffee brewed this way tasted better."

"Knowing you're a coffee addict, she probably just wanted to make sure you were getting the best possible cup."

Yoshitaka smiled faintly and shook his head. He always did that whenever Hiromi started talking about the depth of Ayane's devotion to him or her school or her work.

When he drank his coffee he did admit it tasted much better.

As he sipped his coffee, Hiromi got her things together. Anne's House was closed on Sundays, but Hiromi worked as a part-time instructor at a traditional arts school in Ikebukuro, another job she'd taken over from Ayane.

On her way out, Yoshitaka asked her to call him when she was done so they could have dinner together. Hiromi had no reason to say no.

It was after seven o'clock by the time she was done at the art school. She picked up her phone and called while she was getting ready to leave, but he wasn't answering his cell. She let it ring for a while, then hung up and tried the Mashibas' house phone with the same result.

Maybe he's stepped out somewhere? But he never leaves his cell phone behind.

Hiromi decided to go to his house anyway. She tried calling several times on her way there, but there was still no answer.

Eventually, she found herself in front of the house. She looked up from the gate and saw that the light was on in the living room. Still no one answered the phone or came to the door.

Shrugging, she fished Ayane's key out of her bag, unlocked the front door, and went in. The light was on in the entryway.

Hiromi took off her shoes and walked down the short hallway. She detected a faint scent of coffee. Yoshitaka must have made more during the day.

She opened the door to the living room and froze.

Yoshitaka lay, sprawled on the wooden floor, motionless. Dark liquid had spilled from a coffee cup lying next to him, spreading in a small puddle on the wood.

I have to call an ambulance—what's the number, that number they tell you to call, that number? With shaking hands, Hiromi took out her phone. But she couldn't for the life of her remember what the number was.

THREE

Elegant houses lined the gently sloping curve of the road. Even in the thin light from the streetlights it was obvious that no expense had been spared in their upkeep. The sort of people who lived in this neighborhood never had to save to afford a down payment.

Several police cars were parked along the street. Kusanagi tapped the taxi driver on the shoulder. "Right here's good."

He got out, checking his watch as he headed toward the scene. It was already past ten. *Guess I'm not seeing that movie.* He had missed it in the theater, then held off on renting the DVD when he heard it would be on television. When the call came that evening, he left the house in such a hurry that he'd forgotten to set his recorder.

Due to the late hour, there didn't seem to be any onlookers. Not even the news crews had arrived. *Just give me a cut-and-*

dried case, and the movie can wait, he thought without much hope.

A police officer, his face set in an appropriately stern expression, was standing guard in front of the house. Kusanagi flashed his badge, and the officer wished him a good evening.

He paused before going up to the door. It looked like all the lights in the place were on. There were faintly audible voices inside.

He glanced across the front lawn and saw someone standing by a hedgerow. It was too dark to make out her features, but from her stature and the length of her hair, Kusanagi had a pretty good idea who it was. He walked over.

"What are you doing here?"

Kaoru Utsumi turned around slowly, utterly unsurprised to see him. "Good evening, Detective."

"What are you doing outside?" he clarified.

"Nothing much. Just checking out the hedge and the flowers in the garden here. There're some up on the balcony, too."

"Some what?"

She pointed upward. "Flowers."

Kusanagi looked up and saw that there was, indeed, a second-story balcony on this side of the house, with flowers and bushy leaves sticking out through the railings. Nothing about it seemed particularly noteworthy.

He returned his gaze to the young detective. "Let's try this again," he said. "Why aren't you inside?"

"Population density. There's already a crowd in there."

"Not big on mingling, are you?"

"I just don't think there's much point in looking at something everyone else has already seen. I didn't want to get in Forensics' way, so I took it upon myself to examine the exterior of the house."

"But you're not examining anything. You're looking at flowers."

"I've already completed a circuit of the premises."

"Fine. Did you at least check out the scene of the crime?"

"I haven't checked out anything in there. I turned around at the entrance," Utsumi replied.

Kusanagi shot her a quizzical look. In his experience, a detective's natural instinct was to want to examine the scene of the crime first—an instinct that apparently wasn't shared by the department's new recruit.

"I appreciate that you've given this a lot of thought, but you're still coming in there with me. There's a lot of things you need to see with your own eyes if you want to do this job right."

Kusanagi turned and walked back toward the door. Utsumi quietly followed.

Inside, the house was packed. Kusanagi saw officers from the local precinct milling about as well as people from his own department.

Junior Detective Kishitani spotted him and came over. With a wry smile on his lips he said, "Sorry to call you into work this early, sir."

"You got a problem with the hours I keep?" Kusanagi grumbled. Then: "Is this even a homicide?"

"Not sure yet. But it looks likely."

"Explain it to me. And use small words."

"Well, the gist of it is, a man, the owner of the house, died. In the living room. Alone."

"We're sure he was alone?"

"Come over here."

Kishitani led Kusanagi into the living room, with Utsumi trailing behind. It was a big room—over five hundred square feet, he guessed. There were two green leather sofas and a low marble table in the middle.

An outline of the body had been drawn in white tape on the floor next to the table. The body itself was already gone. Kishitani stood looking down at it for a moment before turning back to Kusanagi. "The deceased's name is Yoshitaka Mashiba, married, no kids."

"I heard that before coming over," Kusanagi said. "He was the president of some company, right?"

"Yeah, an IT place. He wasn't at work today, though, it being Sunday and all. We're not even sure yet if he left the house at all."

"The floor was wet?" Kusanagi asked, noting a slight stain on the flooring.

"Coffee. They found it spilled next to the body. One of the guys in Forensics got it with a syringe. There was a coffee cup, too, on its side."

"Who found the body?"

"Er . . ." Kishitani opened his memo pad. "Woman by the name of Hiromi Wakayama. One of the wife's pupils. Actually, more like her apprentice."

"Apprentice what?"

"The wife is a famous patchwork quilter."

"There are famous quilters?"

"Apparently. It was my first time hearing about it, too. Maybe a woman would know?" Kishitani looked over at Utsumi. "You ever hear of an 'Ayane Mita'?" He showed her his memo book where he had written down the characters for her name.

"No," she replied. "And why would you expect a woman to know?"

"It was just a thought," Kishitani said, giving his head a scratch.

Kusanagi suppressed a smile as he looked at his two subordinates. Poor Kishitani had finally got a new recruit of his own to push around—and it was a woman. *He has no idea how to handle her.*

"Tell me about how the body was found," Kusanagi asked.

"Well, his wife had gone to her parents' house up in Sapporo yesterday. Before heading out, she left her house key with Ms. Wakayama. I guess she didn't know when she'd be getting back, so she wanted someone else to have a key in case anything came up. Ms. Wakayama says that she was worried how Mr. Mashiba was getting along by himself and called him, but he wasn't answering his cell or the house phone. So she got all worked up, and came over to the house. She says she first called a little after seven, and it was almost eight when she got here."

"Which is when she found the body?"

"Correct. She used her own phone to call nine-one-one. The ambulance got here right away and determined he was dead. They got a nearby doctor to come and check him out. That's when they decided there was something suspicious about it and called the precinct . . . and here we are."

"Hmph." Kusanagi grunted and glanced at Utsumi, who had wandered away, over toward the cupboard. "So where's this . . . whoever it was who found the body?"

"Ms. Wakayama is resting in one of the cars. The chief is with her."

"What, the old man's here already? I didn't notice him on the way in," Kusanagi said with a frown. "They got a cause of death yet?"

"It's looking a lot like poison. Suicide's always a possibility . . . but we wouldn't be here if there weren't a good chance of it being homicide, would we?"

"Hmph," Kusanagi grunted again, his eyes following Junior Detective Utsumi as she walked into the kitchen. "So when this Ms. Wakayama got to the house, was the door locked?"

"She says it was."

"The windows and sliding-glass doors, too?"

"Everything except the bathroom window on the second floor was locked when the officers from the precinct got here."

"And is that window big enough for a person to go in and out of?"

"I haven't actually tried, but I don't think so, no."

"Okay, why does the precinct think there's a chance it's homicide, not suicide?" Kusanagi sat down on the sofa and crossed his legs. "Why do they think someone poisoned his coffee? If they did, how did they get out of the house? It doesn't add up."

"Well . . . based just on the crime scene evidence, I agree. It's hard to imagine."

"Something here that I'm missing?"

"Well, when the guys from the precinct were examining the scene, Mr. Mashiba's—the deceased's—cell phone rang. The call was from a restaurant in Ebisu. Apparently, he had made reservations for two at eight o'clock tonight. They were calling because no one had shown. According to the restaurant, he made the reservation an hour and a half before, at six thirty. And, like I said, Ms. Wakayama called Mr. Mashiba a little after seven, by which time he wasn't answering. You see what the problem is. It doesn't make sense for someone who calls and makes reservations at a restaurant at six thirty to go and commit suicide at seven."

"Yeah," Kusanagi said with a frown, crooking one finger to scratch the edge of his eyebrow. "It also doesn't make sense for you not to tell me this right away."

"Sorry. You were asking so many questions, I hadn't gotten around to it."

"Right," Kusanagi said, giving his own knees a slap as he stood. Utsumi had come out of the kitchen and returned to her spot in front of the cupboard. "Hey," he called to her. "Kishi's giving us the lowdown. What are you doing wandering around?"

"I was listening to everything. Thank you, Detective Kishitani."

"Er, you're welcome," Kishitani managed.

"Anything I should know about that cupboard?"

"Look here," she said, pointing with her finger inside the open cupboard. "Doesn't this part of the shelf look a little lonely compared to the rest?"

There was a space in the spot she indicated, large enough for a plate to fit.

"I guess."

"I checked in the kitchen and found five champagne glasses in the drying rack."

"So that's probably what went there."

"I think so, yes."

"And? Why do we care about champagne glasses?"

Utsumi looked up at the detective, her lips slightly parting. Then she shook her head, as though she had changed her mind about whatever it was she was going to say. "It's not important," she said. "I was just thinking, they must've had a party recently. When else would you use champagne glasses?"

"Sounds like a reasonable assumption. And a well-to-do couple like this with no kids probably hosts their share of parties.

Still, it doesn't have much bearing on whether this guy committed suicide or not." Kusanagi looked back toward Kishitani before continuing. "People are complicated creatures, who sometimes do seemingly contradictory things. I don't care if they just held a party or made reservations for dinner, when someone wants to die, they die."

Kishitani sighed and gave a noncommittal nod.

"What about the woman?" Kusanagi asked.

"Sorry, woman?"

"The victim . . . er, I mean deceased's wife. Has anyone called her yet?"

"Oh, right. No, they can't get ahold of her. She's all the way up in Sapporo, and a distance outside the city, besides. Even if they do get through, she probably won't be able to get back until tomorrow at the earliest."

"No, I guess not, not from the middle of Hokkaido," Kusanagi said, inwardly relieved. If the wife were on her way, someone would have to wait around for her, and knowing Division Chief Mamiya, that someone would almost definitely be Kusanagi. It was late enough at this point that going around asking the neighbors questions would probably have to wait until tomorrow. Kusanagi had just begun to dream that he might be able to go home when Mamiya's square face appeared in the doorway.

"There you are, Kusanagi. Glad you decided to show up."

"I got here ages ago. Kishitani filled me in."

Mamiya nodded, then turned to look back outside. "Please, come right in," he said, ushering into the living room a slender woman in her mid-twenties. Her hair, just above shoulder length, was natural black—*unusual for a woman her age these days*, Kusanagi thought. The color set off the whiteness of her skin. Although, given the circumstances, it might've been more appropriate to say she looked pale. Either way, she was definitely attractive and knew how to use her makeup.

Hiromi Wakayama, I presume.

"You were saying that you discovered the body as soon as you walked into the room, correct?" Mamiya was asking her. "So you would have been standing right about where you are now?"

The woman stopped looking at the floor long enough to glance in the direction of the sofa, remembering the moment of the discovery.

"Yes," she answered in a thin voice. "Right around here."

Maybe it was the fact that she was skinny, or the paleness of her face, but to Kusanagi it looked as though the woman was having trouble just standing. *She's still in shock*, he thought, *and no wonder.*

"And the last time you were in this room before then was the night before last?" Mamiya asked, confirming.

Hiromi nodded.

"Is anything different about the room now from how you saw it then? Anything at all? Even little details are fine."

She looked almost fearfully around the room for moment, then quickly shook her head. "I'm not sure. There were a lot of other people here the night before, and we'd just eaten dinner . . ." Her voice was trembling.

Mamiya nodded, his eyebrows drawing sympathetically closer together as if to say, *It's all right, of course you don't remember.*

"Well, we won't keep you here any longer tonight. You should go home and get some rest. We'll most likely need to talk with you again tomorrow, if that's all right?"

"That's fine," she said, "but I'm afraid there's really not much I can tell you."

"I know, but we have to be sure we have as much information as possible. I hope you will be able to help us."

"Okay," Hiromi said, without looking up.

"I'll have one of my men take you home," Mamiya said, looking over at Kusanagi. "How'd you get here tonight? Did you bring your car?"

"Taxi, sorry."

"Figures you would choose today to leave your car behind."

"I haven't been driving much recently."

Mamiya was clucking his tongue in disapproval when Utsumi said, "I brought mine."

Kusanagi turned. "You drive? In Tokyo? On your salary?"

"I was out at a restaurant when the call came in. Sorry."

"No need to apologize," Mamiya said. "Maybe you can drive Ms. Wakayama home?"

"Certainly. If I might ask her a question first, though?"

"What question?" Mamiya asked, shocked at the abrupt request from the new recruit.

Hiromi visibly tensed.

"I understand Mr. Mashiba was drinking coffee when he fell, and I was wondering if he was in the habit of not using a saucer with his cup?"

Hiromi's eyes widened slightly and her gaze wandered off to one side. "Well, I suppose he wouldn't, maybe, if he was drinking alone."

"That would mean that he had a visitor either yesterday or today," Utsumi said with confidence. "Any idea who that might be?"

Kusanagi looked up at her. "How do you know he had a visitor?"

"There's an unwashed coffee cup and two saucers still in the kitchen sink. If Mr. Mashiba had been drinking coffee alone, it doesn't make sense that there would be one saucer out, let alone two."

Kishitani went into the kitchen and came right back out. "She's right. One cup, and two saucers."

Kusanagi exchanged glances with Mamiya before turning again to the young Hiromi Wakayama.

"Any ideas?" he asked her.

She shook her head. "I . . . I don't know." There was anxiety in her voice. "I mean, I haven't been here since the party the other night. How would I know if he'd had any visitors?"

Kusanagi glanced at the chief again. Mamiya nodded, a troubled look on his face. "Right, well, we've kept you here long enough. You'll see her home, Utsumi? Kusanagi, you can go with them."

"Yes sir," Kusanagi said, understanding instinctively what Mamiya wanted. The young Ms. Wakayama was clearly hiding something, and it would be his job to get her to spill the beans.

The three left the house together, and Utsumi asked them to wait while she went to get the car, which she had left in a nearby parking lot.

While they were waiting, Kusanagi kept an eye on the woman next to him. She looked crushed—and he didn't think her shock at finding a body was entirely to blame.

"Are you cold?" he asked.

"I'm fine, thanks."

"Were you planning on going out anywhere tonight?"

"Tonight? Are you kidding?"

"I was just wondering if you might've had any prior engagements."

Hiromi's lips moved slightly. She looked hesitant, uncertain.

Kusanagi said: "Sorry if you've already heard this a hundred times, but if you don't mind me asking . . ."

"Yes?"

"What exactly made you call Mr. Mashiba tonight?"

"Oh, well, since Mrs. Mashiba left her key with me, I thought she wanted me to check in now and then. I think she was worried about leaving her husband all by himself, so if there was anything I could do to help . . ." Her voice trailed off.

"So when you couldn't reach him, you came to the house?"

"Yes," she said with a little nod.

Kusanagi raised an eyebrow. "But surely people don't always answer their phone—cell phone or land line. Maybe he was out and couldn't pick up for some reason? Didn't you consider that possibility?"

After a moment's silence, Hiromi shook her head. "I guess I didn't."

"Why not? Were you worried about something in particular?"

"No, nothing like that. I guess I just had a strange feeling . . ."

"A 'strange' feeling?"

"Is it wrong to come to somebody's house because something didn't feel right?"

"No, of course not. I was impressed, actually. Not everyone who is given a house key feels so much responsibility. And, as it turned out, your strange feeling was right on the money, so I think you deserve praise for what you did."

Hiromi looked away, apparently disinclined to take Kusanagi's words at face value.

A dark red Mitsubishi Pajero SUV stopped in front of the house. The door opened and Kaoru Utsumi stepped out.

"Four-wheel drive?" Kusanagi gaped.

"It's a smoother ride than you might expect," Utsumi said. "Ms. Wakayama?" She opened the back door and Hiromi got inside. Kusanagi followed her in.

Utsumi got in the driver's seat and began setting the GPS— apparently she already knew Ms. Wakayama's address. It was an apartment near the Gakugei Daigaku train station. Not long after the car had started moving, Hiromi leaned forward. "Was what happened to Mr. Mashiba not an accident or . . . or a suicide?"

Kusanagi glanced toward the driver's seat. His eyes met Utsumi's in the rearview mirror.

"We can't really say," he told her. "Not without an autopsy report."

"But you're in Homicide, right?"

"True, but we're only here because there's a *possibility* of murder. I can't say any more—which is to say, we really don't know anything more than that."

"I see," Hiromi said in a small voice.

"That reminds me," Kusanagi said as casually as possible, "I wanted to ask you, Ms. Wakayama: if this *was* a homicide, do you have any idea who might have been responsible?"

He thought he sensed her holding her breath. His eyes went to her mouth.

"No," she said, her voice soft and thin in the quiet interior of the car. "I really don't know much more about Mr. Mashiba other than that he's the husband of my quilting teacher."

"Of course. Well, if anything does occur to you, I know we can count on you to let us know."

Hiromi sat in silence, not even nodding.

They dropped her off in front of her apartment building, and Kusanagi moved to the passenger seat.

"Well," he said, looking straight ahead at the road, "what do you think?"

"She's tough," Utsumi replied as she steered the car back into traffic.

"You think?"

"She didn't cry once. At least, not in front of us."

"Maybe she just wasn't that sad."

"No, she was crying before we got there. The entire time she was waiting for the ambulance, I'd say."

"How do you know that?"

"Her makeup. I could tell that she'd had to fix it in a hurry."

Kusanagi looked over at the junior detective. "Really?"

"Without a doubt."

"I guess women notice different things—I mean that as praise, mind you."

"I know," she said with a smile. "What did you think of her, Detective Kusanagi?"

"In a word, suspicious. I have my doubts about a young woman visiting a man's house to 'check up on him,' whether or not she was given a key."

"I agree. I certainly wouldn't have."

"You think she and the deceased might've had something going on? Or am I reaching?"

Utsumi almost snorted. "I wouldn't call that reaching. It's

hard to imagine that they *didn't* have a thing. My guess is that they had plans to dine together tonight."

Kusanagi slapped his knee. "The restaurant in Ebisu."

"They called because no one showed up, and the reservation was for two. Which means that not only Mr. Mashiba but someone he was supposed to be dining with didn't show up as well."

"Which would make sense if that someone were Hiromi Wakayama," Kusanagi agreed.

"If there was a deeper connection between them, we'll have proof shortly."

"How's that?"

"The coffee cups. The ones in the sink might have been from when they drank coffee together, which means that her fingerprints will be on one of them."

"Right, right. But," Kusanagi lifted his finger, "just because they might've been having an affair isn't sufficient grounds to treat her as a suspect."

"Of course not," Utsumi said. She pulled off the road and stopped the car. "Do you mind if I make a phone call? There's something I'd like to check on."

"Who're you calling?"

"Why, Hiromi Wakayama, of course."

Utsumi began pressing the keys on her phone as Detective Kusanagi looked on, open-mouthed. The call went through almost immediately.

"Ms. Wakayama? This is Utsumi from the police department. I'm sorry to bother you again so soon, but it occurred to me that I've forgotten to ask you about your schedule tomorrow." There was a pause while Hiromi spoke, before Utsumi

said, ". . . I see. Thank you. Sorry for the trouble. Good night."
She ended the call.

"What did she say?" Kusanagi asked.

"She doesn't have definite plans, but thinks she'll be at home.
She's going to take the day off from the quilting school."

"Hmph." Kusanagi snorted.

Utsumi glanced sidelong at the detective. "I wasn't calling to
ask about her schedule, you know."

"Do tell."

"She was trying to hide it, but I could tell from her voice she'd
been crying. It was quite obvious. In other words—as soon as she
was alone in her room, the emotions she'd been holding back
came spilling out."

Kusanagi sat up in his seat. "That's why you called her? To
see if she'd been crying?"

"My thought was that the shock of finding someone dead
would be enough to make some people cry whether or not they
knew them well. But to be crying now, hours later . . ."

"Means she was feeling something other than shock at the
fragility of life," Kusanagi finished. He smiled at her. "Not bad,
Junior Detective Utsumi."

"Why thank you, Detective Kusanagi." Utsumi smiled and
released the parking brake.

The next morning, just past seven A.M., Kusanagi woke to the
sound of the phone ringing. It was Chief Mamiya.

"You're early," Kusanagi grumbled into the receiver.

"Be thankful you got to sleep at home. There's a meeting
this morning about the investigation, at the Meguro City Police

Station. We'll probably be moving in, so get ready to sleep there tonight."

"So you're calling me at seven in the morning to remind me to bring my toothbrush?"

"You should be so lucky. No, you're going to Haneda this morning."

"Haneda? What's in Haneda?"

"The airport, stupid. Mrs. Mashiba will be coming back from Sapporo, and I want you to meet her there and bring her back to the station."

"I assume she knows about this already?"

"She should. I want you to go with Utsumi. She'll be driving. The flight gets in at eight."

"Eight A.M.?"

Kusanagi dropped the phone and jumped out of bed.

As he hurried to get ready, his cell phone rang. It was Kaoru Utsumi; she was already waiting in front of his apartment building. Kusanagi grabbed his wallet, put on his shoes, and ran out to meet her.

Utsumi was waiting at the curb. Kusanagi climbed into her Pajero and they headed off toward Haneda airport.

"Looks like we pulled the short straw again. I'll never get used to meeting the bereaved family," he said, putting on his seat belt.

"But the chief says you're the best at handling them."

"The old man said that?"

"He said your face puts them at ease."

"Nice." Kusanagi snorted. "He's just saying I look like an idiot."

They arrived at the airport at five minutes to eight and stood in the arrivals lobby, scanning the crowd for Ayane Mashiba while passengers streamed past. She was supposed to be wearing a beige coat and carrying a blue suitcase.

"Think that could be her?" Utsumi said, nodding toward an approaching figure.

Kusanagi followed her gaze to find a woman who matched the description. Sorrow hung around her slightly downcast eyes; there was an air of something grave and stark about her—solemnity, perhaps.

"That's her all right," Kusanagi said, his voice suddenly hoarse.

It was as if his heart had suddenly leapt into his throat. He stared, unable to take his eyes off her, completely at a loss as to why the sight of Ayane Mashiba should affect him so strongly.

FOUR

Once the detectives introduced themselves, the first thing Ayane Mashiba asked about was her husband's body.

"There's been a court-ordered autopsy," Kusanagi explained. "I'm not sure exactly where the body is at this very moment, but I'll check on it later today and let you know."

"So I won't be able to see him." Ayane blinked. Her eyes were sunken, her skin rough; she was trying to hold back tears.

I doubt she's slept a wink since the call came. "Once they're done, we'll return the remains as quickly as possible." Kusanagi's words sounded strangely leaden to his own ears. He was never completely relaxed when talking to the families, but somehow, this time felt different. Everything was harder than usual.

"Thank you," Ayane replied.

She had a deep voice for a woman—descriptors like *sultry* and *bewitching* came to his mind.

"We'd like to talk to you a little at the Meguro City Police Station, if that's all right?"

"Yes. They told me that on the phone."

"That's good. If you're ready, we'll take you to the car."

Kusanagi helped her into the back seat of Utsumi's SUV, then climbed into the passenger seat.

"They were having trouble locating you last night. Where did they reach you?" he asked, turning to look back at her.

"I was at a hot springs near my hometown—I went there with an old friend. I'm afraid I had turned off my cell phone, so I couldn't hear it ring. I picked up my messages just before going to bed." She paused, letting out a long breath. "I thought it was some kind of prank call at first—I mean, who expects a call from the police?"

"These things happen without warning," Kusanagi agreed.

"That's just it," she said. "*What sort* of things happen? No one's told me anything, except that he's—" Ayane's voice faltered, and Kusanagi felt an ache in his gut. He knew that the question she most wanted to ask was also the question whose answer she most feared.

"What did they tell you over the phone?" he asked.

"They told me that my husband was dead, and that there was some concern about the cause of death, so there would be a police investigation. That's all."

Which was all the officer calling her would have been able to say. Kusanagi felt a tightness in his chest as he imagined again the night she must've spent after hearing the news, and what it must've been like for her getting on the plane that morning. "Your husband died at home," he told her. "The cause is still unknown, but there were no visible injuries. Hiromi Wakayama discovered him collapsed in the living room."

"Hiromi . . ." Kusanagi sensed Ayane's gasp more than heard it.

Kusanagi glanced over at Utsumi in the driver's seat. For just a moment, she glanced back and their eyes met.

We're both thinking the same thing, Kusanagi realized. It was less than twelve hours since they discussed the possibility of a relationship between Hiromi Wakayama and Yoshitaka Mashiba. Ms. Wakayama was, by all accounts, Ayane's favorite student. If they were in the habit of inviting her to parties at their house, she was a friend of the family, too. If she'd been sleeping with Ayane's husband, it would be a classic case of the dog biting the hand that feeds it.

The question was whether Ayane had been aware of what was going on. They couldn't assume that, just because she was close to her apprentice, she would've known. In fact, Kusanagi had seen several cases where just the opposite was true, when people didn't know because they were *too* close.

"Was your husband suffering from any illnesses?" he asked.

Ayane shook her head. "Not that I knew of. He got regular checkups and there were no problems. He didn't even drink that much."

"And he's never collapsed before now?"

"No. Nothing of the sort. I just can't imagine it happening." Ayane put a hand to her forehead, as though trying to stave off a headache.

Kusanagi decided it would be premature to bring up the idea of poison. In fact, until they had an autopsy report in hand, it was best not to mention the possibilities of suicide or murder at all.

"Because of the unusual circumstances," he said, "we have to record every aspect of the place where the body was found—

whether it turns out to be a crime scene or not. We've already done a bit of this last night with Ms. Wakayama's help. We would have preferred it to be you, of course."

"Yes, they mentioned that on the phone as well."

"Do you go back to Sapporo often?"

Ayane shook her head. "It was my first time since getting married."

"Your parents live there, correct? Is everything all right?"

"My father isn't doing as well as he could be, so I thought it was about time to visit. Of course, when I arrived he seemed to be doing much better than I'd been led to believe, thus the trip to the hot springs."

Kusanagi nodded. "And why did you leave your key with Ms. Wakayama?"

"I thought it would be prudent, in case something came up while I was away. She helps me a lot with my work, and I keep a lot of materials and finished pieces at home that she might need to use in class."

"Ms. Wakayama tells us that she was concerned about your husband and, when he didn't answer his phone, she went over to make sure everything was all right. I was wondering"—the detective chose his words carefully—"had you at any point specifically asked her to check in on him?"

Ayane gave a little frown. "I don't think so, but maybe I did give her that impression. She's always so thoughtful, and it was my first time leaving him on his own since we got married . . . Did I—" She paused a moment before saying: "Was it wrong of me to leave my key with her?"

"No, not at all. I just wanted to confirm what Ms. Wakayama told us yesterday."

Ayane buried her face in her hands. "I just can't believe it. He was fine, in perfect health. We just had some friends over on Friday night. He was . . . he was so happy." Her voice was trembling.

"I know it's hard," Kusanagi said as gently as possible. "And I'm sorry I have to ask these questions, but—this party on Friday . . . who were the friends?"

"A college friend of my husband's and his wife." She gave him the names of Tatsuhiko and Yukiko Ikai. Then, Ayane let her hands drop into her lap, a look of determination on her face. "I have a request."

"Sure," Kusanagi said. "Anything."

"Do we have to go straight to the Police Station?"

"Is there something you need to do?"

"I want to see the house first, if I can. I want to know where he was when . . . I want to know how he died. If that's okay?"

Kusanagi glanced at Utsumi again. This time, their eyes didn't meet. The junior detective seemed focused intently on the road ahead.

"I'll have to ask the lead detective on the case," Kusanagi said, fishing his cell phone out of his pocket.

Mamiya answered, and Kusanagi relayed the request. He heard the chief groan for a moment, then: "Fine . . .

"In fact, the situation's changed a little bit. It might even be preferable to talk to her on site. We'll see you at the house."

"How has the situation changed?" Kusanagi asked.

A pause. "I'll fill you in later."

"Right." Kusanagi ended the call and turned back to look at Ayane. "We'll be taking you home."

Under her breath, she said: "Thank you."

Kusanagi returned his gaze to the road. A moment later he heard Ayane calling someone on her cell phone.

"Hello, Hiromi? It's me."

Kusanagi tensed. He hadn't expected her to call anyone, much less Ms. Wakayama—but he couldn't just tell her to hang up.

". . . I know, I know," Ayane was saying. "I'm with the police now. We're heading to the house. Oh, I can't imagine what you've been through, Hiromi."

Kusanagi's mind was racing as fast as his heart. For the life of him, he couldn't imagine how Ms. Wakayama was responding to the call. He envisioned her overcome with grief at losing her lover, perhaps even spilling the beans. If that were the case, he had a pretty good idea of how Ayane would react.

". . . That's what they tell me. Are you okay? Please tell me you're eating . . . Well, that's good. You know, if it's not too much trouble, do you think you could come over? I'd really like to talk."

Kusanagi hadn't expected her to invite Ms. Wakayama to the house, either. From this half of the conversation, it sounded like the younger woman was keeping her composure.

"You're sure it's all right? Okay, see you soon . . . Yes, thanks. You take care of yourself, too." It sounded like the call was over. Kusanagi heard a sniffle from the backseat.

"Will Ms. Wakayama be joining us?"

"Yes. Oh! I hope that's all right?"

"It's fine. She was the one who found him, it might be best if you heard it straight from her," the detective said, inwardly growing excited. On one hand, he was interested, out of pure curiosity, to see how the husband's lover would go about describing the discovery of his body to the wife. On the other, he hoped that by carefully observing Ayane, he'd be able to determine whether she had known about her husband's infidelity.

They got off the highway onto the local road as they neared the Mashiba residence. Utsumi seemed to know the way without checking—maybe she had committed it to memory.

They arrived at the house to find Chief Mamiya waiting for them. He was standing with Kishitani in front of the gate.

They got out of the car and walked over to the other two detectives, and Kusanagi introduced Ayane.

"I'm sorry for your loss," Mamiya told her. He turned to Kusanagi. "You've told her the particulars?"

"For the most part."

Mamiya gave Ayane a sympathetic look. "As you might expect, we have a lot of questions we'd like to ask. I'm so sorry to put you through this right as you've returned home."

"I don't mind."

"We should go inside. Kishitani, the key."

Kishitani pulled a key from his pocket and handed it to Ayane, who accepted it with a perplexed frown.

She used the key to unlock the door, opened it, and stepped in. The others followed, with Kusanagi bringing up the rear, the widow's suitcase in one hand.

Inside, Ayane asked: "Where was he?"

"This way," Mamiya said, walking down the hallway.

The tape was still stuck to the floor in the living room. Ayane saw the outline and stopped, her hand over her mouth.

"According to Ms. Wakayama, he was lying here, on the floor when she came in," Mamiya explained.

Ayane shook, then her legs buckled and she fell to her knees. Kusanagi saw her shoulders trembling, and a quick hiccuplike sob escaped her lips. She caught her breath and asked in a thin voice: "Around what time was it?"

"Near eight when she found him," Mamiya answered.

"Eight . . . What could he have been doing?"

"Apparently, he was drinking coffee. We've cleaned it up, but there was a coffee cup on the floor, and a little coffee had spilled."

"Coffee . . ." She looked up. "Did he make it himself?"

"Excuse me?" Kusanagi asked.

Ayane shook her head. "It's just, he doesn't do that. I've never seen him make his own coffee."

Kusanagi noticed Mamiya's eyebrows twitch.

"He never made coffee?" the chief asked.

"Well, I know he used to before we got married. But he had a coffeemaker back then."

"And you don't have one now?"

"No. I didn't need it so I threw it out. I use a single-cup dripper."

A hard light came into Mamiya's eyes. He spoke: "Ma'am, I can't say anything for sure without the autopsy results, but it's likely that your husband was poisoned."

Ayane's face went blank for a moment, then her eyes opened wide. "Poison? Like, food poisoning?"

"No. A very potent poison was discovered in the coffee found at the scene—though we don't yet know exactly what kind of poison it was. Which is to say that your husband's death was not due to illness or a simple accident."

Ayane covered her mouth again, blinking repeatedly. Her eyes were growing redder by the moment.

"Why would he . . . How could that happen?"

"We don't know. Which is why I wanted to ask if you had any ideas."

This, apparently, was what Mamiya had been talking about when he'd said that the situation had changed, Kusanagi thought. Now it made sense that the chief showed up in person.

Ayane pressed her fingers to her forehead and sat down on the nearest sofa. "No. No idea at all."

"When was the last time you spoke with your husband?" Mamiya asked.

"On Saturday morning. We left the house together on my way to the airport."

"Was there anything unusual about him, or his behavior, at that time? Even the smallest details can help."

Ayane sat still for a moment, as though searching inwardly; then she firmly shook her head. "No. I can't think of anything."

No wonder, Kusanagi thought. Having to bear the shock of her husband's death, knowing only that he'd died under suspicious circumstances—and then to learn that he'd been poisoned . . .

"Maybe we should let her rest a bit, Chief," Kusanagi said. "She's probably tired after the trip from Sapporo."

"Yeah, you're probably right."

"No, I'm fine," Ayane said, straightening. "Only, if I could change, that would be nice. I've been in the same clothes since last night." She was wearing a dark-colored suit.

"Since last night?" Kusanagi asked.

"Yes, I was hoping to find a quicker way back to Tokyo, so I got dressed for the trip ahead of time."

"Then you haven't slept at all?"

"I couldn't have even if I'd tried."

"Well, that won't do," Mamiya said. "You should probably rest before we continue."

"No, I'm fine. I'll change and come right back down," Ayane said, standing.

Kusanagi watched her leave the room, then turned to Mamiya. "What do we know about the poison?"

Mamiya nodded. "There were traces of arsenous acid in the coffee."

Kusanagi's eyes opened wide. "Arsenous acid? Like in that school curry poisoning case?"

"Forensics thinks the particular compound used here was sodium arsenite. From the concentration in the coffee, Mr. Mashiba drank well over a lethal dose. We should have more accurate autopsy results by the afternoon, but arsenous acid poisoning fits with the condition that the body was found in."

Kusanagi nodded, sighing. The possibility of this being an accidental death was rapidly approaching zero.

"But if it's true that Mr. Mashiba never made his own coffee, who made that cup?" Mamiya said, half to himself, but loud enough that everyone could hear.

Utsumi suddenly spoke up: "I think he did make his own coffee."

"How do you know that?" Mamiya asked.

"Because we have a witness who says he did," Utsumi continued, after a glance in Kusanagi's direction. "Ms. Wakayama."

"Oh yeah, what was she saying about the coffee?" Kusanagi thought back on their conversation the day before.

"Remember the saucers? I asked her if Mr. Mashiba wasn't in the habit of using a saucer when he drank coffee. Ms. Wakayama indicated that she didn't think he did use a saucer when he was drinking alone."

"Now that you mention it, I overheard that conversation myself," Mamiya said, nodding. "The question now becomes, assuming Ms. Wakayama wasn't making things up, how does the wife's apprentice know something about the husband that the wife does not?"

"There's probably something I should tell you," Kusanagi

said, leaning over to whisper to him about their hunch that Hiromi Wakayama and Yoshitaka Mashiba had more than a passing acquaintance.

Mamiya's glance flicked back and forth between his two subordinates, and he grinned. "You both think so, too?"

"What, you knew about it, Chief?" Kusanagi raised an eyebrow.

"When you've been doing this as many years as I have, you notice things. I was pretty sure something was up yesterday." Mamiya tapped the side of his head with a finger.

"Um, would someone mind explaining what's going on?" Kishitani asked.

"I'll tell you later," Mamiya said, turning back to Kusanagi. "Nobody says anything in front of the wife, agreed?"

Kusanagi and Utsumi nodded.

"So the poison was in the coffee on the floor?" Kusanagi asked.

"And one other place as well."

"Do tell."

"The paper filter still in the dripper. Specifically, in the used coffee grounds."

"So they mixed the poison in with the coffee while they were making it?" Kishitani asked.

"That's one possibility. There is one other possibility to consider, however," Mamiya said, raising a finger.

"They could have mixed the poison in with the ground coffee beans ahead of time," Utsumi said.

Mamiya beamed at her. "Exactly. The ground coffee was in the refrigerator. Forensics couldn't find anything in the bag, but that doesn't mean it wasn't there. There could have been just enough poison on the top layer for him to scoop out with the coffee."

"So, when was the coffee poisoned?" Kusanagi asked.

"Don't know. Forensics snagged a bunch of used filters out of the trash, but there wasn't any poison in them. Not that I would expect to find any in them, because that would mean someone had already used a poisoned filter, and we'd have another body."

"There was an unwashed coffee cup in the sink," Utsumi said. "I'd like to know when *that* coffee was drunk. And who drank it, for that matter."

Mamiya wet his lips. "We already know. Fingerprints got two matches. One was Yoshitaka Mashiba, the other was exactly who you think it was."

Kusanagi and Utsumi exchanged glances. Apparently, their theory already had backing evidence.

"Chief, I should mention that we're expecting Ms. Wakayama to come here at any moment," Kusanagi said, and told him about the phone call in the car.

Long wrinkles formed in the space between Mamiya's eyebrows. He nodded. "Sounds like an opportunity, then. You can ask her when she drank that coffee. And get specifics. None of this 'Oh, the other day' stuff."

"On it," Kusanagi said.

The four fell silent at the sound of footsteps on the stairs.

"Thanks for waiting," Ayane said as she reached the living room. She was wearing a light blue shirt over black pants. She didn't look quite as pale as she had on the way from the airport, though that may have been due to a little makeup retouch.

"If you're sure you're not too tired, we'd like to ask a few more questions," Mamiya said.

"Certainly. What else can I help you with?"

"Please, take a seat." The chief waved in the direction of the sofa.

Ayane sat down, her gaze wandering to the garden beyond the sliding-glass doors.

"Look at them, all wilted," she said. "I asked my husband to water them, but he was never that interested in flowers. I should have known."

Kusanagi joined her in looking at the garden. Flowers of various colors were blooming in pots and long planters.

"I'm sorry," Ayane said, half standing from the sofa. "Could I water them? I don't think I'll be able to focus otherwise."

Mamiya looked taken aback for a brief moment, then smiled. "Of course. We're not in any hurry here."

She rose and went not over to the glass doors, but into the kitchen. Kusanagi glanced in after her and saw that she was filling a large bucket with water from the tap.

"No hose in the garden?" he asked.

Ayane looked around and smiled. "This is for the flowers on the balcony," she said. "There's no sink on the second floor."

"Oh, right." Kusanagi recalled how, the day before, he had seen Utsumi looking up at the potted plants on the second-floor balcony.

Full of water, the bucket looked rather heavy. Kusanagi offered to carry it.

"It's all right, I can manage."

"No, really, allow me," the detective insisted. "Up the stairs here, right?"

"Thank you," Ayane said in a voice so quiet he almost didn't hear her.

The master bedroom wasn't quite as big as the living room

downstairs, but it was still large. A wide patchwork tapestry hung over the bed. Kusanagi found his eyes drawn to the vivid bands of color.

"This one of yours?"

"From a while back, yes."

"It's really impressive. It's probably just my own ignorance, but when I heard 'patchwork' I was picturing something simple, like embroidery. But this, this is fine art."

"I like to think of it as a practical art. Patchwork is about making things that are of use in our daily lives. And why not make everyday items look beautiful?"

"You have quite a talent. I can only imagine how much work it is."

"It does take a lot of time, and a certain amount of persistence. But it's fun, making them. In fact, if you don't have fun doing it, you wind up with something that isn't fun to look at."

Kusanagi nodded, looking back at the wall hanging. Though at a glance it looked like the colors that made up the patchwork had been chosen on a whim, he imagined he could see the mind of the quilter at play in the curves and arrangement of the pieces, and it brought a smile to his face.

The balcony ran the length of one side of the room and was fairly wide, though the tightly packed planters made it difficult for even one person to navigate.

Ayane picked up an empty aluminum can from the corner. "Isn't this neat?" she said, holding it out to Kusanagi where he waited by the sliding glass door.

Several small holes had been opened in the bottom of the can. She used it to scoop water out of the bucket, then held the can over the planters, letting the water trickle from the holes like a shower.

"Ha! A homemade watering can."

"Exactly. It would be hard to get water out of the bucket into a real watering can, so I used an awl to punch holes in this soda can."

"Good idea."

"Isn't it? Of course, he never could understand why I'd even bother having flowers up here in the first place . . ." Ayane's face tensed and she squatted down on the balcony. The water from the little can was drizzling on her slipper.

"Ms. Mashiba?" Kusanagi called out.

"I'm sorry. I . . . I just can't believe he's gone."

"No one expects to you to."

"We were only married a year. One year. I'd just gotten used to my new life . . . started to figure out those things couples know. What he likes to eat, what he drinks . . . We had so many things planned."

Kusanagi watched her, one hand over her face, her head hanging. He couldn't think of anything to say. The bright flowers around her suddenly looked garishly out of place.

"Sorry," she mumbled. "I know I'm not much help to you like this. I should be . . . I need to be stronger."

"We can come back to ask our questions another day," Kusanagi said without thinking. Immediately he saw Mamiya in his mind's eye, grimacing.

"No, that's all right. I need to know what happened myself. I just can't understand it. Why would he have drunk poison—?"

She was interrupted by the chiming of the doorbell. Ayane stood, startled, and looked over the balcony railing.

"Hiromi!" she called out, giving a little wave of her hand.

"Ms. Wakayama's here?" Kusanagi asked.

Ayane nodded and moved back inside.

Kusanagi followed her down the stairs. Utsumi was in the hallway, going to answer the door. Kusanagi caught up to her by the entrance foyer and whispered, "It's Hiromi Wakayama."

Ayane walked past them and opened the door. Hiromi Wakayama was standing outside.

"Hiromi, come in," Ayane said, her voice choking.

"Are you okay, Ms. Mashiba?"

"I'm all right. Thanks . . ."

Ayane stepped out through the door to embrace her visitor. Then she began to cry out loud, sobbing like a child.

FIVE

Ayane stepped away from Hiromi. "Sorry," she murmured, wiping at her eyes. "I thought I could hold it back, but when I saw you . . . I'm fine now. Sorry."

Kusanagi felt his stomach knotting as he watched the widow attempt a smile. *She needs to be alone.*

"Is there anything I can do?" Hiromi asked.

Ayane shook her head. "Just being here is enough. And honestly, I'm having trouble thinking of anything at all right now. Please, come in. I'd like to hear about what happened."

"Actually, Ms. Mashiba," Kusanagi broke in, flustered. "We'd also like to speak with Ms. Wakayama. Things were a little rushed last night, and there are some gaps that need filling."

Hiromi looked confused.

"You'd be welcome to join us," Ayane said.

The detective cursed inwardly. *She's missed the point en-*

tirely. "Actually, we'll need to speak with her first, if you don't mind."

Ayane blinked. "But I want to hear what happened, too. That's why I asked her here."

"Mrs. Mashiba?" Mamiya joined in. Kusanagi wasn't sure how long the chief had been standing behind him. "I'm sorry, but there are certain police procedures that need to be followed. If you could let Detective Kusanagi speak with her first . . . ? This is really all just about filling in the blanks, taking care of paperwork, but if we don't do things in the proper manner, we might run into trouble later on."

Classic passive-aggressive cop, Kusanagi thought bemusedly.

Ayane frowned. "All right. So, where should I be?"

"You can stay here, Mrs. Mashiba. We'd also like to speak with you." Mamiya turned to Kusanagi and Utsumi. "Maybe you can find someplace quiet to talk with Ms. Wakayama?"

"I'll get the car." Utsumi strode purposefully out the door.

Twenty minutes later, Kusanagi was sitting beside Utsumi in a quiet corner of a twenty-four-hour restaurant. Across the table from them, Hiromi Wakayama looked tense.

"Did you get some sleep last night?" the senior detective asked after a sip of coffee.

"Not much."

"I understand. You must have been in shock." *And in tears, if Utsumi called it right.* "It's not every day you see a dead body." *Especially your lover's.*

Hiromi was looking down at the table, chewing her lip.

"I was hoping we could ask a few questions we didn't get around to yesterday, if you don't mind?"

Hiromi took a deep breath. "I really don't know anything more than what I've already said. I can't imagine how I'd be able to answer any more questions."

"You might be surprised. The questions aren't that difficult. That is, as long as you're willing to answer them honestly."

Hiromi looked up, her gaze almost a glare. "I haven't lied."

"Then we'll be just fine. So, I was wondering: you've told us that you discovered Yoshitaka Mashiba's body at eight o'clock last night, and the last time you were in the Mashibas' house before that was the party on Friday. Is this correct?"

"It is."

"Are you sure? Ms. Wakayama, the shock of seeing someone dead can play with our memories in strange ways. Try relaxing and thinking about it a little harder. Are you *sure* you didn't visit the Mashiba household from the moment you left on Friday night until yesterday evening?" Kusanagi watched Hiromi's face.

Her long eyelashes fluttered. After a few moments of silence, her lips parted. "Why are you asking me this? Why do you keep asking me when I've told you the truth?"

Kusanagi smiled slightly. "Let's keep it to just me asking questions, if we could. Do you have an answer?"

"But—"

"Think of it as a simple confirmation. I'm asking you again because I want you to very carefully consider your answer. If it turned out later that there was an inaccuracy or omission in what you've told us, well, then it would be a bit of a difficult situation for both of us."

Hiromi's mouth snapped shut. Kusanagi could almost hear the cogs whirling in her head, as she ran the calculations. *She's considering the possibility that her lie will be uncovered, wondering whether it might be better to admit everything here and now.*

She maintained her silence, the scales in her head refusing to settle to one side or the other. Kusanagi was growing impatient.

"When we arrived at the scene yesterday, in the sink there was a single coffee cup and two saucers. When we asked you if you knew why, you said you didn't know. Yet, your fingerprints were found on the coffee cup. So naturally I wondered, when did you touch the cup?"

Hiromi's shoulders slowly rose and fell with her breathing.

"You saw Yoshitaka Mashiba over the weekend, didn't you . . . ? When he was still alive."

Hiromi put her hand to her forehead, her elbow on the table. *Trying to find a way out of this one?* Kusanagi was confident that she wouldn't be able to slip free, no matter how much she squirmed.

She nodded, eyes following her hand down to the table. "Yes. I did. I'm sorry."

"You saw Mr. Mashiba?"

A pause, then: "Yes."

"When?"

Her reply didn't come immediately. *She's a sore loser,* Kusanagi thought, growing irritated.

"Do I have to answer that?" Hiromi looked up again at the two detectives. "It doesn't have anything to do with what happened. Isn't this an invasion of privacy?"

She looked ready to cry, but there was also growing anger in her eyes, a sharpness to her words. Kusanagi remembered something another detective once told him: *no matter how soft she may look, never underestimate the power of a cheating woman.*

They didn't have time to do this carefully. Kusanagi played his next card.

"We know the cause of death," he said slowly. "Mr. Mashiba was poisoned."

Hiromi flinched. "What?"

"Traces of poison were found in the coffee he was drinking when he died."

Her eyes opened wide. "I don't—that's impossible!"

Kusanagi leaned slightly forward, staring her directly in the eye. "Why do you say that?"

"Because . . ."

"Because when you drank coffee with him earlier, nothing was wrong?"

She blinked, then, after a moment's hesitation, slowly nodded.

"You see our problem, Ms. Wakayama. If Mr. Mashiba put the poison in the cup himself, that's one thing—it would either be suicide or an accident. But the possibility of either of those things is extremely low. We're forced to consider a scenario in which someone intentionally poisoned Mr. Mashiba's coffee. Traces of the poison were also found in a used paper coffee filter. Our best guess at present is that someone mixed poison in with the ground coffee beans."

Now considerably flustered, Hiromi shook her head. "I don't know anything about it."

"Surely you can at least answer some of our questions? It is extremely important that we know exactly *when* you drank that coffee at the Mashiba household if we are going to be able to determine the time at which the coffee was poisoned. Well?"

Kusanagi straightened in his chair, staring evenly at the woman across the table, perfectly ready to sit there in silence as long as was necessary.

Hiromi covered her mouth with both hands. Her eyes wandered, unfocused. Then, abruptly, she said: "It wasn't me."

"Huh?"

"It wasn't me." Her voice was pleading. She shook her head. "I didn't poison the coffee. Really. You have to believe me."

Kusanagi and Utsumi exchanged glances.

Hiromi Wakayama was a suspect, of course, and their most likely suspect at that. She'd had plenty of opportunities to poison the coffee. If she was having an affair with Yoshitaka Mashiba, then it was fairly easy to imagine some rift between lovers providing the motivation. Poisoning him, then "discovering" the body, could have been merely an attempt to camouflage her role.

At this stage, however, Kusanagi intended to avoid any preconceived notions, in order to get as unfiltered a story from her as possible. He had deliberately chosen not to say anything that might sound accusatory. All he had asked was when she had drunk that coffee with Yoshitaka Mashiba. So why *was* she claiming innocence all of a sudden? Was she, in fact, the guilty party? Had she just skipped ahead, anticipating where all this was leading?

"We are not accusing you of poisoning him," Kusanagi said, with a gentle smile. "As I said, all we're trying to do is establish the timing. If you met with Mr. Mashiba and drank coffee, then can you tell us when that was, who made the coffee, and exactly how?"

A pained expression rose on Hiromi's pale face. Kusanagi still couldn't tell whether she was simply hesitant because she was unwilling to admit she was having an affair or whether it was something more than that.

"Ms. Wakayama?" Utsumi put in abruptly.

Hiromi looked back up, startled.

"We've already made certain assumptions about your relationship with Yoshitaka Mashiba," the younger detective continued, with all the disinterest of a government official explaining how to fill out a form. "You can deny it if you like. At which point, we will have to start asking more questions in order to determine the truth. When we set our minds to it, we can usually bring the truth to light . . . but as part of that process, we have to talk to a lot of people. You understand?

"I'd like you to give what I just said some thought. If you can be completely honest with us now, we may be able to be a bit more circumspect with our investigation. Say, for instance, if you wanted to tell us something that you'd rather we didn't repeat to anyone else outside of our office."

Utsumi glanced toward Kusanagi, nodding her head slightly.

Was that her idea of an apology for speaking out of turn? Kusanagi wondered.

Her advice seemed to have a remarkable effect on Hiromi, however. *Perhaps it was easier hearing it from a woman.* She hung her head for a moment, then looked up again, blinked slowly, and took a breath. "You promise to keep it a secret?"

"As long as it isn't directly related to the case, we keep all personal information private. It's standard procedure," Kusanagi explained.

Hiromi nodded. "Then . . . as you suspect, Mr. Mashiba and I did have a . . . special relationship. That, and I visited him earlier over the weekend."

"Exactly when was this?"

"Saturday night. A little after nine o'clock, I think."

A rendezvous while the wife was away, then.

"Had this been arranged in advance?"

"No. He called me at work—I was teaching a patchwork class. He called right about when the class was finishing up. He invited me over."

"So you went, and what happened next?"

Hiromi thought for a moment, then with growing determination, she looked back at Kusanagi. "I spent the night and left the next morning."

Utsumi had begun taking notes. Kusanagi glanced at her but couldn't read anything from her expression. *She's on to something,* he thought, resolving to ask her about it later.

"When did you drink coffee together?"

"In the morning. I made it. Oh, but we also had coffee the night before."

"On Saturday night? So you had coffee twice?"

"Yes."

"Did you make the coffee the night before as well?"

"No. Mr. Mashiba had already made it when I arrived. He poured a cup for both of us," Hiromi continued, looking down at the table. "It was the first time I'd ever seen him make his own coffee. 'It's been a while,' he said."

"But you didn't use saucers that evening?" Utsumi asked, looking up from her notebook.

"No," Hiromi confirmed.

"But you made the coffee the next morning—yesterday morning?" Kusanagi asked.

"Mr. Mashiba's coffee was a little too strong, so he asked me to make it in the morning. He stood there watching me while I did it." She looked up at Utsumi. "We used saucers with our cups that time. Those were the ones in the sink."

Kusanagi nodded. So far, her story was checking out. "Just to be certain, I should ask whether the coffee you drank on Saturday night and Sunday morning was made from the ground beans at his house?"

"I think so. At least when I made it, I used the coffee in the refrigerator. I don't know about the coffee Mr. Mashiba drank

Saturday night. But I don't see why he would've used anything different. There was plenty left."

"Have you ever made coffee at the Mashibas' before this weekend?"

"Only rarely, when Ayane asked me to. She was the one who showed me how to make it without a coffeemaker. That's how I knew what to do yesterday."

"Did you notice anything different when you were making the coffee? Was the bag in a different place than usual? Was it the same brand?"

Hiromi let her eyelids fall closed and gave her head a shake. "I don't remember anything different. It was the same as always." When she opened her eyes again they had a gleam of curiosity in them. "But I don't see why it should matter how anything was when *I* made the coffee."

"Why's that?"

"Well, because—" She lowered her face, eyes looking up at them. "There wasn't any poison in the coffee when I made it, right? If someone poisoned the coffee, it would've had to have been after I used it."

"That's true, unless there was a trick to it, one that involved doing something to the coffee earlier."

"A trick?" Hiromi didn't look convinced. "Well, I didn't notice anything out of the ordinary."

"You drank coffee that morning. What next?"

"I left. I teach a patchwork class at an arts school in Ikebukuro."

"What time does the class run?"

"Well, there's one in the morning, which goes from nine to eleven, and one in the afternoon, which goes from three to six."

"What do you do between classes?"

"Mostly clean up from the first class, eat lunch, and get ready for the next class."

"Do you bring a lunch?"

"Not usually. Yesterday I went out and ate at a noodle place in a department store that's nearby . . ." She narrowed her eyes. "I think I was away from the school building for about an hour. I wouldn't have been able to go to the Mashibas' and back in that amount of time."

Kusanagi chuckled, waving a hand. "Don't worry, we're not checking your alibi. According to what you told us yesterday, you gave Mr. Mashiba a call as soon as your class was finished. Would you care to amend that statement in any way?"

Hiromi frowned and looked away. "I did call him. That's true enough. But my reason was a little different from what I said."

"I believe you told us that you were worried about how he was getting along without his wife there?"

"Actually, when I left that morning, he asked me to call him when I was through with class."

Kusanagi stared at her. "He invited you out to dinner, didn't he?"

"I think that was the plan, yes."

"Well, honestly, that makes a lot more sense. It would take an extremely devoted student to worry that much about her teacher's husband, and a champion worrier to go to someone's house just because they didn't answer the phone."

Hiromi's shoulders sagged. "I was afraid it sounded suspicious. But I couldn't think of what else to say."

"Mr. Mashiba didn't answer the phone, so you went to his house—any adjustments that need making there?"

"No. Everything else happened just like I said it did. I'm sorry I lied."

Next to Kusanagi, Utsumi was furiously taking notes. He glanced over at her before returning to Hiromi. Everything in her story thus far made sense. All of the doubts they'd had the night before had been largely defused. Not that this was reason enough to trust her completely.

"Like I said, we're fairly certain that this is a homicide. I believe I asked you last night if you had any suspicions as to who might have been responsible. You told me you didn't—that you knew nothing about the deceased other than that he was your teacher's husband. I wonder if you might be able to elaborate now that we know about your connection with him?"

Hiromi raised her eyebrows. "I really don't know who it could have been. I can't believe anyone would want to kill Yoshitaka."

Kusanagi mentally noted her shift from "Mr. Mashiba" to "Yoshitaka."

"Try to recall any recent conversations. If this was a homicide, then it was clearly premeditated. That means that there will be a definite motive, and in most cases, the victim is well aware of it. Even if he was trying to keep it from you, he may have said something inadvertently."

Hiromi rubbed her temples with her fingers and shook her head. "I don't know. Work seemed to be going fine, he didn't have any big worries, and he never spoke ill of anyone."

"Please, take a moment now to think it over again."

She looked at Kusanagi with sad, defiant eyes. "I did think about it. I cried all night thinking about it, wondering how this could've happened. I thought about everything we said to each other, everything we did, over and over again. I still have no idea. Detective, I want to know why he was killed, too. More than anything else, I want to know."

Kusanagi noticed a redness in her eyes, a pink blush in the skin around them.

She really loved him, Kusanagi thought. *Or if this is just an act, she's really good.*

"When did your relationship with Mr. Mashiba begin?"

Hiromi opened her reddening eyes wide. "Does this have something to do with the case?"

"It's not for you to decide whether it does or whether it doesn't. It's for us to decide. Again, we won't mention it to anyone; and, once we're satisfied it has nothing to do with the case, we won't pry any further."

Her lips formed a tight line and she took a deep breath. She reached out and took a sip of her surely-cold-by-now tea.

"About three months ago."

"Thank you." Kusanagi looked down, wondering how to broach the topic of how the affair had started. "Does anyone else know?"

"Not that I'm aware of."

"But you'd gone out to eat together before? Somebody might've seen."

"We were very careful. We never ate at the same place together twice. And Yoshitaka often ate with women he'd met through business, or hostesses at bars, so I don't think anyone would have thought twice, even if they did see us together."

So Yoshitaka Mashiba had been something of a playboy. Kusanagi considered the possibility that he had other lovers in addition to Ms. Wakayama. Which, of course, would provide the woman sitting across the table from him with a motive.

Utsumi's pen stopped on the page and she looked up. "Did you ever rendezvous at hotels?" she asked coolly. Kusanagi gave her a sidelong glance. He'd been meaning to ask the same question, but hadn't been able to bring himself to be so direct.

Hiromi looked displeased. "Is that really necessary for your investigation?"

Utsumi's expression remained blank. "Of course it's necessary. In order for us to solve this case, we'll need to know everything about Yoshitaka Mashiba's daily life. We need to know what he was doing, when, and with whom, in as much detail as possible. If we ask enough people, we may be able to fill most of it in, but there will certainly be blanks remaining. I don't need to know what you did there, but I do need to know if you went to any hotels."

Why don't you go ahead and ask her what they did while you're at it, Kusanagi wanted to interject, but restrained himself.

Hiromi's lips curled downward. "Yes. But mostly regular hotels. Not those cheap places people use for . . ." Her voice trailed off.

"Did you always go to the same hotel?"

"We went to three different places. But you won't be able to find him on the registers. He always used a false name."

"Just in case, could you tell me the names of the hotels?" Utsumi asked, pen held at the ready.

Her face wilting, Hiromi gave the names of three hotels. They were all first-class places in the city, and large hotels at that. Unless the trysting couple had gone there every day, none of the people on staff were likely to remember their faces.

"Did you meet on predetermined days?" Utsumi continued.

"No—we figured out what would work over e-mail."

"How often did you meet?"

Hiromi shrugged. "Once a week or thereabouts."

Utsumi finished writing and gave Kusanagi a quick nod.

"Well," he said, "thanks for your time. We don't have any more questions for you today."

"I doubt I have anything else I could tell you even if you did," Hiromi said gloomily.

Kusanagi smiled at her and picked up the check.

The three left the restaurant and were headed toward the parking lot when Hiromi suddenly stopped.

"Umm . . ."

"Something wrong?" Kusanagi turned to look at her.

"Can I go home?"

The detective blinked. "Didn't Mrs. Mashiba ask you over?"

"Yes, but I'm really tired, and honestly, I don't feel very good. Could you tell her that for me?"

"Sure. It's fine by us."

"Would you like a lift?" Utsumi asked.

"No, thanks. I'll get a cab."

Hiromi turned and walked away. A taxi rounded the corner; she hailed it and got inside. Kusanagi stood watching as the car rejoined the flow of traffic.

"Do you think she thought we were going to tell Mrs. Mashiba about their affair?"

"I can't say," Utsumi replied, "but after she told us all that, she probably didn't want to be seen talking to the wife as if nothing had happened."

"Hmm. Good point."

"Still, I wonder if she really hasn't noticed."

"If who hasn't noticed?"

"Mrs. Mashiba. Do you really think she doesn't know what was going on?"

"I'm guessing no."

"Why do you think that?"

"From the way she acted earlier. Practically the first thing she did when she saw Ms. Wakayama was burst into tears and hug her."

"I guess." Utsumi looked down.

"What? If you've got something to say, say it."

She looked back up, straight at Kusanagi. "Something occurred to me when I saw the two of them in front of the house. I thought, what if she *wants* us to see her crying like that? Crying in front of the last person in the world she wanted to cry with."

"Excuse me?"

"Sorry, never mind. I'll get the car."

Dumbfounded, Kusanagi watched Utsumi dash off.

SIX

Back at the Mashiba residence, Mamiya had already finished questioning Ayane. Kusanagi informed the widow that Ms. Wakayama had been feeling out of sorts and had gone home.

"I understand," Ayane said. "I'm sure she's in as much shock as I am." She was holding a teacup in both hands, a far-off look in her eyes. She was still frowning, but as she sat on the sofa there was a certain poise to her posture, a rigidity in her spine that spoke of inner strength.

A cell phone rang in the handbag that lay beside her. She took it out and glanced toward Mamiya, seeking his approval.

He nodded.

She checked the display on the phone before answering.

"Yes? . . . Yes, I'm fine . . . The police are here right now. They're not sure yet. They found him lying in the living room . . . Of course, I'll tell you as soon as I know. And tell Dad

not to worry. Yeah. Bye." She hung up and informed Mamiya
that the call had been from her mother.

"Have you told her what happened?" Kusanagi asked.

"Only that he died suddenly. She wanted to know why, but I
wasn't sure what to say." Ayane put a hand to her forehead.

"Have you told your husband's office?"

"Yes. I told the legal consultant this morning before leaving
Sapporo. That's the Mr. Ikai I told you about."

"The one at the dinner party on Friday?"

"Yes. Their office is a mess with the CEO gone . . . I only
wish there was more I could do to help." A pained look came
over Ayane's face; she stared at nothing, eyes focused on a single
point in space. *She's trying to appear strong*, Kusanagi thought.
*But I can see the tension in her. The façade might crumble at any mo-
ment.* He felt impelled to help her.

"Maybe you should have a relative or another friend come to
keep you company until Ms. Wakayama's feeling better? Even
simple day-to-day things can seem overwhelming at times like
these."

"I'm all right. And you probably don't want a lot of people
tromping around just yet, do you?"

Mamiya turned to Kusanagi, a discomfited look on his face.
"Forensics is coming in again this afternoon—we have Mrs.
Mashiba's okay."

So she wouldn't even be given a chance to mourn in peace.
Kusanagi lowered his head to the widow in silence.

Mamiya stood. "Sorry to take up so much of your time this
morning, Mrs. Mashiba. Kishitani will be staying behind, so if
you need something—chores, anything—just let him know."

Ayane thanked him in a small voice, as Mamiya and Kusanagi
took their leave.

———

"So how'd it go?" Mamiya asked Kusanagi as soon as they were outside.

"Ms. Wakayama confirmed that she was in a relationship with the deceased, starting about three months ago. She says no one knew."

Mamiya's nostrils flared. "And the coffee cup in the sink?"

"Was from when they had coffee Sunday morning—made by Ms. Wakayama, apparently. She said nothing seemed out of the ordinary."

"So the coffee was poisoned after that," Mamiya concluded with a scratch at the stubble on his chin.

"Get anything from Mrs. Mashiba?"

A sour look came over the chief's face and he shook his head. "Nothing good. I don't even know if she was aware he was having an affair. I asked her pretty directly if there were any other women, but she denied it, and looked pretty surprised that I'd asked. No indecision, no wandering eyes. It didn't look like an act. If it was, she's a pro."

Kusanagi stole a sidelong glance at Utsumi, who clearly was of the opinion that Ayane's tearful embrace with Hiromi Wakayama had been a performance. She'd said she wanted to ask the chief what he thought, but now the young detective seemed intent only on taking notes.

"Think we should tell Mrs. Mashiba her husband was cheating on her?"

Mamiya immediately shook his head. "No need for us to let that particular cat out of the bag. I can't see how it would help the investigation. I'm guessing you two will be seeing a lot more of her in the coming days, so be careful what you say."

"So we hide it."

"No, we just don't go out of our way to tell her. If she figures something out on her own, well, there's nothing we can do about that. Assuming she doesn't know already." Mamiya pulled a piece of paper from his pocket and glanced at it. "I want you to go to this address."

The name Tatsuhiko Ikai was written on the paper, along with a telephone number and an address.

"Ask him how the deceased was doing lately, and about that party on Friday."

"I hear Mr. Ikai's a busy man trying to keep Mr. Mashiba's business afloat."

"Then talk to his wife. Call first. Ms. Mashiba says she just had a baby two months ago, so we should go easy on her."

Apparently Ayane was told about their intention to question the Ikais. Kusanagi was honestly impressed that she'd had the presence of mind to be concerned about the strain on anyone but herself.

Utsumi brought the car around and they headed toward the Ikai residence. Kusanagi called while they were on the way. The moment he introduced himself as a policeman, Yukiko Ikai's voice took on a grave tone. Kusanagi emphasized that all they needed was to ask some simple questions, and she finally relented and invited them over, but asked them to give her an hour. The two detectives spotted a coffee shop where they could wait and went inside.

"What you were talking about earlier—you really think that Mrs. Mashiba knows her husband was cheating on her?" Kusanagi asked, picking up his cup of hot cocoa. He'd reached his limit on coffee for the day when they were talking to Ms. Wakayama.

"I just said that's how it felt."

"But you do think she knows."

Utsumi stared into her cup and didn't reply.

"If she did know, then why didn't she confront her husband or Ms. Wakayama? She even invited Hiromi to her dinner party. People don't normally do that, do they?"

"I'm sure your average woman would lose her head the moment she found out."

"But Mrs. Mashiba isn't your average woman?"

"It's too early to say, but I have a feeling she's very smart. Not just that, but she's patient too."

"Patient enough to endure a husband's infidelity?"

"I think she understands that she had nothing to gain by going on the offensive. In fact, she would lose two important things: a stable married life and a talented apprentice."

"Sure, but she couldn't just put up with her husband's lover hanging around forever. You think a marriage of pretenses is that valuable?"

"I think everyone's idea of value is different. There's no evidence of domestic violence, for one, and things were apparently smooth enough within their marriage—on the surface, at least—for them to host a party. She had no financial worries and she could spend all the time she wanted to on her patchwork—she's not stupid enough to throw all that away on an impulse. Maybe she thought that, ultimately, it made more sense to wait for the affair between her husband and her student to run its course and end naturally.

"At least—that's what I imagine, anyway. I could be wrong."

Kusanagi took a sip of his hot cocoa and grimaced. It was too sweet. He quickly chased it with a swig of water. "She doesn't look like the calculating type."

"It's not a calculation. It's a smart woman's instinct for self defense."

Kusanagi wiped his mouth with one hand and looked at the junior detective. "Do you have those instincts, too, Utsumi?"

She chuckled and shook her head. "I'm afraid not. If my husband were cheating on me I'd probably go ballistic."

"I feel sorry for the guy already. Anyway, I don't understand how anyone can go on living a regular married life when they know their partner's unfaithful."

He glanced at his watch. It had already been thirty minutes since his conversation with Yukiko Ikai.

The Ikai residence was as upper-class as the Mashibas', with a large gate sporting decorative posts covered in brick-shaped tiles. Right next to the gate was an extra garage for visitors, which saved Utsumi the trouble of having to find parking.

Yukiko Ikai and her husband, Tatsuhiko, were waiting for their visitors inside. Apparently, she had called her husband after Kusanagi talked to her and he had hurried home.

"Everything all right at the office?" Kusanagi asked.

"We've got a great team, so I'm not worried. I'm not looking forward to explaining this to our clients, though. Speaking of which . . ." He looked up at the two detectives. "What did happen? What's going on?"

"Yoshitaka Mashiba passed away at home."

"I know that. But if the Tokyo Metropolitan Police Department is involved, then this is something more than an accident or suicide, isn't it?"

Kusanagi gave a little sigh, remembering that he was talking to an attorney who likely wouldn't settle for the usual vague explanations—and who, if he really wanted to, would have other ways of finding out what he wanted to know if they tried to stonewall him. After emphasizing that all facts pertaining to the case were to be kept secret, Kusanagi told the Ikais about the poisoning, and that arsenous acid had been found in the coffee Mr. Mashiba had been drinking.

Yukiko, sitting next to Tatsuhiko on the sofa, put both hands to the sides of her round face. Her eyes were wide and a little red. She was somewhat on the plump side; Kusanagi wondered whether she had always been that way, or whether it was because she had just had a baby.

Tatsuhiko ran his hands back across his head. His hair was slightly curly, as though he had gotten a perm some time ago and it was beginning to fade. "Well, that explains that," he said. "When I heard that the police had been called, and there was going to be an autopsy, I thought something was up. That, and I couldn't imagine him committing suicide."

"But you could imagine him being murdered?"

"I don't know what other people might think of him. Still, poison's no way to go . . ." He frowned and shook his head.

"Is there anyone who might have had ill will for Mr. Mashiba?"

"If you're asking me whether he ever butted heads with people, then I couldn't say no. As far as I'm aware, though, what conflicts he had were strictly about business. I doubt he ever gave anyone reason to dislike him personally. Whenever there was trouble, it tended to be me they pushed out to the front lines, not him," Tatsuhiko explained, jabbing his thumb toward his own chest.

"What about outside the office? Did Mr. Mashiba have any enemies in his personal life?" Kusanagi asked.

Tatsuhiko leaned back on the sofa and crossed his legs. "I

can't say. He and I were close business partners, but we tended not to pry into each other's private lives."

"But he did invite you to parties at his home."

Tatsuhiko shook his head dismissively. "He invited us to his parties precisely because we don't pry. It's more convenient that way. These are the lengths to which we busy people have to go in order to attain some semblance of a normal life."

In other words, he didn't have time to lounge around with mere "friends."

"Did you notice anything out of the ordinary when you were at the Mashibas' house Friday night?"

"If you mean did I expect something like this would happen, then the answer is no. It was a good party. We had fun." Tatsuhiko furrowed his brow. "Hard to believe that was only three days ago."

"Did Mr. Mashiba mention any plans to meet with anyone over the weekend?"

"Nothing I heard," Tatsuhiko said, looking over at his wife.

"I didn't hear anything, either. Just that Ayane was going back home . . ."

Kusanagi nodded, scratching his temple with the back of a ballpoint pen. He was growing increasingly certain he wasn't going to get any useful information from the Ikais.

"Did you go to parties with the Mashibas often?" Utsumi asked.

"Once every two or three months."

"Was it always at their house?"

"We invited them here once, right after they got married. Since then, the parties were always at their house, with Yukiko being pregnant and all."

"Did you know Ayane before she married Mr. Mashiba?"

"Sure. I was there when they first met, actually."

"Where did they meet?"

"Mashiba and I were at this little party that she happened to be at—they started dating after that."

"When was this?"

"Well . . ." Tatsuhiko scratched the back of his neck. "About a year and a half ago? No, maybe a little more recently."

"But they married a year ago," Kusanagi cut in. "That was fast."

"I suppose it was."

"Mr. Mashiba wanted kids," Yukiko put in. "It took him a while to find the right person, and I think he was getting a little impatient."

"That's really none of their business," Tatsuhiko said to his wife. He looked back at the detectives. "Or is how they met, and their marriage, somehow related to the case at hand?"

"I didn't mean to suggest that," Kusanagi said with a wave of his hand. "We just don't have many leads at present, and I thought it might behoove us to learn a bit about the Mashibas' married life."

"I understand why you'd want to gather as much information as you can about the victim . . . but pry too far and you could get into trouble," Tatsuhiko said, putting on his lawyer face. There was a look in his eye that Kusanagi interpreted as a mild threat.

"I'm aware of that," the detective said, lowering his head in an apologetic bow before looking back up at the attorney. "Apologies in advance for my next question—but to satisfy our standard operating procedures, I'll need to ask you how both of you spent your weekend, if you don't mind."

Tatsuhiko nodded slowly, the corner of his mouth curling upward. "You want our alibis? I suppose that's to be expected."

He pulled a small, leather-bound organizer out of his jacket pocket.

Tatsuhiko Ikai had gone to work at his own office on Saturday, after which he went out drinking with one of his clients. On Sunday, he went to play golf with another client, returning home sometime after ten in the evening. Yukiko had been at home the whole weekend, and on Sunday her mother and sister had come to visit.

That night, an investigation briefing was held at local precinct headquarters, the Meguro City Police Station. The head officer from the First Investigation Division of the Metropolitan Police Department opened by repeating that they were, in all likelihood, looking at a homicide. It would be hard to explain the presence of the particularly virulent arsenous acid found in the used coffee grounds any other way. If it had been a suicide, the deceased probably wouldn't have bothered mixing the poison into his coffee—and even if he had, it would have been far more typical for him to mix it into an already brewed cup.

Someone from Forensics had a report on the ongoing investigation to determine how the poison had gotten into the ground coffee, but there was nothing Kusanagi hadn't heard before; it could all be summed up with "we don't know." Forensics had gone back to the Mashiba residence that afternoon, with the intent of examining everything in the house that Yoshitaka Mashiba might have put in his mouth: food, spices, drinks, medicine. The same attention was given to all of the flatware and silverware in the house. At the time of the briefing, they had already checked eighty percent of the items; so far they hadn't found traces of poison on anything. The liaison from Forensics suggested that it was unlikely they would find anything in the remaining twenty percent.

This meant that the guilty party had specifically targeted the coffee Yoshitaka was going to drink. This, Forensics informed them, could have been accomplished in one of two ways: the killer could have put poison in the ground coffee, the paper filter, or the cup in advance; or they could've mixed it in when the coffee was being made. There no way of telling which it had been at this point, without finding arsenous acid anywhere else in the house, and with no way of knowing whether someone had been with Yoshitaka when the coffee was made.

Someone else had gone around questioning the neighbors. No one had seen anyone visit the Mashiba residence on that day prior to the time of death. Of course, in a quiet residential neighborhood like the one in question, people tended not to pay attention to anything that didn't affect them directly, so they might not have noticed a visitor's presence.

Kusanagi reported on what he'd learned from talking to Ayane and the Ikais, without mentioning the relationship between Hiromi and Yoshitaka. Before the briefing, Mamiya had told them to keep that under wraps for now, though he had included it in his own report to the head officer from Division. Apparently, the higher-ups felt it was too delicate a matter to spread beyond those directly involved in the investigation until it was proved to have some connection to the case. If word leaked out to the press, it would mean headaches for everyone.

After the briefing, Mamiya called Kusanagi and Utsumi into his office. "I want you to go to Sapporo tomorrow," he told them.

"You want us to check on Mrs. Mashiba's alibi?" Kusanagi asked.

"You got it. A man having an affair was killed. That makes his lover and his wife both suspects, and we've already established that the lover doesn't have an alibi. Division wants us to narrow in on our perpetrator as quick as we can. Speaking of which, you've only got a day up there to do your thing. I'll make sure the Hokkaido police are ready to help you out any way they can."

"The wife said the police contacted her at a hot springs resort—we'll probably have to go there, too."

"Yeah, Jozankei Hot Springs. It's about an hour out of Sapporo by car. The wife's family home is in Nishi Ward, right in the city. You can split up and get it all done in a few hours."

I guess so, Kusanagi thought, scratching his head. *Shame on me for even imagining that he'd put us up at the hot springs for a night.*

"What is it, Utsumi? You look like you want to say something," Mamiya said.

Kusanagi glanced over to see the junior detective standing with her lips pressed together as if she could barely contain a question.

"Are we only checking out her alibi for the weekend?"

"What do you mean?" Mamiya asked.

"Mrs. Mashiba left Tokyo on Saturday morning, and returned on Monday morning. I was wondering, is that the only time period for which we need an alibi?"

"You don't think that's enough."

"I'm not sure. But it seems to me that as long as we don't know how the poison was mixed into the coffee, or when, we can't remove her from the list of suspects just by knowing where she was over the weekend."

"Wait a second," Kusanagi said. "We might not know how it was done, but we do know the time. Hiromi Wakayama drank coffee with Yoshitaka Mashiba Sunday morning and neither of them died then. The coffee must have been poisoned after that."

"Are you sure we can say that?"

"Can't we? When else could the poison have put in?"

"Well . . . I don't know."

"You think Hiromi Wakayama's lying to protect the wife?" Mamiya asked. "That would suggest that the lover and the wife were in cahoots, which seems unlikely."

"I agree. I don't think that's it."

"So what's the problem?" Kusanagi said, a little roughly. "All we need is her alibi from Saturday to Sunday. Actually, we only need it on Sunday to clear the wife. Is there something wrong with that train of logic?"

Utsumi shook her head. "No, nothing. It seems perfectly reasonable. I was just wondering if there wasn't some way of poisoning the coffee that we haven't thought of, something that wouldn't require the guilty party to be present at the house on Sunday. Maybe a way to get Mr. Mashiba to poison it himself?"

Kusanagi's eyebrows drew together. "You mean someone compelled him to commit suicide?"

"Not that. They didn't have to tell him it was poison. What if he thought it was something to make the coffee taste better? A secret ingredient?"

"A secret ingredient? In coffee?"

"Like garam masala for curry—you sprinkle on a little before you eat, and it improves the flavor and aroma. Whoever it was could've told Mr. Mashiba the poison was like that, but for coffee. I know it's a bit of a stretch . . . but he could've not used it when he was taking coffee with Ms. Wakayama, then only remembered it later when he was brewing a cup for himself."

"Yeah, that's stretching it a bit too far for me," Kusanagi declared.

"Is it?"

"I've never heard of anyone mixing something in with their ground coffee to make the brewed stuff taste better. And I don't think Yoshitaka Mashiba's the kind of guy who would believe them if they did. If he did believe it, why wouldn't he have told Ms. Wakayama? *He had a conversation with her about how to make coffee!* Besides, if he had put it in himself, there would be traces of it somewhere else. Arsenous acid is a powder. You'd have to carry it in a baggie or a paper sack, but nothing of the sort has been found on the scene. How do you explain that?"

Utsumi nodded as Kusanagi quickly dismantled her theory.

"I'm afraid I don't have a way to explain it. I think what you're saying is probably right, sir. I'm just worried that there might be some other way we haven't thought of yet."

Kusanagi sighed. "You want me to trust your female intuition?"

"I said nothing of the sort. But maybe women do have a different way of thinking—"

"Hold it right there," Mamiya butted in, a weary look on his face. "I don't mind lively discussions, but let's not lower this to hunches and intuition. Utsumi, you suspect the wife?"

"Yes, though I'm not completely sure."

Sounds like intuition to me, Kusanagi thought, but he resisted the urge to say it.

"What's your reasoning, then?" Mamiya asked.

Utsumi took a deep breath before saying: "The champagne glasses."

"Champagne glasses? What about them?"

"When we arrived at the scene, there were five recently washed champagne glasses in the kitchen." She looked at Kusanagi. "You remember?"

"Yeah, I remember. They were left over from the party on Friday."

"The champagne glasses were usually kept in a cupboard in the living room. That's why when we got to the house there was an empty space on the shelf."

"And?" Mamiya asked. "Maybe I'm just slow, but I don't see what the problem is with the glasses."

Neither could Kusanagi. He studied her profile, seeing a steady determination.

"Why didn't the wife put them away before she left?"

"Huh?" Kusanagi grunted. A moment later, Mamiya echoed him.

"So what if she didn't put them away?" Kusanagi demanded.

"I just think that normally she would have. You saw the cupboard, right? It was perfectly organized—so well that the space for the missing champagne glasses was obvious. I'm guessing she's the kind of person that can't relax if her important glassware isn't exactly where it should be. Which makes the fact that she didn't return the champagne glasses to their proper place rather curious."

"Maybe she just forgot?" Kusanagi suggested.

Utsumi firmly shook her head. "Impossible."

"How so?"

"Maybe on any old day she might forget for a little while, but she was heading away on a trip that weekend. It is very hard to imagine that she would have left those champagne glasses out."

Kusanagi glanced over at Mamiya, wondering if his own face looked as astonished as the chief's. Utsumi had raised a question that hadn't even occurred to him.

"I can only think of one reason why the wife wouldn't have put away the champagne glasses," the young detective continued. "If she knew she wouldn't be away for very long, she wouldn't have felt the need to rush and clean them up."

Mamiya sat down in his seat, crossing his arms. He looked up at Kusanagi. "Your rebuttal?"

Kusanagi scratched his head. He didn't have a rebuttal. Instead, he turned to Utsumi and asked: "Why didn't you bring this up sooner? Didn't it occur to you as soon as we got to the house?"

She shrugged, an unusually demure smile rising to her lips. "I didn't want to get scolded for obsessing over details. And I figured that, if the wife really was guilty, we'd probably find out some other way eventually . . . Sorry."

Mamiya breathed out a deep sigh. "We've got some work to do, Kusanagi," he said. "What's the point having our new detective on the team if she doesn't feel at ease sharing her observations with us, hmm?"

"Oh, it's not like that—" Utsumi began, but Mamiya lifted his hand.

"Don't be afraid to speak what's on your mind any time you like. There's no rank and no gender when we're on the case. I'll pass what you just told us on to Division, but don't get too comfortable, no matter how keen your observation may be. It is a little odd that she didn't put those glasses back, but it's not exactly incriminating evidence. What we need is something we can prove. So right now, what I want both of you to do is find proof that Mrs. Mashiba's alibi holds, if it does. It's not your job to worry about how we're going to use that information. Understood?"

Utsumi lowered her eyes for a moment and blinked several times before she looked back up. "Understood," she said, staring the chief straight in the eye.

SEVEN

Hiromi opened her eyes to the sound of her ringing cell phone.

She hadn't been asleep—just lying on her bed with her eyes closed, ready for yet another sleepless night. She still had some sleeping pills that Yoshitaka had given her, but she was scared to take them.

She sat up, her body leaden, a vague ache in her temples. She was scared even to pick up the phone. *Who could be calling me at this hour?* She glanced at the clock. It was almost ten.

When she saw the name on the digital display, it woke her like a splash of frigid water. It was Ayane. She quickly pressed the talk button.

"Yes? Hiromi speaking." Her voice was hoarse.

"Hi, it's Ayane. I'm sorry, were you asleep?"

"No, just lying down. I'm sorry about not coming back over this morning."

"It's okay. Are you all right?"

"I'm fine. How about you? You must be exhausted," Hiromi asked, wondering if the detectives had told Ayane about her affair with Yoshitaka.

"A little, yes. It's all so confusing . . . I still can't really believe it happened."

The same was true for Hiromi. It was like an interminable nightmare. "I know," she said to her phone.

"Are you sure you're okay, Hiromi? You're not sick?"

"No, I'm fine. I should be able to go to work tomorrow."

"Don't worry about that. Actually, I was wondering if we could get together?"

"Now?" Hiromi asked, a sudden unease rising in her chest. "What is it?"

"This is something I want to talk to you about in person. I don't think it will take very long. If you're tired, I can come over there."

Phone pressed to her ear, Hiromi shook her head. "No, I'll come over. Give me about an hour, I have to get dressed."

"Actually, I'm at a hotel now."

"Oh?"

"The police wanted to check some more stuff in the house, so they have me staying here. I just swapped some of the things in the suitcase I took to Sapporo and brought it along."

Hiromi's boss explained that she was staying in a hotel close to Shinagawa station on the southern side of Tokyo.

"I'll be right there," Hiromi said, ending the call.

While she was getting ready to go, her mind spun, trying to imagine what Ayane wanted to talk about. *If she was so worried about how I'm feeling, why did she want me to come over right away?* Maybe she was feeling that time was tight—or that what she had to say was so important it couldn't be put off.

On the train to Shinagawa, Hiromi sat nervously, unable to refrain from imagining what Ayane was going to tell her. Maybe she'd heard about the affair. Her voice hadn't sounded harsh over the phone, but what if she'd been hiding her feelings?

Hiromi tried to imagine how Ayane would react if she heard that her husband was having an affair with her apprentice. She had no idea. She had never seen her teacher angry before, not for any reason. She was always so quiet—so unemotional. *But she has to have the capacity for anger in her somewhere. Everyone does.*

Hiromi's own inability to predict how Ayane would act toward the woman who'd stolen her husband terrified the apprentice. She had decided that if Ayane asked about it, she wouldn't make some lame attempt to hide the truth; she would just apologize, though she had little hope of being forgiven. Or, for that matter, of holding on to her job. If it came to that, making a clean break was the most important thing she could do.

Hiromi called Ayane when she arrived at the hotel, and was invited up to her room. The older woman met her wearing a beige hotel bathrobe.

"Sorry to drag you over here when you're so tired."

"That's all right. What did you want to talk about?"

"Have a seat," Ayane said, waving toward one of the two overstuffed sofa chairs in the room.

Hiromi sat down and looked around the room. It was a twin. Ayane's suitcase was lying open next to one of the beds. From the looks of it, she had brought half her wardrobe. She was ready for an extended stay.

"You want something to drink?"

"No thanks."

"Well, there's some if you want any," Ayane said, pulling a

bottle of oolong tea from the hotel refrigerator and filling two glasses.

"Thank you." Hiromi reached out for her glass, suddenly realizing how thirsty she was.

"What did the detectives ask you?" Ayane began, her tone as soft as always.

Hiromi set down her glass and licked her lips. "They asked me how he was when I discovered him. They asked me if I had any idea who did it."

"What did you say?"

Hiromi waved a hand in front of her. "Of course I don't have any idea."

"Of course. Did they ask you anything else?"

"Nothing, really. Not that I remember." Hiromi looked down at the floor. *They asked about me drinking coffee with your husband Sunday morning.*

Ayane nodded and reached for her own glass. She took a sip and pressed the glass to her forehead, as though trying to cool a fever.

"Hiromi, there's something I have to tell you."

Hiromi's eyes darted upward. They met Ayane's. For a second, she thought her teacher was glaring, then, a moment later, her expression changed. There was no hatred or anger at all in those eyes. Just sadness and loss, made more poignant by the thin smile floating on her lips.

"He asked me to leave him," Ayane said, her voice flat.

Hiromi looked back down at the floor. She knew she might be expected to feign surprise, but she didn't have it in her. She couldn't even look Ayane in the face.

"It was on Friday. He told me just before the Ikais arrived.

He said there was no point being married to a woman who couldn't have children."

Hiromi hung her head. Yoshitaka had told her he'd asked Ayane for a divorce, but she'd had no idea he had said it like that.

Ayane continued. "He also said something else . . . something along the lines of having already found the next woman. He wouldn't tell me her name, but he said she was someone I didn't know."

Hiromi tensed. *She knows. She's trying to trap me by appearing not to care.*

"I think he was lying," Ayane said. "I think I know who it is. I think I know her very well. That's why he wouldn't tell me the name."

Hiromi was starting to feel physical pain just listening to her speak. She looked up, tears welling in her eyes.

Ayane showed no surprise at all. She was still wearing the same vacant smile on her face when she said, as if she were scolding a little child: "It was you, wasn't it, Hiromi?"

Hiromi closed her mouth to hold back a sob. A tear ran down her cheek.

"It *was* you . . . wasn't it?"

There was no point denying it now. Hiromi gave a little nod.

Ayane breathed out a slow sigh. "I thought so."

"Ayane, I . . ."

"No, don't say anything. I knew it the moment he told me we were over. Or maybe from a little while before, though I didn't want to admit it to myself. How could I not notice, being so near you all the time? That, and he's not as good a liar or an actor as he thinks he is."

"You must be furious."

Ayane tilted her head. "Maybe. Maybe I am upset. I'm sure he was the one who made the advances, but I could be angry with you for not refusing him. Yet I don't feel like you stole him away from me. Really. It wasn't a fling, you see. He stopped loving me first, and then went to you. I feel a little responsible for not being able to hold onto him."

"I'm so sorry," Hiromi blurted. "I know I shouldn't have done it, but he kept asking and asking—"

"Say no more." Ayane's voice cut the air with a sudden cold sharpness. "Or I might even start hating you a little, Hiromi. Do you really think I want to hear how you fell for his charms?"

She's right. Hiromi shook her head, still looking down at the floor.

"We made a promise to each other when we got married," Ayane said, the softness returning to her voice. "We said if we went a year without having children, we'd reconsider. The truth is, neither of us is that young, and neither of us wanted to go through lengthy infertility treatments if it came to that. To be honest, learning you were the other woman came as a shock—but for him, I think he was just acting on that promise."

"He may have mentioned it," Hiromi said without looking up.

He had spoken of it again when she'd seen him on Saturday. He'd used the word "rules"—*those were the rules*—*that was why Ayane had accepted the situation.* Hiromi hadn't been able to understand, but listening to Ayane now, the younger woman thought it might actually have been true.

"I went back to Sapporo to think things over. I couldn't bear staying in the house after he told me we were through. That's why I gave you my key—so I wouldn't have to interact with him again. I knew you two would meet while I was away; why not give you the key and make it official?"

Hiromi remembered that morning when Ayane had appeared at her apartment. She'd had no idea what had been going on in her teacher's head. *I thought she was showing her trust in me. How stupid could I be?* When she thought about how Ayane must have felt seeing her clutching that key, it made her shrivel inside.

"Did you tell the detectives about you and Yoshitaka?"

Hiromi gave a little nod. "I think they already knew somehow. I didn't really have a choice."

"I see. That makes sense, I guess. It would be strange for you to let yourself into the house just because you were worried about him. That's how they must've figured it out. They didn't say a word about it to me, you know."

"Really?"

"I think they were pretending not to know so they could observe how I acted. They must suspect me, after all."

"What?" Hiromi looked up at her teacher. "You mean, you're a suspect?"

"Well, sure. If you think about it, I have a motive. My husband betrayed me."

Right again. But Hiromi hadn't suspected Ayane at all. For one, she had been in Sapporo when Yoshitaka was murdered. That, and she had believed it when Yoshitaka told her that everything was going smoothly. *Maybe I was being stupid again.*

"Not that I mind. They can suspect me all they want." Ayane pulled her bag closer to her and fished out a handkerchief, daubing with it beneath her eyes. "All I want to know is what happened. Why that had to happen to him . . . Hiromi, are you sure you have no idea who could've done it? When was the last time you saw him?"

She didn't want to answer the question, but lying didn't seem like an option. "Yesterday morning. We had coffee together. The detectives asked me all about it, but all I could tell them was that I didn't notice anything unusual at the time. Not about the house, or . . . Mr. Mashiba."

"Right," Ayane said, tilting her head in thought for moment before looking at Hiromi. "You haven't kept anything a secret from the detectives, have you? You told them everything, right?"

"I think so."

"Well, okay then. But if you remember anything that you might've forgotten, you should tell them as soon as you can. They might suspect you, too, you know."

"I think they already do suspect me. I'm the only one who saw him over the weekend."

"That's true. I suppose that is where they would start looking."

"Should I tell them about this, too? That we met here tonight?"

Ayane nodded, putting a hand to her forehead. "I don't see any reason why you shouldn't. I certainly don't care. And if you tried to hide it, they might take it the wrong way."

"Okay."

Ayane's lips softened into a smile. "It's funny, don't you think? Here we are, the woman abandoned and her husband's lover, in the same room, talking. And instead of being at each other's throats, we're at our wits' end. Maybe it's because it doesn't matter anymore, now that he's dead."

Hiromi didn't have an answer for that, though she realized that she felt the same. She only knew that if Yoshitaka were to spring back to life, she wouldn't care about her teacher's anger. She understood instinctively that her own loss right then was even greater than Ayane's, just as she knew that this was the last thing she could tell anyone.

EIGHT

Ayane Mashiba's parents lived in a tidy, organized residential quarter of Sapporo, and their house was a squat, square three-story structure. The ground floor was a garage, but was treated as a basement for zoning purposes, with two regular stories above it. A stairway led up to the front entrance on the second story.

"There are lots of houses like this around here," Ayane's father, Kazuhiro Mita, explained, putting out some rice crackers for his guests. "We get a lot of snow in the winter, so the front door has to be a ways off the ground."

Kusanagi nodded. *It's a different world up here.* He reached for the steaming cup of tea that Ayane's mother, Tokiko, had just brought. She sat down next to her husband, the empty tea tray resting on her lap.

"We were very surprised to hear the news about Mr. Mashiba. We didn't know what to make of it when they said it wasn't an accident or an illness, but a police investigation was the last thing we expected." Kazuhiro's speckled white eyebrows formed little inverted Vs above his eyes.

"It's not been officially ruled a homicide yet," Kusanagi said.

Kazuhiro frowned, the wrinkles running deep on his thin face. "That man had his share of enemies. Most capable businessmen do. Still, you'd like to think that people were a little more decent than that . . ."

Kazuhiro had been employed at a local credit union until his retirement five years earlier. He'd seen his share of businessmen in his day, and no doubt he knew the type.

"I was wondering," Tokiko said, looking up. "How is Ayane doing? On the phone she says she's fine, but then again, I'm sure she doesn't want to worry us."

"Surprisingly well, actually. Of course, it was all a great shock," Kusanagi explained, "but throughout it all she's been very helpful with our investigation."

"Well, then, that's a relief." The woman's words belied the worry that lingered in her face.

"Ayane says she came home on Saturday? She told us that she had concerns about your health." Kusanagi fixed his gaze on Kazuhiro. The older man was thin, and a bit pale, but he didn't seem to be suffering.

"Yeah, my pancreas," the older man explained. "Got an inflammation about three years ago, and haven't really felt right since. I get a fever sometimes, and some days my stomach and back hurt so much I can't move. But I've been carrying on. That's what you do, you know. Carry on."

"Did you need Ayane's help for any specific reason this time?"

"No, nothing like that," Kazuhiro said with a glance toward his wife.

Tokiko shook her head. "She called us on Friday night. Said

she'd be here the next day. She said she was worried about her father and she hadn't visited us since getting married."

"Did she have any other reasons for her visit?"

"Not that she told us."

"How long did she say she was going to stay?"

"Well, she didn't say anything in particular—when I asked her when she'd be going back to Tokyo, she told me she hadn't decided yet."

Kusanagi took a mental note: *no urgent reason to rush home.* So why had she gone to visit her parents? Nine times out of ten, when a married woman suddenly took a trip back home, it was because of marital troubles.

"Er, Detective?" Kazuhiro said a bit hesitantly. "You seem awful interested in why Ayane came up to see us. Care to tell us why?"

Kusanagi smiled. *The old banker's still sharp.* "If, in fact, Mr. Mashiba's death *was* a homicide, there's a chance that the guilty party intentionally picked a time when Ayane wouldn't be at home to strike." The detective spoke slowly and precisely. "If that is the case, then we have to ask how the guilty party knew where Ayane would be. That's why I'm afraid we have to cover all the bases. Please understand, it's all part of standard procedure."

"Is that so," Kazuhiro said, nodding. It was unclear whether he bought the detective's story or not.

"How did she spend her time when she was here?" Kusanagi asked, looking at both parents.

"She stayed at home the whole day on Saturday. At night, we went out to a local sushi place, just the three of us. One of her favorite places when she was growing up," Tokiko told him.

"What's the name of the restaurant?"

A suspicious look crossed Tokiko's face, mirrored in the expression of her husband beside her.

"Sorry." Kusanagi smiled again. "We don't know what might become important as the investigation continues, so I need to take down every detail, no matter how trivial. We'd prefer not to have to make the trip up here again, if possible."

Tokiko looked unsatisfied, but she still told him the name of the restaurant: "Lucky Sushi."

"And she went with a friend to a hot springs on Sunday?"

"Yes, her friend Saki—they've been close since middle school. Her parents live not a five-minute walk away from here. Saki moved down to the south end of town when she got married, but Ayane gave her call Saturday night and the two went out—to Jozankei, I think it was."

Kusanagi nodded, glancing at his notepad. Mamiya had previously gotten the name of the friend from Ayane: Sakiko Motooka. Utsumi was scheduled to pay her a visit on her way back from the springs.

"You mentioned that this was Ayane's first trip since her marriage. Did she happen to say anything about Mr. Mashiba while she was here?"

Tokiko cocked her head. "Just that he was busy as always with work, but still managed to find time to play golf. That sort of thing."

"Nothing about how things were going at home?"

"Not a word. She was so busy asking us questions I could barely get a word in edgewise. She wanted to know how father was doing, how her brother was doing. —Oh, she has one brother, he's working in the United States."

"So, if she had never visited home," Kusanagi went on, "I guess you didn't see much of Mr. Mashiba?"

"That's true. We went to visit him at his home just before the wedding, but that was the last time we talked at any length. He invited us to visit any time, of course, but with Kazuhiro's health not being so great, we never seemed to get the chance."

"I doubt we met him more than four times in all," Kazuhiro said, shrugging.

"It sounds like they made the decision to get married rather quickly?"

"I should say. Ayane was thirty, and we were just starting to worry whether she would ever find someone, when she gives us a call to say she's tying the knot." Tokiko displayed a mother's pout.

According to her parents, Ayane had left for Tokyo eight years earlier—and before that she had gone to a junior college for two years, and spent some time as an exchange student in the UK. Her interest in patchwork started during high school; by graduation she had already received some recognition at professional contests. Her popularity soared when, upon her return from England, she had published a book about patchwork quilting that caught on with a core group of enthusiasts.

"She was so interested in her work, whenever we'd ask her when she was planning on getting married, she'd tell us she didn't have any time to be someone's wife," Tokiko said. " 'I'm so busy, I want a wife of my own,' she'd tell us."

"Really." Kusanagi chuckled, a bit surprised. "She seemed quite good at managing the affairs of the house."

Kazuhiro shook his head. "Being good at crafts doesn't mean you're good at housework. When she was still living here, I don't think she did a single thing around the place, did she, Mama? I don't think she even cooked for herself when she was living in Tokyo. Alone, I mean, before she got married."

"You don't say?"

"It's true," Tokiko said. "We visited her there a few times, and I've never seen a stove that clean. I think she ate out or bought boxed lunches at the convenience stores."

"But according to their friends, they put on parties quite regularly, with your daughter cooking."

"We heard that, too. Ayane told us. I guess she went to a cooking school before she got married, and picked up a few tricks. We used to say 'I guess she must have found the right man, for her to pick up a pot and spoon.'"

"And now he's gone," Kazuhiro said, lowering his gaze.

"Would it be all right for us to visit her?" the mother asked. "We'd like to help out with the arrangements for the funeral and such."

"Of course, that's no problem at all," Kusanagi told them. "However, I can't say at this point when we will be able to release the body."

"Oh . . ." Tokiko muttered.

"Give Ayane a call and talk to her about it later on," Kazuhiro suggested to his wife.

Kusanagi thanked his hosts and prepared to leave. As he was putting on his shoes, he noticed a patchwork vest hanging from a coat rack in the entryway. It was very long, long enough to reach the knees of an average adult.

"She made it for us several years ago," Tokiko told him. "It's for Kazuhiro to wear in the winter when he goes out to pick up the papers and the mail."

"I only wish she hadn't felt the need to make it so bright," Kazuhiro said, though his pleasure was evident.

"His mother went out once during the wintertime and fell so

hard she broke her hip bone. Ayane remembered that story, so she sewed a cushion halfway down," Tokiko explained, showing them the inside of the long vest.

Considerate as always, Kusanagi thought.

Leaving the Mita household behind, he made his way to Lucky Sushi. There was a "closed" sign on the door, but the chef was inside, getting ready for the day. He was a man of about fifty with a crew cut, and he remembered Ayane's recent visit.

"It's been a long time since I've seen her around, so I wanted to make it a special night for them. I think they were here until around ten o'clock . . ." The chef raised an eyebrow at Kusanagi. "Did something happen?"

There was no point in telling the whole city what had happened, so Kusanagi shook his head and gave some vague excuses before leaving. He was scheduled to meet with Utsumi back in the lounge of the hotel by supper. He found her there, in the middle of writing something in her notebook.

"Did you get anything?" he asked, sitting down across from her.

"Well, Ayane did stay at an inn in Jozankei Hot Springs. I talked to one of the caretakers there who said she and her friend seemed to have had a good time."

"And Ms. Sakiko Motooka?"

"Met her."

"Anything that didn't fit with what Mrs. Mashiba told us?"

Utsumi looked down at the floor for a moment before shaking her head. "Nothing at all. Everything happened just like she said."

"Same here. She didn't have time to go to Tokyo and back."

"Ms. Motooka said that she met up with Mrs. Mashiba in the A.M. on Sunday. And her story also confirmed that Mrs. Mashiba didn't notice the message on her phone until later that night."

"Sounds pretty ironclad to me," Kusanagi said, leaning back in his chair with an eye on the junior detective. "Ayane Mashiba's not our killer. It's impossible. I know you're not satisfied with that, but we have to look at the objective truth here."

Utsumi looked away for a breath, then turned back to Kusanagi. "There *were* a few things that worried me about Ms. Motooka's story."

"Such as?"

"She said it had been a very long time since she last saw Mrs. Mashiba. Since at least before she was married."

"That fits what her parents told us."

"She said she thought her friend had changed. Before she'd been energetic, edgy, even—but this time she seemed calm. Maybe even a little lackluster."

"So?" Kusanagi said. "It's likely that Mrs. Mashiba was aware of her husband's infidelity. Maybe she came home to recuperate? I don't see why any of that should be cause for worry. Like the chief said, we're only here to find out whether her alibi holds or not, and it does. What else is there?"

"One other thing," Utsumi said, her expression unchanging. "She said that she saw Mrs. Mashiba turn on her cell phone several times. She would check it for messages, then turn it right off again."

"Saving the batteries. I do that all the time."

"You think that's what it was?"

"You got another theory?"

"Maybe she was expecting a call, but she didn't want to answer it. She preferred to get a message, then call back."

Kusanagi shook his head. *This Utsumi's a sharp cookie*, he thought, *but a little stubborn.* He looked down at his watch and stood. "Let's go. We're going to miss our plane."

NINE

The air in the building was cool down around her feet. The place seemed deserted; her footsteps sounded alarmingly loud despite her soft-soled sneakers.

Climbing the stairs, she finally passed someone—a kid wearing glasses. He glanced at her with a look of mild surprise. *Probably not a lot of strange women visiting here*, Kaoru Utsumi reflected.

It'd already been several months since her previous visit, which had come just after she'd been assigned to the First Investigation Division at the department. They needed a tricky physics question answered to solve a case, and Kusanagi had sent her here for advice. She traced the path from memory.

Laboratory 13 was right where Utsumi had left it. A familiar whiteboard hung on the door, showing the whereabouts of everyone associated with the lab. Next to the space marked "Yukawa," a red magnet had been stuck in the "IN" column. She breathed a light sigh of relief. *At least he didn't skip out on me.*

The board seemed to indicate that all the assistants and students were out at classes. This was another relief. She'd rather that no one listened in on their conversation.

She knocked on the door and a voice inside said, "Yes." She waited.

"Sorry, it's not automatic," the voice said after a few moments had passed.

Utsumi pushed open the door. Straight ahead a man was sitting with his back to her, wearing a black T-shirt. He was staring at a large monitor on which a structure composed of large and small spheres was displayed.

"Think you could press the switch on the coffeemaker next to the sink?" the man asked without turning. "It's all ready to go."

The sink was directly to her right. She spotted the coffeemaker. It looked brand-new. Utsumi pressed the switch and heard the sound of steam being generated.

"I'd heard you like instant coffee," she said.

"They gave me that coffeemaker as a prize for winning the badminton tournament. Thought I'd give it a spin. It's quite convenient, you know. And the price per cup is *very* reasonable."

"Bet you wish you'd had one before."

"Not really. It has one major flaw."

"What's that?"

"It doesn't taste like instant coffee," Manabu Yukawa said, banging out something on the keyboard before swiveling around in his chair. He looked up at Utsumi. "Getting used to Division yet?"

"A little."

"Ah, a 'little.' That's good to hear. I have a theory that getting used to detective work is essentially the same thing as losing your humanity."

"Have you told Detective Kusanagi this theory?"

"Several times. Not that he ever listened." Yukawa looked back at the monitor, hand reaching for the mouse.

"What's that?"

"A model of a ferrite crystalline structure."

"Ferrite . . . Like in a magnet?"

The physicist's eyes widened slightly behind his glasses. "Ferromagnetic material, more properly . . . but still, you know your stuff."

"I think I read about it once. They use that to make magnetic heads, right?"

"Kusanagi doesn't know what he's got, does he," Yukawa muttered, flicking off the monitor and looking back up at Utsumi. "So, question time. Me first. Why am I supposed to keep your coming here a secret from Kusanagi?"

"In order for me to explain that, I'll have to tell you about the case first."

Yukawa slowly shook his head. "When you called me, I initially refused because I'm really not that interested in working on police cases. What made me change my mind was when you said you weren't telling Kusanagi you were coming. That was intriguing, which is why I've set aside time out of my busy schedule. So, explain that to me first. And be aware I'll only decide whether or not I'll listen to whatever else you have to say afterward."

Utsumi watched the professor's face while he talked. Kusanagi had said that the man they called "Detective Galileo" had always been very helpful when it came to working on a case. But something to do with one particular investigation had caused a rift between the detective and the physicist. Since then, the two had grown apart, though no one had told her any of the details.

"It would be difficult to explain the need for secrecy without describing the case."

"Unlikely. Tell me, when you go out questioning people, do you describe the whole case to everyone you question? Just use whatever streamlining techniques you would use then. And please be quick about it. The more time we waste, the more likely it is that one of my students will return."

Utsumi didn't like the professor's acerbic tone, and it almost showed on her face. She was struck with an irrational desire to ruffle the cool physicist's feathers.

"Something wrong?" He narrowed his eyes. "Don't feel like talking?"

"That's not it."

"Then, swiftness is your ally. I'm really short on time here."

"Right," Utsumi said, gathering herself. "Detective Kusanagi . . ." she began, staring Yukawa in the eye, ". . . is in love."

"Huh?" The cool light in Yukawa's eyes faded and his focus softened, so that he looked like a little lost boy for a brief moment until he looked back up at Utsumi. "Did you just say 'love'?"

"Yes," she said. "Detective Kusanagi is in it."

Yukawa leaned back, straightening his glasses. When he again returned his gaze to Utsumi, there was wariness in his eyes. "With whom?"

"Our suspect," Utsumi replied. "He's in love with the suspect in our current case, which is affecting his view of certain details. That's why I didn't want him to know I was coming here."

"So he's not expecting me to offer you any advice about the case?"

"Not in the least." Utsumi nodded.

Yukawa crossed his arms and let his eyelids fall shut. He

leaned back in his chair, breathing out a long breath. "I think I underestimated you. In fact, I was ready to refuse as soon as you'd said whatever it was you were going to say, but this . . . was unexpected. Love, is it? You sure we're talking about the same Detective Kusanagi?"

"Can I tell you about the case?" Utsumi said, tasting victory.

"First, we drink coffee. I need to let things settle a bit before I can focus."

Yukawa stood and poured coffee into two mugs.

"This is perfect, actually," Utsumi said as he handed her one of the mugs.

"What is?"

"This coffee. You see, the case begins with a cup of coffee."

"'From a cup of coffee what dreams may bloom . . .' There was a song about that once. So, what's your story?" Yukawa sat back in his chair, sipping at his mug.

Utsumi proceeded to tell him everything she knew about the Yoshitaka Mashiba murder, in chronological order. Officially they weren't permitted to divulge the details of the case outside of Division, but Kusanagi once told her it was the only way to get Yukawa's assistance. More importantly, Utsumi trusted him.

Yukawa drank his coffee and stared down into the empty mug while she finished talking.

"So your point is: you suspect the wife, and Kusanagi doesn't, but since he's is in love with her, his judgment is flawed."

"I might've been overstating it when I said 'love.' I was just trying to get your attention. However, it's true that Detective Kusanagi holds a special affection for the wife. He acts strangely when he's around her, or talking about her."

"I won't ask how it is that you're so certain. I'm a great believer in female intuition about such things."

"I'll take that as a compliment."

Yukawa furrowed his brow and placed his coffee mug on the desk. "Still, just listening to your story, it doesn't sound as though Kusanagi's thinking about the case is all that off the mark. Ayane Mashiba, was it? Her alibi sounds perfect."

"If the murder weapon were something direct, like a knife or a gun, I would agree. But this is a poisoning, and it's possible to commit the act before the actual murder happens."

"So you want me to figure out how she did it?"

Utsumi waited in silence.

A knowing smile spread on the physicist's lips. "Perhaps you've gotten the wrong impression somewhere along the line, but physics is not magic."

"But you've solved plenty of cases before now involving tricks that seemed like magic."

"Criminal tricks are different from magic tricks. Do you know what the difference is?" He waited for Utsumi to shake her head before continuing: "They both contain a secret, but the fate of that secret is not the same. With a magic trick, as soon as the show is over, the opportunity for the audience to perceive the secret is gone. However, with a criminal trick, investigators can pore over every detail of the crime scene until they're satisfied. If a trick was used, some trace always remains. The most difficult thing when committing a crime is to perfectly cover one's tracks, wouldn't you agree?"

"What if the tracks *were* covered?"

"Going on what you've told me, I would have to say that the possibility is extremely low. What was the other girl's name again, the lover?"

"Hiromi Wakayama."

"She's testified that she drank coffee with the victim, correct?

Not only that, but she made the coffee. If the coffee had already been poisoned, why didn't it kill both of them? That's the biggest mystery here. I liked your conjecture about the magic powder that makes coffee taste better—in other words, setting the victim up to poison himself. That sort of thing makes for an excellent murder mystery, but it's not a method a real criminal would choose."

"How do you know?"

"Imagine that you were the guilty party. What if you gave him the poison and he used it somewhere outside the house? What if he went over to a friend's place and told them about this great powder his wife had given him, and they drank it together?"

Utsumi bit her lip. He had a point. Worse, she realized she had been clinging to the theory as a real possibility.

"If the wife was indeed the murderer, there would be at least three hurdles for her to clear," Yukawa said, holding up three fingers. "One, no one must notice or have reason to believe that the poison had been placed before it was ingested. Otherwise, there'd be no point in constructing an alibi. Two, she would have to be sure that it was Mr. Mashiba who took the poison. She might not mind getting the lover, too, as collateral damage, but she would have to be sure to also get her mark. Third, the whole plan would have to be something easily prepared in a short amount of time. There was a dinner party at their house the night before she left for Hokkaido, correct? If she'd placed the poison before then, there'd be too much danger of someone else taking it. I think she would've placed it afterward." He raised his hands. "And I can't think of how anyone would be able to do that. Sorry."

"Are those hurdles all that difficult?"

"They seem pretty difficult to me. The first, in particular. I think it makes far more sense to assume that the guilty party is not the wife."

Utsumi sighed. If the physicist, the so-called Detective Galileo himself, was telling her it was impossible, then maybe it was.

Her cell phone rang. She picked up, watching Yukawa refill his coffee mug out of the corner of her eye.

"Where are you?" It was Kusanagi. There was a roughness in his voice.

"Asking questions at a pharmacy. I was told to investigate possible routes for obtaining arsenous acid. Is something wrong?"

"Forensics came through. They found poison somewhere other than the coffee."

Utsumi gripped her phone tighter. "Where?"

"The hot water kettle on the stove."

"The kettle? Really?"

"Just a trace amount, but it was definitely there. I'm going to be taking Hiromi Wakayama in for questioning."

"Her? Why?"

"Her prints were on the kettle."

"Of course they were. She made coffee on Sunday morning."

"Which means she had the opportunity to put poison in it."

"Were hers the only fingerprints they found?"

"No, the victim's were on there, too."

"What about the wife's fingerprints?"

She heard a deep sigh on the other side of the line. "Of course they were, she lives there. But she wasn't the last one who touched it. They can tell by the way that the fingerprints overlap. Also, there was no indication that anyone had touched it wearing gloves."

"I understand that glove marks don't always remain."

"I know that. But look at the circumstantial evidence as a

whole: no one but Ms. Wakayama could have put the poison in. We're going to be questioning her down at Division, and I want you there. Now."

He hung up before she could answer.

"Sounds like a development," Yukawa said, standing while he drank.

Utsumi related to him what Kusanagi had told her. He listened, lips on his mug, not even nodding while she spoke.

"The kettle? Really?"

"That's what I said. Maybe I have been thinking too much. On Sunday morning, Hiromi Wakayama used the same kettle to put on coffee, and drank it with the victim. That has to mean that there was no poison in the kettle at that point. Ayane Mashiba couldn't have done it."

"Why not go a little further and say that there was no reason for the wife to put poison in the kettle? There's no trick to that at all."

Utsumi cocked her head, unsure of what he was saying.

"Just now, you admitted that it couldn't have been the wife," he explained. "But you can only say that because there was someone who used the kettle—without dying—after she left, but before the crime was committed. What if no one else had used the kettle? Then the police would have gone straight to the wife as the most obvious suspect. Surely she would have known that, so why would she go out of her way to make an alibi at all? It wouldn't have held up."

"Oh. That's true," Utsumi said, her head drooping, her arms folded across her chest. "Either way, this removes Ayane Mashiba from the list of suspects, doesn't it?"

Yukawa didn't answer. He was staring at her.

After a moment, he said: "So, where does this leave you? If

the wife wasn't the murderer, are you going to join Kusanagi in suspecting the lover?"

She shook her head. "No. I don't think so."

"Such confidence. Mind telling me why? Please don't tell me you don't think she could kill the man she loved." Yukawa sat in his chair and crossed his legs.

Utsumi panicked—she had been about to say that very thing. Other than that, she couldn't think of any reason why it hadn't been Hiromi Wakayama.

But the more she stood there, looking at Yukawa, the more she started to believe that maybe *he* didn't think it was Hiromi Wakayama, either, and that *he* had some reason why he thought she was innocent. The only details he knew about case were what she'd just told him. So somewhere in there had to be a hint that it wasn't the young apprentice who put the poison in the kettle.

With a little gasp, she looked up.

"Something on your mind?"

"She would've washed the kettle!"

"Oh?"

"If she put the poison in the kettle, she would have washed it before the police came. She was the one who discovered the body, after all. She had plenty of time!"

Yukawa nodded, a satisfied look on his face.

"Precisely. We might add that, were she the murderer, she wouldn't have just washed the kettle, but also disposed of the old coffee grounds and the paper filter. Then, if I were she, I would have placed a little baggie of poison next to the body. To make it look like a suicide."

Utsumi gave a little bow with her head. "I'm glad I came. Thank you."

She turned and started walking toward the door when Yukawa called out, "Oh, Detective." She stopped.

"I'm guessing I won't be able to view the crime scene, but if you had some photos . . ."

"Photos of what?"

"The kitchen where the coffee was poisoned, for starters. And a picture of the flatware and kettle in evidence."

Utsumi's eyes widened. "You're going to help?"

Yukawa frowned and gave his head a scratch. "I might think about it a bit, in my spare time. I'm curious to know how someone in Hokkaido was able to poison someone in Tokyo, a thousand kilometers away."

Utsumi grinned despite herself. Reaching into her shoulder bag, she produced a folder. "Here."

"What's this?"

"The photos you asked for. I took these this morning."

Yukawa opened the file and pulled back a little.

"If we figure out how she did it," he said with a grin, "we can serve Detective Kusanagi a lethal dose of humble pie."

TEN

When Kusanagi called Hiromi Wakayama, she was in Ayane Mashiba's patchwork classroom. He jumped in the car with Kishitani behind the wheel and they headed for the school. The place was a white apartment building with tiled walls, nestled in amidst a row of trendy stores. There was no lock on the building's main door, unusual for that area. They took the elevator up to the third floor, where a sign on room 305 read "Anne's House."

Kusanagi pressed the doorbell and, almost immediately, the door opened. Hiromi looked out, a worried expression on her face.

"Sorry to barge in like this," Kusanagi said, stepping inside. He squared his shoulders. "Actually—" The words died on his lips. Ayane Mashiba was behind Hiromi, seated in the center of the room.

"Did you find anything out?" Ayane got up and came toward the detectives.

"I'm sorry, Mrs. Mashiba, I didn't know you were here, too."

"Hiromi was helping me make some decisions about what to do now. Did you need her for something? I'm sure she's told you everything she knows."

Her voice was low and calm, but it held a definite tone of irritation directed toward Kusanagi. Her eyes fell on him, and the sorrow in them made him shrink back.

"Actually, there's been a slight development in the case," Kusanagi said, turning toward Hiromi. "I'd like you to come with us back to the station."

Hiromi's eyes opened wide and she blinked several times.

"What's all this about?" Ayane asked. "Why does she have to go with you?"

"I'm afraid I'm not at liberty to talk about that right now. Ms. Wakayama, if you wouldn't mind? Don't worry, we're not here in a marked police vehicle," he added.

Hiromi glanced worriedly toward Ayane, then nodded to the detective. "Fine. But I don't have to stay there? I mean, I'll be free to go home?"

"As soon as we're finished."

"I'll get ready."

Hiromi disappeared into the back for a moment, then reappeared wearing a jacket and carrying her bag. While she was gone Kusanagi found himself unable to look at Ayane. He could feel her eyes on him, glaring.

Hiromi stepped out into the hallway, following Kishitani. Kusanagi had turned to join them when Ayane grabbed him by the arm. "Wait." Her grip was surprisingly strong. "Hiromi's not a suspect, right?"

Kusanagi hesitated. Kishitani was waiting with Hiromi just outside the door.

"You go on ahead," he said, closing the door before turning to face Ayane.

"I . . . I'm sorry," she said, letting go of his arm. "But there is no way that she could have done this. If you're suspecting her for whatever reason, you're making a horrible mistake."

"I'm afraid it's our job to look into every possibility, no matter how slight."

Ayane firmly shook her head. "The possibility that she did it is zero, do you understand? She couldn't have killed my husband. I'm sure you understand that."

"Why couldn't she?"

"You know, don't you? About their relationship?"

Kusanagi gaped. "So you knew?"

"Yes. I spoke with Hiromi about it the other day—that is, I figured it out and confronted her, and she admitted to it."

Ayane began to describe their exchange at the hotel. Kusanagi was astonished by what she was telling him, but not as amazed as he was to have found the two of them here, today, working in the same room. He assumed the fact that her husband was dead had something to do with it; yet he found himself utterly baffled by a woman who would maintain a working relationship with someone who had betrayed her the way her apprentice had.

"I went home to Sapporo because I couldn't bear to stay in the same house with him. I'm sorry I lied." Ayane lowered her head. "But you have to understand that she had absolutely no reason to kill my husband. You can't suspect her of this."

Kusanagi blinked. What kind of person went to such lengths to protect the woman who stole her husband? "I understand what you're telling me," he said. "But we can't make decisions based on how we feel about the suspect. We need objectively verifiable physical evidence."

"Physical evidence? So you have evidence proving Hiromi poisoned my husband?" Ayane's eyes flashed with a hard light.

Kusanagi sighed. He debated with himself under the weight of her stare. At last he decided that revealing the latest evidence wouldn't cause any further complications in the investigation. "We found out how the poison got into the coffee," he said, and told her about the traces found in the kettle in the kitchen. "And no one is known to have been in the house on Sunday, other than Hiromi herself."

"Poison, in the kettle? How does that incriminate her?"

"It's not conclusive," the detective explained, "but as long as there exists a possibility that Ms. Wakayama did put the poison into the coffee, she will remain a suspect."

"But—" Ayane said, then faltered, at a loss for words.

"Sorry, but I need to get going." Kusanagi gave a curt bow and left the room.

As soon as they got Hiromi back to the station, Mamiya brought her into an interrogation room to begin questioning. Though normally this would have been done at the local pre-cinct headquarters, Mamiya had chosen the Metropolitan Police Department instead—a sure sign he believed she would confess and turn herself in. Once she'd confessed, they would write up a warrant for her arrest, and only then take her to the Meguro sta-tion. It was a setup to give the press the photo op they wanted: a criminal being led off to justice.

Kusanagi was waiting at his desk for the results when Ut-sumi returned. The first thing she said when he looked up was that Hiromi Wakayama was not the criminal.

When Kusanagi heard her evidence, he frowned. Not because it was another ridiculous theory—in fact, it was exactly the opposite. It made complete sense. If Hiromi Wakayama had put the poison into the coffee, the junior detective explained, she wouldn't have left the kettle on the stove after discovering the body.

"So then who put the poison in the kettle?" Kusanagi asked. "And don't tell me it was Ayane Mashiba, because we've already established that that's impossible."

"I don't know who it was. I can only guess that somebody must have gone into the Mashiba residence after Hiromi Wakayama left on Sunday morning."

Kusanagi shook his head. "There's no indication that anyone else went in there. It was just Yoshitaka Mashiba. Alone."

"We can't say that for sure. We just haven't found out who it was yet. In any case, there's no point questioning Ms. Wakayama any further. Not only is there no point, it might be a violation of her rights," Utsumi said with unusual forcefulness.

Kusanagi was at a loss. He was contemplating the situation when his cell phone rang. Feeling saved by the bell, he relaxed as he looked down at the phone display, only to tense up again immediately. It was Ayane.

"Sorry to bother you when you're busy. But there is something I have to tell you."

"Yes?" Kusanagi gripped his phone tightly.

"Finding poison in the kettle doesn't necessarily mean that somebody actually put poison in the kettle."

Kusanagi was flustered again. "Why's that?"

"Well, perhaps I should've mentioned this earlier, but my husband was extremely health conscious, and never drank water straight from the tap. Even when cooking, I always used water from a filter. He only ever drank bottled water, and he asked me to use it when I made coffee, too. I'm sure he used water from a bottle on Sunday."

"So you think the poison could have been in the bottled water?"

At the desk next to him, he saw one of Utsumi's eyebrows go up.

"I just thought that it might be a possibility. It just doesn't make sense for Hiromi to have done it. And if the poison was in the bottled water, somebody else could've done it. Anyone."

"Well, that's true, but . . ."

"For instance," Ayane went on, "it could even have been me."

ELEVEN

It was just past eight o'clock when Utsumi drove Hiromi Wakayama home. Hiromi had been in the interrogation room for only two hours, far less than Mamiya had anticipated.

Ayane Mashiba's call was the main reason he'd cut off the questioning. The widow was very clear about her husband's instructions: the dead man had insisted that bottled water be used exclusively for all coffee making. If that was true, then all the killer had to do was poison one of the bottles ahead of time—which meant Hiromi Wakayama was no longer the only suspect.

In any case, Mamiya had been unable to press her into making a confession. After two hours of the young woman's tearful professions of innocence, he nodded with reluctant resignation when Utsumi suggested sending Ms. Wakayama home for the time being.

Now she sat in the passenger seat, emphatically silent. *She's probably exhausted*, Utsumi thought. She had seen strong men wilt under the heat of the hard-faced detective's interrogations. It would take a while for the tears to fade from Hiromi's eyes. Utsumi settled in for a quiet ride. Her passenger was too worked up to say anything. *And why would she, anyhow, when she knew that she was now a suspect?*

Hiromi's cell phone rang. She pulled it out of her purse.

"Yes?" she said in a quiet voice. "We just finished. I'm getting a ride back now . . . No, the lady detective . . . No, not the station in Meguro, the Metropolitan Police Department. It might take a little longer to get home . . . Yes, thank you."

She ended the call.

Utsumi took a few steady breaths, then asked, "Was that Mrs. Mashiba?"

She could feel Hiromi tense in her seat. "Yes. Is there a problem?"

"She called Kusanagi while you were being questioned. She seems very worried about you."

"She is."

"You talked about your relationship with Mr. Mashiba?"

"Where did you hear that?"

"Mrs. Mashiba told Kusanagi when he came to bring you down to the department."

Hiromi fell silent, and Utsumi stole a glance at her. Her eyes were downcast, lips curled into a thin frown.

"I don't mean to be rude," Utsumi went on, "but it's very strange to me that the two of you remain so close, when most people in your situation would be at each other's throats."

"Well, he *is* dead."

"Still, it's strange."

There was a pause before Hiromi nodded. "I guess it is."

She doesn't understand it herself, Utsumi realized. She waited several seconds before she spoke again. "Actually, there are two or three things I wanted to ask, if you don't mind."

Hiromi sighed. "What else could you possibly need to know?"

"I know you're tired, and I'm sorry, but these are very simple questions. And the last thing I want to do is cause you any pain."

"It's a little late for that. What did you want to ask?"

"On Sunday morning, you and Mr. Mashiba drank coffee, correct? And you made the coffee?"

"That again?" Hiromi asked, tears in her voice. "I didn't do anything. I don't know anything about any poison."

"I'm not asking about that, just about how you made the coffee. Do you remember what water you used?"

Hiromi blinked. "Excuse me?"

"Did you use water from one of the plastic bottles in the fridge, or water from the tap?"

"From the tap." Hiromi sighed again.

"Are you sure?"

"Yes. Why does it matter?"

"Why did you use water from the tap?"

"I didn't have any deep reason, if that's what you're suggesting. I just thought using hot water would make it boil quicker."

"Was Mr. Mashiba there when you made the coffee that time?"

"He was. Didn't I already say this a few times? I taught him how to make coffee." There was an echo of irritation through the tears in her voice.

"Try to recall the moment as clearly as you can. I don't mean when you were making the coffee, I mean when you were pouring water into the kettle. Was Mr. Mashiba standing there?"

Hiromi fell silent, and Utsumi knew that this wasn't one of the questions Mamiya had asked her.

"Oh," she whispered after a few moments had passed. "You're right. He wasn't in the room yet when I put the kettle on. I'd just turned up the burner when he came in to the kitchen and asked me to show him how it was done."

"You're sure?"

"Yes, very sure."

Utsumi pulled over and stopped the car. She put on the hazard lights and turned to face Hiromi directly.

"What is it?" she asked, shrinking away from the detective.

"Ayane taught you how to make coffee at her house, yes?"

Hiromi nodded.

"Well, Ayane told Kusanagi that her husband was very health conscious, and never drank water directly from the tap. Mr. Mashiba had insisted that she always use bottled purified water, even for making coffee. Were you aware of that?"

Hiromi's eyes went wide and she blinked. "She *did* tell me about that. But she said not to worry about it too much."

"Oh?"

"Yes. She didn't think it was very economical to use so much bottled water, and besides it takes longer to boil that way. But she told me if Mr. Mashiba ever asked, I was to tell him I had been using bottled water." Hiromi put a hand to her cheek. "I completely forgot about all that!"

"So Ayane was using tap water, too?"

"Probably." Hiromi looked into Utsumi's eyes. "It didn't even occur to me to mention it when I was talking to the other detectives."

Utsumi nodded, smiling. "It's okay. Thank you." She turned off the hazard lights and released the brake.

"Could you tell me why it matters?" Hiromi asked. "Was there a problem with me using water from the tap?"

"Not a problem. But, since there's reason to suspect that Yoshitaka Mashiba was poisoned, we need to make sure we know every detail about what he ate on the day he died."

"I see . . ." Hiromi lowered her gaze, then looked back up at the detective. "Ms. Utsumi, you have to believe me. I really didn't do anything."

Utsumi swallowed, her eyes on the road. She was about to say *I believe you*, but instead she told her, "You're not the only suspect in this case. In fact, at this point, we have to suspect everyone in the world. If anyone ever told you police work was fun, they lied."

Hiromi fell silent.

Not the answer she was expecting.

Utsumi stopped her car by Gakugei Daigaku Station, not far from Hiromi's apartment. She watched as Hiromi got out and walked toward the apartment building. Then Utsumi glanced at the building itself, quickly turned off the engine, and got out of the car. Ayane Mashiba was waiting just inside the glass front door of Hiromi's apartment building.

Hiromi looked surprised to see her. As surprised as Utsumi was. Ayane gave her apprentice a consoling look; then she noticed Utsumi running over and her face hardened. Hiromi turned around and frowned.

"Is there something else?" she asked the detective as Ayane came out to join them.

"I just saw Mrs. Mashiba there and thought I should say hello," Utsumi said. "I'm sorry to have kept Hiromi at the station for so long." She bowed apologetically.

"I take it Hiromi is no longer a suspect?"

"She was very forthcoming with details. And I hear you provided very valuable information to Detective Kusanagi as well. Thank you."

"I hope it was helpful," Ayane said. "But I should think you have enough to go on without questioning her any further. Hiromi is innocent."

"I'm afraid that's a decision for us to make, Mrs. Mashiba. I hope we can count on your continued cooperation."

"I'll be happy to cooperate, but please leave the poor girl out of this."

Utsumi looked up, flustered by the harsh tone in the older woman's voice. This was not the Mrs. Mashiba she had seen on the night her husband's body was discovered.

Ayane turned to Hiromi. "You have to tell them the truth. You know that, right? If you keep things to yourself, no one will be able to protect you. You understand what I'm saying? It's not good for you to be holed up in that interrogation room for so long."

Utsumi noticed Hiromi's face tense at those words. *That hit a sore spot.* Suddenly, a light went off in her head. She stared at the younger woman. "Wait, you're not . . ."

"You might as well come clean now," Ayane broke in. "It looks like the lady detective has figured it out anyway, and if even *I* know—"

"Did . . . Mr. Mashiba tell you?" Hiromi asked.

"Not a word. But I am a woman, and I'm not blind."

The situation was now clear to all three, but Utsumi still had to hear it in words.

"Ms. Wakayama, are you pregnant?"

There was a pause, then Hiromi gave a slight nod. "Two months."

At the edge of Utsumi's vision, she saw Ayane twitch. *She really is hearing this for the first time. I guess woman's intuition does count for something.*

A moment later Ayane turned to Utsumi with an implacable look on her face. "I hope you're satisfied? Hiromi has to take care of herself. She can't be hanging out at the Police Station for hours on end. You're a woman. You understand."

Utsumi had no choice but to nod. The list of required precautions detectives had to observe when interrogating a pregnant suspect was long and detailed.

"I'll let my superiors know. I'm sure they'll be able to arrange something."

"I certainly hope so," Ayane said. She turned to Hiromi. "This is all for the best. If you had kept it hidden, you wouldn't even be able to go to the hospital."

Hiromi leaned toward Ayane, her lips trembling as though she were about to cry. Utsumi couldn't clearly make out what she said, but it sounded like "Thank you."

"There's another thing worth mentioning." Ayane squared off against the detective again. "The child's father is Yoshitaka Mashiba. There's no question of that. That was why he decided to separate from me and go to her. Now, let me ask you: what possible reason could she have to kill the father of her own child?"

Utsumi agreed, but she held her tongue. She wondered how the woman would take her lack of response.

Ayane shook her head. "It's a complete mystery to me what you detectives are thinking. She has no motive. If anyone has a motive here, it's me."

Utsumi returned to headquarters to find Kusanagi and Mamiya still there, sipping vending-machine coffee, frowns on their faces.

"What did Ms. Wakayama have to say about the water she used when she made the coffee?" Kusanagi asked Utsumi when he saw her. "You asked her, right?"

"She said she used tap water."

Utsumi related everything Hiromi had told her about that morning in the kitchen.

"Which is why nothing happened when they drank their morning coffee together," Mamiya concluded. "The poison still could've been in one of the bottles in the fridge."

"We can't know for sure she's telling the truth," Kusanagi put in.

"True, but as long as there aren't any glaring contradictions in what she's told us, we don't have much to follow up on. We'll just have to wait for Forensics to give us a little more dirt."

"Did you ask Forensics about the plastic bottles?" Utsumi asked.

Kusanagi picked up a report from his desk and scanned it. "They found only one bottle of water in the Mashibas' fridge. The seal on the cap was broken. The water inside was clean."

"Okay," Utsumi said. "What did you mean about waiting for more dirt?"

"The situation isn't quite so simple." Mamiya's lips curled into a frown.

"Oh?"

"They found a one-liter bottle in the fridge," Kusanagi continued with a glance at the papers in his hand. "But there were nine hundred milliliters of water left in it—only one hundred milliliters were gone. That's not enough to make even one cup of coffee, and there were enough grounds in the dripper for two."

"So there was another bottle of water in the fridge that's gone missing?" Utsumi asked.

Kusanagi nodded. "That's what it looks like."

"And it might've been poisoned?"

"Seems likely," Mamiya said. "Here's the scenario: The killer opens the refrigerator. They find two bottles—one open, one sealed. If they put poison in the brand-new one, they'd have to break the seal, which might alert the victim. So they poison the one that's already open. Now, when Mashiba goes to make his coffee, he takes the open bottle, uses it up, and tosses it. But that's not enough water for two cups of coffee, so he opens the other bottle and adds a little to the dripper, then puts it back in the fridge."

"So we need to look in the garbage—check the empties."

"Forensics did," Kusanagi said, shaking the report in his hand. "You'd think that'd be enough."

"It wasn't?"

"They went over every empty bottle they could find. No poison anywhere. But, they also couldn't prove that any of the bottles *weren't* used in the crime."

"What's that supposed to mean?"

"What it means is we're not really sure about anything yet," Mamiya said. "The trace amounts of water they got from the bottles didn't give them enough to test properly. Which I guess makes sense; they *were* empties, after all. They've sent them all to a different lab for further testing."

Utsumi nodded, finally understanding the frowns she'd seen when she walked into the room.

"Not that finding poison in one of the bottles would change our case much at this point," Kusanagi said, replacing the papers on his desk.

"It would widen the range of possible suspects," Utsumi said.

Kusanagi raised an eyebrow. "Were you listening to what the chief just said? If our killer put the poison in one of the plastic bottles, he or she would have put it in one that was already open. Which means there was an open bottle of water in the fridge that the victim *didn't* drink from until he made that final cup of coffee. Which means that not a lot of time passed between the poisoning of the water and the victim's death."

"I don't see why the victim not drinking from the water should indicate that not much time had passed. There were other things for him to drink besides bottled water if he got thirsty."

Kusanagi flared his nostrils in a sort of triumphant display. "You seem to have forgotten that Mr. Mashiba didn't just make coffee on Sunday night. According to Ms. Wakayama, he made his own coffee on Saturday night, too. That coffee was too strong, so she showed him how to make it the next morning, right? So we know that as late as Saturday night, there was no poison in that bottle."

"How do we know that Mr. Mashiba used water from one of the bottles when he made coffee on Saturday night?"

Kusanagi leaned back in his chair and spread his arms wide. "Are you suggesting we throw out our assumption that Mr. Mashiba demands bottled water for his coffee? His wife's statement to that effect is the whole reason we're talking about this at all."

"Not throw it out, exactly," Utsumi said, keeping her voice even. "I just think it's dangerous to assume what she told us is an absolute. We don't know how consistent Mr. Mashiba was about only using bottled water. It could've been a preference, not something he insisted on or even practiced with any kind of regularity. Maybe the whole bottled water thing started with an offhand comment that his wife took more seriously than he intended. Not to mention that it was the first time he had actually made coffee in a long while. I can imagine him using water from the tap without thinking about it. They did have a filtration system on their sink."

Kusanagi shook his head. "Twist reality to fit your guesswork too much and you'll break something, Detective."

"All I'm saying is, we have to judge the case based on objective facts." She turned to Mamiya. "As long as we don't know who last drank bottled water from that fridge safely, or when, we won't be able to determine when the poison was added."

Mamiya grinned, rubbing his chin. "You know," he said, "I like this kind of open discussion. At first I was firmly on Kusanagi's side, but as I listen to the two of you go on, I find myself slowly leaning toward the challenger's position."

"Chief!" Kusanagi looked a little wounded.

"However." Mamiya turned a stern gaze toward Utsumi. "We're not completely in the dark about the timing of the poisoning. You recall what took place on Friday night at the Mashiba house?"

"Of course. A dinner party," Utsumi replied. "During which several people in the house likely drank bottled water."

Mamiya raised his index finger. "So the water was poisoned after the party—or perhaps during it."

"I agree. However, I don't believe either of the Ikais would have had a chance to poison the bottle. For one thing, they were the guests; it would be difficult for either of them to go into the kitchen at all—let alone do their work in there undisturbed."

"Which leaves the two ladies as our suspects."

"Now just wait a minute," Kusanagi broke in. "I understand suspecting Hiromi Wakayama, but Mrs. Mashiba? She's the one who told us the victim used bottled water for his coffee. Why would she go out of her way to give us information that could incriminate her?"

"Because she knew we'd find out eventually?" Utsumi said. "If she suspected that, given enough time, poison would be found in one of the bottles, she could have told us in advance to deflect suspicion."

Kusanagi frowned. "Talking with you gives me a headache sometimes. Why are you so determined to make the wife the bad guy?"

"It sounds pretty logical to me," Mamiya said. "Utsumi's idea's as good as any we've got going right now. And there are serious problems with the assumption that Ms. Wakayama is the killer, most notably the fact that she didn't dispose of the tainted kettle. As far as motivation goes, Ayane Mashiba *is* the most logical suspect."

Kusanagi opened his mouth to protest, but Utsumi headed him off. "Speaking of motivation, I have some new information that strengthens the wife's motive for killing her husband."

"From whom?" Mamiya asked.

"Hiromi Wakayama."

Frowns became looks of complete astonishment as Utsumi began to explain.

TWELVE

"Hold on—" Tatsuhiko Ikai lowered his cell phone and picked up the ringing phone on his desk, launching immediately into another conversation. "What?—Yes. That's why I want you to take care of it—all of it. I think that was made pretty clear in the second clause of the contract . . . Yes, I'll handle that part, of course . . . Right. Thanks." He put down the receiver and lifted the cell phone back to his ear. "Sorry. I just talked to them . . . Right. Just like we discussed at the meeting . . . Got it."

At last the phones were silent. Ikai began scribbling a memo, still standing over his desk—the CEO's desk—which until recently had belonged to Yoshitaka Mashiba.

Only when he had stuffed the memo in his pocket did Ikai look over at Kusanagi, who was sitting on a nearby sofa. "Sorry to keep you waiting."

"No problem. You seem pretty busy."

"It's all details, really. Yes, we lost our CEO, but from the way they're acting, you'd think all of our section directors had their heads cut off. I always had misgivings about Mashiba's one-man-show style of management. I only wish we'd done something about it sooner," Ikai concluded as he joined Kusanagi on the sofa.

"Will you continue as CEO?"

The lawyer waved the suggestion away. "I'm not fit for management. I'm a firm believer that everyone is born to do a specific job, and me—I'm at my best pulling the strings behind the scenes. I will happily leave that big desk to someone else." Ikai looked the detective in the eye. "Don't think I killed Mashiba to take over his company, because, believe me, I don't want it."

Kusanagi's eyes widened and Ikai laughed. "I'm sorry, that was a joke. Not very funny, I'm afraid. I've been too busy to let it sink in that he's gone."

"I'm sorry to take up more of your time," Kusanagi said.

"Don't be. I'm interested in how the investigation is proceeding. Any new developments?"

"Some things are coming into focus, I guess you could say. In particular, the route by which the poison got into the coffee."

"That's interesting."

"Were you aware that Mr. Mashiba was excessively health conscious to the point of not drinking tap water?"

Ikai raised an eyebrow. "I wouldn't call that *excessive*. I don't drink tap water, either. Haven't for years."

"Oh?" Kusanagi asked. *Rich people.* "Any particular reason?"

"Not really, now that you mention it," Ikai said, his gaze wandering back to the desk. "I can't even remember when I stopped. It wasn't that tap water tastes bad. Maybe I'm the victim of some bottled water company's advertising campaign? But once you fall into a pattern . . ." He looked sharply back up. "The water was poisoned?"

"We don't have a definitive answer yet, but it's a possibility. Did you drink any mineral water when you visited the Mashibas Friday night?"

"We did. Quite a bit of it. Poisoned water, huh?"

"We've been led to understand that Mr. Mashiba used bottled water when he made coffee. Were you aware of this?"

"I suppose so." Ikai nodded. "So that's how the poison got into the grounds."

"The question is: when exactly did the killer poison the water? I was wondering if you could think of anyone who might've visited the Mashibas over the weekend, possibly in secret?"

Ikai shot the detective a sharp look. "In secret?"

"Yes. Unfortunately we haven't been able to identify any visitors. But it's probable that someone did visit during those two days—perhaps even with Mr. Mashiba's knowledge."

"You're asking me if another woman came to see him while his wife was away?"

"That's one possibility, yes."

Ikai uncrossed his legs and leaned forward. "Let's be frank, Detective. I understand that you have to keep some aspects of your investigation a secret—I'm not new to criminal inquiries. So I assure you, anything you say stays here. In return, I won't hold anything back."

Kusanagi raised an eybrow and remained silent.

Ikai leaned back on the sofa. "You've found out that Mashiba had a lover."

The detective kept his expression neutral. "How much do you know?" he asked.

"He confessed to me about a month ago. Said he was thinking about making a 'change in partners.' It occurred to me he might already have someone on the side." A gleam came into the man's eyes. "Surely you have the resources to figure out something as obvious as that. Which you have, which is why you're here talking to me. Isn't it?"

Kusanagi chuckled. "Well, yes. Mr. Mashiba was seeing someone."

"I won't ask who it was, though one obvious candidate comes to mind."

"You noticed something?"

"It was simply a process of elimination. Mashiba wasn't the type to hit on girls at a bar. And he was a firm believer in keeping business and romance separate. Which would leave only one woman conveniently available." Ikai shook his head. "I still have trouble believing it. Better not tell my wife!"

"We have it from the woman in question that she visited the Mashibas' house on the weekend he died. What we need to determine is whether he was seeing anyone else."

"You mean you're wondering if he took advantage of his wife's absence to invite over *multiple* lovers? What a Casanova!" Ikai slapped his knee. "But I'd have to say, I really doubt it. Mashiba might've been a chain-smoker, but he wasn't the type to smoke two cigarettes at once."

"By which you mean?"

"He might've gone from one woman to the next, but he wasn't a two-timer. I'm willing to bet that once he started seeing this new woman, he even neglected his 'nightly duties' with his wife. In fact, I recall him once saying that sex 'for pleasure's sake' could wait until later."

"So he was mainly interested in procreation?"

"Dedicated to it, you might say," Ikai said, his lips curling upward into a smile.

Sounds like his dedication paid off, Kusanagi thought. "Would you say having children was his primary reason for getting married?"

Ikai stretched out expansively. "Not even primary. It was his *only* reason. He's been talking about having kids—and the sooner the better—since his bachelor days. It was all about finding the perfect mother for his children. And he did his research, earning a bit of a reputation as a playboy in the process, too. But believe me, he wasn't playing around. He just wanted to be sure he got the right one."

"What about finding the perfect wife? Doesn't that come first?"

Ikai shrugged. "I'm pretty sure he wasn't actually that interested in a wife at all. 'I need a woman who can bear me children,' he told me, 'not some household manager or expensive trophy.'"

Kusanagi's eyes widened. "Trophy . . . ? I can imagine how most women would react to that."

"No kidding. Actually, that was what he said to me when I praised Ayane's devotion to him. She was the perfect wife, you know. Utterly dedicated to him. Whenever he was home, she would sit there on the living room sofa, doing her patchwork, ready to serve if he needed anything. Not that he ever appreciated her. To him, a woman who couldn't bear children was no more useful than a trophy on the wall—just taking up space."

"Nice. I take it Mr. Mashiba wasn't much of a feminist. Why was he so obsessed with having kids?"

"I can't say. I mean, I wanted kids, too, but I wasn't pathological about it. Of course, once you actually have a kid, you can't think of much else." Ikai allowed himself the warm smile of a new father; then his mouth straightened and he continued. "I would guess it had something to do with his upbringing."

"Really? What about it?"

"Did you know that Mashiba didn't have any family growing up?"

"I heard. But tell me what you know."

Ikai nodded. "Well, Mashiba's parents divorced when he was an infant. The father got custody, but he was a real workaholic who was hardly ever home. So Mashiba was mostly raised by his grandmother. Then, tragedy struck. His grandmother died, followed by his father a short time later. His father was still in his twenties, but he developed something called a subarachnoid hemorrhage, and was gone in the blink of an eye. Mashiba was left all by himself. He got a decent inheritance, and he started working in his teens, so he didn't want for much—but he pretty much missed out on what you'd call familial love."

"And he wanted to make up for that with kids of his own?"

"He probably wanted someone close to him by blood—true kin. After all," Ikai added coldly, "no matter how much you love your girlfriend or your wife, genetically she's a total stranger."

It occurred to Kusanagi that Ikai might share Mashiba's outlook to some degree. Which made his take on the deceased's psychology all the more convincing.

"I heard the other day that you were there when Mr. Mashiba met Ayane. At a party, was it?"

"Yes. It was a social gathering for people from various different industries—a matchmaking shindig for successful professionals, really. I was already married, but Mashiba invited me along so I went with him. He said he was obliged to go because of a client. Of course, he ended up meeting his wife there. It just goes to show that you never know what life will bring. I suppose the timing was good, too."

"How's that?" Kusanagi asked.

A slight shadow passed over Ikai's face. *He said more than he intended*, Kusagani thought.

"He was seeing someone before he met Ayane," the lawyer said after a moment. "The party was right after they split up. I think having just hit a dead end gave him a sense of urgency. Maybe that's what pushed him to actually seal the deal." He laid a finger to his lips. "Please don't tell Ayane. Mashiba made me swear not to say anything."

"Do you know why he broke up with the other woman?"

Ikai shrugged. "We had an unspoken agreement not to get too involved in that sort of personal matter. If I had to guess, though, I'd say he probably found out the other girl didn't want children, or couldn't have them."

"But they weren't married yet."

"At the risk of repeating myself, children were literally the most important thing to him. In fact, marriage after conception— the classic shotgun wedding—would probably have been preferable."

So he switched to Ayane and then to Hiromi . . .

Kusanagi considered himself a good judge of people in all their varieties, but he was having trouble understanding Yoshitaka Mashiba. Ayane seemed like a loving woman, and certainly not a bad match for a man like Mashiba. Why couldn't he have been happy just with her?

"What sort of person was she, the girl Mashiba was seeing before?"

Ikai shrugged again. "I don't really know. I never met her.

Mashiba was a man who liked to keep secrets. He might have decided not to introduce her until he was sure he was going to marry her."

"Did the breakup go smoothly?" Kusanagi asked.

"Smoothly enough. Though we never talked about it at any length." Ikai looked at the detective quizzically. "You don't think she might somehow be involved in his death?"

Kusanagi shook his head. "Nothing like that. We just need to know as much as possible about the victim."

Ikai chuckled and waved a hand. "If you're thinking that Mashiba might've invited his ex-girlfriend over, I'd say you're barking up the wrong tree. I can say with total confidence that that's not his style. Not at all."

"Because he never smoked two cigarettes at the same time, was it?"

"Precisely." Ikai nodded.

"I'll take that into consideration." Kusanagi glanced at his watch, then rose to his feet. "Thanks for your time."

Kusanagi was headed for the exit; but Ikai hurried past him, opened the door, and stood waiting beside it.

"Er . . . Thanks."

"Detective Kusanagi," Ikai said, a serious look in his eyes. "I don't mean to comment on the way you're conducting your investigation, but there is one request I'd like to make if possible."

"What's that?"

"Mashiba didn't exactly lead the life of a saint. Keep looking under stones and you're sure to find some dirt. But if you want my opinion, I don't think his death the other day has anything to do with his past. If you can, I'd rather you didn't dig too deeply. It's a sensitive time for the company."

Worried about the company's public image? "Even if we do dig something up, I promise we won't go telling it to the press," Kusanagi said, then slipped out the door.

He headed for the elevators, a sense of vague disgust toward the deceased growing inside him. *So women were nothing more to him than baby factories!* He was surprised at his own anger.

What if Mashiba had applied the same kind of thinking to everyone in his life? Were employees nothing more to him than gears to keep his company moving, consumers no more than targets for exploitation? It was easy to imagine how many casualties the man had left by the side of the road during his lifetime. It certainly wouldn't be surprising if more than one person wanted him dead.

Of course, Hiromi Wakayama wasn't entirely free from suspicion yet—though Ayane did have a point: there seemed to be no motive for her to kill the father of her unborn child. Yet based on what Kusanagi had just heard, it seemed dangerous to assume anything when it came to women and Yoshitaka Mashiba. The deceased intended to leave his wife and go to Hiromi, but only because she was pregnant, not necessarily because he loved her. Who knew what kind of selfish proposal he might've made to the girl and earned her hatred?

Still, as Utsumi had pointed out, it wouldn't make much sense for the first one on the scene to leave traces of poison lying around if she had actually committed the murder. Kusanagi had no rebuttal to that argument; "maybe she just forgot" wasn't going to fly.

The detective decided to see what he could discover about the woman Mashiba was dating before he met Ayane. As he left the building, Kusanagi was contemplating where to begin.

———

Ayane Mashiba's eyes went wide. Kusanagi detected the wave of surprise in her pupils.

"His ex-girlfriend?"

"Another sensitive subject, I know." The detective bowed his head apologetically.

The two sat in the lounge of the hotel where Ayane was staying. Kusanagi had called her to arrange the meeting.

"Does that have something to do with your investigation?"

"Well—we can't say for certain yet. But because there's a very high likelihood your husband was murdered, we need to track down everyone with a probable motive. We're just covering all the bases."

The rigid line of Ayane's lips softened and a lonely smile came to her face. "Well, knowing my husband, I'm sure that the end of her relationship with him was as abrupt and inconsiderate as the end of mine."

"Er . . ." Kusanagi hesitated. "It's our understanding that your husband was . . . primarily searching for a woman to bear him children. Men like this have a tendency to focus too much on the goal at the expense of the partner. We wondered if a previous partner who'd also been spurned might still bear him some ill will."

"Like I do?"

"I wasn't suggesting that—"

"No, it's all right." Ayane took a careful breath. "What was the lady detective's name? Ms. Utsumi? I'm sure you heard from her that Hiromi was successful in fulfilling my late husband's 'goal,' as you put it. That's why he chose her, and discarded me. I would be lying if I said I didn't bear him ill will because of that."

"But it would have been impossible for you to commit the crime."

"You sound so sure."

"Nothing's been found in any of the plastic water bottles, so it seems most likely that the poison was put directly into the water in the kettle. You couldn't have done that. So . . . the only possible answer is that someone came over on Sunday and put the poison in the kettle. It's unlikely that they entered without your husband's knowledge, so we can assume whoever it was came by invitation. We checked his work contacts, and found no likely leads there. That leaves someone close to your husband, whom he invited over in secret—which suggests a very specific sort of relationship."

"A lover or former lover?" She brushed aside her bangs. "Well, I'd love to help you, but I'm afraid he never spoke about such things to me. Not even once."

"Not even a suggestion? No detail is too small, Mrs. Mashiba."

She shrugged. "He wasn't the kind of man who talked about his past. He was very circumspect in that regard. He even made a point of never going to any restaurants or bars he had frequented with previous girlfriends."

"I see," Kusanagi said, frowning inwardly. He'd been planning on following up by asking around at the restaurants the Mashibas had frequented.

Yoshitaka Mashiba certainly was a cautious man. They hadn't caught so much as the scent of a woman other than Hiromi from any of the personal effects he'd left behind at his home and office. All of the numbers on his cell phone were either work contacts or male friends. He hadn't even entered Hiromi's number.

"I'm sorry I couldn't be of more help."

"There's no need to apologize."

"But—" Ayane broke off her next sentence when her phone

rang in her handbag. She quickly took it out, then hesitated. "Do you mind if I answer it?"

"Of course not," Kusanagi said.

"Hello? Ayane speaking."

She began the conversation calmly, but a moment later, her eyebrows twitched and she glanced tensely at Kusanagi. "Of course, I don't mind. But what are you—Oh, I see. All right. Thank you." She hung up the phone, then put her hand to her mouth, her lips forming an *oh*. "Maybe I should have mentioned you were here?"

"Who was it?"

"Detective Utsumi."

"What did she have to say?"

"That she wanted to examine the kitchen again, and wondered if it would be all right to go inside the house. She said she wouldn't be long."

"Reexamining the kitchen? What's she up to?" Kusanagi muttered, giving his chin a scratch.

"Perhaps finding another way the poison could have gotten into the coffee?"

"That would be the most obvious answer." Kusanagi looked at his watch, then reached for the bill on the table. "I think I'll join her, if you don't mind."

"Not at all," Ayane said. Then she looked up. "Actually, I have a request."

"Yes?"

"I know this isn't really your job as a detective, but . . ."

"Don't worry about that. What is it?"

She smiled. "I was just thinking that it's time to water the flowers at home. When I left, I assumed I would only be here for a day or two at most."

"I'm sorry for the inconvenience," Kusanagi said. "And I think you should be able to move back into your house any time now. Forensics is done, and our reexamination should be finished today. I'll let you know."

"No, that's all right. I think I'd prefer to stay here for now, actually. It's . . . hard to imagine being alone in that big house."

"I can understand."

"I know I can't just run away from the truth forever, but all things being equal, I think I'll stay here at least until the date of the funeral is set."

"On that note . . . we should be able to return the remains to you shortly."

"Thank you. I suppose that means I should be making arrangements . . ." Ayane blinked. "About the flowers at the house—I was planning on watering them when I went there tomorrow to pick up some more things. But the sooner the better. I know it sounds silly, but it's been weighing on my mind."

Kusanagi smiled. "Don't worry about a thing. I'll be happy to water the flowers for you. The garden as well as the ones on the balcony, correct?"

"You're sure you don't mind? I hate forcing anyone to do my chores."

"It's the least we can do in return for all of your assistance. I'm sure I can find someone else to take care of it if I can't, so don't worry about a thing."

Kusanagi rose and Ayane stood with him. She stared into his eyes. "It would be a shame if the flowers there were to wither," she said, an unexpected softness slipping into her voice.

"I understand they're very important to you." Kusanagi recalled how she had watered them the day she got back from Sapporo.

"I've been keeping those flowers on the balcony since before I got married. Each one of them brings back a different memory . . ."

Ayane's gaze wandered into the distance before returning to the detective. The look in her eyes tugged at something in Kusanagi's chest, and he found himself unable to meet her stare. "I'll be sure to water them. Don't worry." He turned and went to pay the bill.

Out in front of the hotel he caught a taxi and headed over to the Mashiba residence. The expression on Ayane's face as he left her still burned in the back of his mind.

Kusanagi let his gaze wander outside the window until he spotted a large sign for a home repair center. A thought came to him, and he told the driver to stop.

"Wait for me here."

Kusanagi hurried into the store, then returned to the taxi with a spring in his step.

A police cruiser was parked outside the Mashiba house. *Just what she needs*, Kusanagi thought. *More for the neighbors to talk about.*

A uniformed officer was standing next to the front gate, the same one who'd been stationed at the house the day Mashiba died. He acknowledged the detective with a silent nod.

Kusanagi spotted three pairs of shoes in the entrance way. The sneakers belonged to Utsumi. The other two pairs were men's shoes: one pair cheap and worn nearly to the ground, the other new and bearing an Armani logo.

He walked down the hallway toward the living room. The door was open; he stepped inside and found the room empty. A man's voice sounded from the kitchen.

"I'm not seeing any signs this was touched at all."

"Right?" Utsumi's voice answered. "Forensics said the same thing, that no one had touched it for at least a year."

Kusanagi peeked into the next room. Utsumi was standing in front of the sink, a man kneeling next to her. He had his face stuck into the cabinet beneath the basin, so Kusanagi couldn't see who he was. Kishitani was standing next to them.

It was Kishitani who noticed the new arrival first. "Hey, Detective Kusanagi."

Utsumi turned around, a flustered look on her face.

"What are you doing?" Kusanagi asked.

She blinked. "Why are you . . ."

"Answer me first. I asked what you're doing here."

"Is that really the tone to take with someone so devoted to their work?" came the voice of the man beneath the sink. He extracted himself and looked around.

Kusanagi took a step back, startled. "Yukawa!? What are you—" He stopped and looked back at Utsumi. "You were talking to him behind my back, weren't you?"

Utsumi bit her lip.

"Well, that's an odd thing to say. Does she need permission from you before she talks to everyone, or am I a special case?" Yukawa stood and smiled at the detective. "Long time no see. You look well."

"I thought you weren't helping with investigations anymore."

"As a rule, I'm not. But every rule has its exceptions. For instance, when I'm presented with a mystery that piques my scientific curiosity. Although, I will admit that this particular case interests me for other reasons as well . . . but I see no need to go into that with you," Yukawa added with a meaningful glance at Utsumi.

Kusanagi looked at the female detective. "Is this what you meant by a reexamination? Bringing him in?"

Utsumi's mouth opened halfway in surprise. "Mrs. Mashiba told you?"

"I was with her when you called. Oh, I almost forgot. Kishitani, you don't look like you're doing much."

Kishitani stiffened. "I was asked to accompany Utsumi and the professor, so we wouldn't miss anything."

"Great. Then, in the interest of thoroughness, go water the flowers."

"Water?" Kishitani blinked several times. "Flowers?"

"Mrs. Mashiba has vacated the premises of her own accord to make our investigation as easy as possible. We can at least water the flowers for her. Just get the ones in the garden. I'll take care of the balcony."

Kishitani frowned, his eyebrows drawing together for a moment, before he nodded and walked out of the kitchen.

Kusanagi turned back to Utsumi and the physicist. "So, sorry to make you go over this again, but can you tell me exactly what it is you're reexamining? Start from the beginning." He set down the paper bag he'd been carrying.

"What is that, anyway?" Utsumi asked with a glance at the bag.

"It's not related to the case so it's nothing for you to worry about. Well?" Kusanagi crossed his arms and looked at Yukawa.

Yukawa hitched his thumbs in the pockets of his pants—*Armani too, no doubt*, the detective surmised—and leaned back against the sink. He was wearing gloves. "The young detective here presented me with a puzzle: 'Is it possible to poison the drink of a specific person from a distance, using a method that leaves no trace?' Quite the mystery, right? Even in physics it's hard to find problems as worth solving as that." He shrugged.

"From a distance, huh?" Kusanagi said with a glare at Utsumi. "You still suspect the wife. You've decided that she's the one, and you want Yukawa to tell you what kind of magic trick she had to pull off in order to do it."

"It's not just Mrs. Mashiba that I suspect. I just want to be sure that no one with an alibi for Saturday and Sunday could have done it."

"Same difference. You're after her." Kusanagi looked back at Yukawa. "So why were you looking beneath the sink?"

"According to what Ms. Utsumi here has told me, the poison in question was found in three locations." Yukawa lifted three fingers of his gloved hand. "The victim's coffee cup. The ground coffee beans and filter used to make the coffee. And last but not least, the kettle used to boil the water. But what I can't figure out is what comes next. There are two possibilities: the poison was either inserted directly into the kettle, or it was mixed with water. If it was mixed with the water, we have another two possibilities: bottled water or water from the tap."

"Tap water? Are you suggesting that the water line was poisoned?" Kusanagi asked with a snort.

Yukawa's expression did not change as he continued. "When multiple possibilities exist, the most logical course of action is to use a process of elimination. Forensics tells us that nothing was amiss with the water line or the filtration system, but I like seeing things for myself. Thus my expedition under the sink here. If you were going to do anything to the water line, that's where you would have to do it."

"Find anything?"

Yukawa slowly shook his head. "No signs of anything unusual on the water line, the connector for the filtration system, or the filter itself. It might be worthwhile to take the whole thing apart and examine the inside, but I'm guessing we would still come up empty-handed. This leads me to conclude that if the water was poisoned before the coffee was made, it was water from a bottle."

"But no poison was found in any of the empty bottles."

"We're still waiting on a further report from the lab," Utsumi reminded him.

"They won't find anything. Our Forensics unit does good work," Kusanagi said, uncrossing his arms and putting his hands on his hips. He looked at Yukawa. "What's your conclusion, then? For all your effort, leaving your ivory tower and trekking all the way out here, you've got precious little to show."

"We've covered the water; next comes the kettle. Didn't I just say the poison could have been put directly into the kettle?"

"That's what I've been saying," Kusanagi replied. "But we know that there was nothing in the kettle as of Sunday morning. If we're to believe Hiromi Wakayama's testimony."

Without answering, Yukawa reached out and picked up a kettle that sat beside the sink.

"What's that?" Kusanagi asked. "You brought your own kettle?"

"This is the same brand of kettle as the one Mr. Mashiba used. Ms. Utsumi requisitioned it at my request." Yukawa poured hot water from the tap into the kettle, which he then emptied into the sink. "Nothing special, no tricks, just a regular kettle."

He refilled the vessel with water and lit the gas stove.

"What are you doing now?"

"Watch and learn," Yukawa said, leaning nonchalantly on

the edge of the sink. "So: you're thinking our killer came here on Sunday and put poison into the kettle?"

"I don't see any other explanation."

"That seems like an awfully risky strategy. They must have been sure that Mr. Mashiba wouldn't tell anyone they were coming. Or is your hypothesis that Mr. Mashiba stepped out for a moment and they snuck in?"

"Breaking and entering seems unlikely. I'm thinking the killer knew that Mr. Mashiba wasn't the type to talk about his guests."

"I see. So this guest wasn't someone he wanted the neighbors to know about, then." Yukawa nodded and turned to Utsumi. "You don't have to worry. Your boss is still capable of rational thought."

Kusanagi scowled. "What's that supposed to mean?"

"Nothing in particular. I was just making the point that, if both parties are rational, then any difference of opinion is probably a good thing."

There he goes again—that charming way of making me feel like a complete idiot. Kusanagi glared at the physicist. Yukawa grinned, completely unperturbed.

The water in the kettle came to a gradual boil. Yukawa turned off the stove, opened the lid, and looked inside. "Exactly what I was looking for," he said, tipping the kettle over the sink.

When Kusanagi saw the liquid spilling out into the sink he almost jumped. The water was bright red.

"Is this some kind of joke?"

Yukawa placed the kettle in the sink and turned toward Kusanagi with a smile. "When I said there were no tricks, I lied. There was red powder in the bottom of the kettle, covered with a layer of gelatin. As the water boiled, the gelatin gradually dissolved, allowing the powder and water to mix." His smile faded and he nodded toward Utsumi. "Am I correct in my understanding that the kettle was used at least two times before the victim died?"

"Yes," Utsumi replied. "On Saturday night and Sunday morning."

"By adjusting the type and amount of gelatin, it is theoretically possible to keep the poison from getting into the liquid until the third time the water is used. You might want to have Forensics look into that. They should also consider where on the kettle the gelatin was placed. Oh, and they'll also want to consider alternatives to gelatin."

"Right," Utsumi said, making a memo in her book.

"What's wrong, Kusanagi?" Yukawa chided. "You look unhappy."

"My happiness has nothing to do with it. I was just wondering whether your average murderer would use such an elaborate method of poisoning."

"Elaborate method? There's nothing elaborate about it. Anyone who has any familiarity with gelatin would have no trouble doing something like this. Say, for instance, a wife who fancied herself a good cook."

Kusanagi began grinding his molars—a bad habit he had developed in moments of stress. It was becoming clear that the physicist, too, suspected Ayane Mashiba. *What has Utsumi been putting in his head?*

Just then the junior detective's cell phone rang. She answered it, said a few words, then looked up at Kusanagi. "A report from the lab. You were right—they didn't find anything in the empties."

THIRTEEN

"We will now observe a moment of silence."

Hiromi closed her eyes and bowed her head at the emcee's announcement. The Beatles' song "The Long and Winding Road" filled the room, nearly making her gasp. Yoshitaka was a Beatles fan and had often played their CDs in the car. This was one of his favorite songs, with its slow rhythm and poignant melody. *Ayane's choice, no doubt*, Hiromi thought bitterly. The mood of the song fit the occasion far too perfectly.

Hiromi felt a tightening in her chest, and tears she thought had long run dry began to spill from her closed eyes. How could she not remember him? Yet she knew she mustn't be seen crying here. *What would people think if they saw me, the deceased's wife's assistant, crying my eyes out? What would Ayane think?*

After the moment of silence, there was a presentation of flowers. The guests approached the altar in order and laid their bouquets in a pile. Yoshitaka hadn't been a religious man; the church ceremony was Ayane's choice. She stood beside the altar, keeping her head bowed as people shuffled forward.

The police had released the body to the funeral home the day before, and Tatsuhiko Ikai had made the arrangements for the ceremony as soon as he received word. This presentation of flowers took the place of a traditional wake; the company would hold a more formal, upscale ceremony the following day.

Now it was Hiromi's turn. She took her flowers from the attendant waiting in the aisle and laid them at the altar. Then she looked up at the photo of the deceased and pressed her hands together in prayer. In the photo, Yoshitaka was smiling, looking tan and fit.

Hiromi struggled to hold back a fresh wave of tears. Her stomach gave a sudden brutal lurch. *Morning sickness.* She unclasped her hands and pressed them to her mouth.

Nauseous, she turned to leave; her eyes met Ayane's and she stiffened. Ayane's face was devoid of emotion as she stared down at her. Hiromi bowed quickly and began to walk past her.

"Hiromi?" Ayane called out in a soft voice. "Are you okay?"

"I'm fine, thanks," Hiromi managed.

Ayane nodded and turned back toward the altar.

Hiromi left the room. *I need to get out of here.* She hurried for the exit, but she had just reached the door when someone touched her on the shoulder from behind. It was Yukiko Ikai.

"Oh . . . h-hello."

"Poor dear." Yukiko sighed. "You've had a rough time. With the police asking you all those questions . . ." Though her expression was one of genuine concern, Hiromi detected a glimmer of curiosity in the woman's eyes.

"It's over now," Hiromi told her.

"You have to wonder what those detectives are doing, anyway. I hear they don't even have a suspect yet."

"I know," Hiromi agreed.

"My husband was saying he hoped they solved the case quickly, before the company's clients start worrying. I hear Ayane's not going back home until they figure it all out—which I completely understand, by the way. Talk about creepy."

Hiromi nodded and mumbled agreement.

"Hey," said Tatsuhiko Ikai, walking toward them. "What are you two doing out here? There's food and drink in the guest hall."

"Oh?" his wife replied. "Well, Hiromi, shall we?"

"No, I think I'm fine, thanks."

"You should come! You'll be waiting for Ayane anyway, won't you? With all those people in there, she won't be getting out for a while."

"No," Hiromi insisted, "actually, I'm leaving early today."

"Oh, you should come, just for a little while. Keep me company."

"Don't be so pushy," Mr. Ikai said, frowning. "Other people have lives, too, you know."

Something in the way he said "lives" sent a chill down Hiromi's spine. Ikai stared coolly at her for a moment before looking away.

"I'm sorry. Maybe next time . . . Excuse me." Hiromi nodded to the couple and turned to leave without looking up. *He knows about me and Yoshitaka,* she thought. *Ayane wouldn't have told him. Maybe he heard it from the police?* She guessed that he hadn't told Yukiko, at least. *What must he think of me?*

Hiromi's thoughts churned. What was going to happen to

her? People were bound to learn the truth about her and Yoshi-taka eventually. And once they did, she couldn't remain so close to Ayane. She would eventually have to distance herself from the social circle that had once included the Mashibas.

I doubt she's really forgiven me, anyway. She probably never will.

The look Ayane had given her by the altar was seared into her memory. She regretted putting her hands over her mouth when she went up to offer her flowers. Of course Ayane knew what that meant. *Why else would she ask if I was okay?*

If she and Mashiba had merely had a fling, maybe Ayane could have forgiven her. *Dirty water under the bridge.* But a pregnancy changed all of that.

Sure, her boss probably suspected the truth; but suspecting something and hearing it from your husband's lover's mouth were two different things. It had already been several days since Hiromi admitted she was pregnant in front of Detective Utsumi. Since then, Ayane hadn't spoken a word about it. *Her feelings toward me must've changed since that time in the hotel room,* Hiromi thought, but she wasn't sure exactly how.

Thinking about the future made her head swim. *What do I do?*

She knew she should have an abortion. What kind of home could she provide for the child? The father was already dead, and Hiromi was on the brink of losing her job. She doubted that Ayane would give her any more work if she chose to keep the child.

The more she thought about it, the more she realized she didn't have a choice—and yet it seemed an impossible decision to make. Maybe it was the love she still felt for Yoshitaka that made her unwilling to let go of this last remnant of him. Maybe it was something more primal, a female need to bear a child. She wasn't sure.

Either way, there wasn't much time. She had at most two weeks left to decide.

She was walking away from the funeral hall, looking for a taxi, when she heard a voice call out, "Ms. Wakayama?"

She looked over her shoulder and frowned. Detective Kusanagi was making his way down the sidewalk toward her.

"I was looking for you—are you headed home?"

"Yes. I'm a bit tired."

Hiromi figured the man must know about her pregnancy by now. She considered telling him to leave her alone, so as not to place undue strain on her at such a delicate time.

"I know you're tired, and I'm really sorry, but I was hoping for a word or two? It will only take a few minutes, I promise."

Hiromi stopped trying to hide her displeasure. "Now? Must you?"

"Yes. I'm really sorry."

"Do I have to go to the station again?"

"No, any place we can talk quietly is fine." Without waiting for her to answer, the detective hailed a cab.

Kusanagi told the driver to take them to restaurant near Hiromi's apartment. *Maybe he really will let me go soon*, she thought with relief.

They took a table in the back of the nearly empty restaurant.

Tea and coffee were self-service at this place, and Hiromi, not wanting to get up, ordered milk. Kusanagi ordered hot cocoa.

"Luckily, these places are mostly nonsmoking these days. I thought that might be better for you," the detective said with a pleasant smile.

Hiromi was sure the comment was made to indicate that he knew about her condition; but despite his discretion, her own inner debate about the pregnancy made the remark feel harsh and insensitive.

"What did you want to ask me?" she said, looking down at the table.

"Of course, you're tired. I'll skip the small talk." Kusanagi leaned forward. "I want to know about Yoshitaka Mashiba's female relations."

Hiromi looked up. "What do you mean by that?"

"Well . . . was he seeing any other women? Other than you, I mean?"

Hiromi straightened in her chair and blinked. She felt her head spinning. "Why would you ask me that?"

"Was there another woman?"

"Are you asking me because you heard there was?" Hiromi countered, her voice sharp.

Kusanagi smiled wanly and waved a hand. "No, we haven't heard anything concrete. It just seemed like a possibility, which is why I wanted to ask you."

"Then I'm sorry but I don't know. And I don't know why you'd think there was someone else."

Kusanagi's smile faded and he clasped his hands together, resting them on the table. "As you know," he said, "Mr. Mashiba was poisoned. From the specific circumstances of the poisoning, the killer had to be someone who had access to the Mashiba house on the day he died. That makes you the prime suspect."

"I've already told you, I didn't—"

"I understand." Kusanagi cut her off. "But if it wasn't you, then who else? Who else had access to the house? We've looked into Mr. Mashiba's work connections and his private life, and haven't found a single likely person. This leads us to think that there might've been someone—someone else—with whom Mr. Mashiba had a secret relationship."

Hiromi finally understood what the detective was driving at, but she couldn't bring herself to acknowledge it. The whole idea was completely ridiculous.

"Detective, I think you have him all wrong. He may have done and said some outrageous things, and he did have a relationship with me, so I can understand why you might suspect him of being less than morally upright—but he was no playboy. He was very serious about his relationships, including with me."

Hiromi had intended to sound strong and decisive, to put the detective in his place, but Kusanagi's expression barely changed.

"So you didn't suspect the presence of any other woman in his life?"

"No. Not at all."

"What about any ex-girlfriends? Do you know anything about them?"

"Ex-girlfriends? You mean people he saw before getting married? I know there were a few, but he never talked much about them."

"Do you remember anything at all? About what they did for work, or where he met them?"

Hiromi frowned, sifting back through her memories. Yoshitaka had said a few things about the women he used to see—and one or two of them still lingered in her mind.

"He did say something about being with a woman in publishing once."

"Publishing? Like, an editor?"

"No. A writer, I think."

"A novelist? Something like that?"

Hiromi shrugged. "I'm not sure. All he said was that whenever she put out a book, he would always have to give her his opinion, and he couldn't stand doing that. I asked him what kind of books they were, but he avoided the topic. He didn't like talking about his exes, so I didn't push him on it ."

"Anything else?"

"He did say he was never drawn to prostitutes or performers. He didn't like those matchmaking parties where the organizers would slip in a few models to drum up interest. That was a turn-off for him."

"But he met his wife at a party like that?"

"So I hear," Hiromi said, lowering her eyes.

"Did you ever get the sense that he was still in contact with any of his exes?"

"Not as far as I was aware." Hiromi looked up at the detective. "Do you think some old flame might've killed him?"

"It's a possibility, which is why I'd like you to try and remember anything you can. Men tend to be less guarded about their relationships than women. Perhaps he let something slip in the middle of some other conversation?"

"I'm sorry," Hiromi said, pulling her cup of milk toward her. "I don't remember much else." She took a sip, wishing she had gotten tea instead. Picking up a napkin to wipe her lips seemed an impossibly onerous task.

Then an old memory surfaced, and she met the detective's stare.

"What is it?" he asked.

"Yoshitaka always drank coffee, but he was very knowledgeable about tea, too. I asked him about it once, and he said it was because of one of his exes. She was a real tea lover, and always bought her tea from the same store. A specialty place in Nihon-bashi, I'm pretty sure."

Kusanagi scribbled a note on his memo pad. "Do you remember the name of the store?"

"No. Sorry. He might not even have told me."

"A tea specialty store, then," Kusanagi muttered, frowning slightly.

"I'm sorry I can't give you more."

"Not at all." Kusanagi smiled again. "This is quite a lot to go on, actually. We asked Mrs. Mashiba the same questions and didn't get anything from her. Maybe he felt more comfortable talking with you than with his actual wife."

The detective's comment irritated Hiromi. Maybe he'd intended to be comforting, but he was an idiot if he thought it could possibly make her feel better.

"Are we done here?" she asked. "I'd really like to go home."

"Yes. Yes, and thank you for your time. If you remember anything else that might help, please don't hesitate to call."

"I'll be sure to," Hiromi said.

"Right. I'll see you home."

"It's okay. I can walk from here."

Hiromi stood, leaving the bill on the table, not even bothering to thank him for the milk.

FOURTEEN

Steam poured from the mouth of the kettle. In sullen silence, Yukawa lifted it and emptied the boiling water into the sink. Then he took off the lid and, after removing his glasses so they wouldn't fog, peeked inside.

"How does it look?" Utsumi asked.

Yukawa replaced the kettle on the burner and slowly shook his head. "No good. Exactly the same as last time."

"The gelatin?"

"Still there."

The physicist pulled up a metal folding chair and sat down. Linking his hands behind his head, he looked up at the ceiling. Instead of his white lab coat, he was sporting a black, short-sleeved cutsew revealing slender but well-muscled arms.

Utsumi had come to visit him at the laboratory to watch him try to mix poison into the kettle using the trick he had come up with the other day. So far, the results were less than impressive.

In order for the trick to work, he would have to use the kettle twice without melting the gelatin and allowing the poison to mix with the water. This required a thick layer of gelatin. But when he layered on a sufficient amount, the gelatin would fail to completely melt, leaving traces inside the kettle. Traces of the sort that had not been found by the Forensics investigation.

"I guess it wasn't gelatin," Yukawa said, scratching his head with both hands.

"Forensics said the same thing," Utsumi said. "They were of the opinion that even if the gelatin melted completely, it would still leave a small amount on the inside of the kettle. Also, no traces of gelatin were found in the used coffee grounds. At least Forensics liked your idea, though. They tried several other materials."

"I'm guessing they tried wafers, then?" Yukawa asked.

"The ones for taking powdered medicine? Yes. Wafers leave a trace of flour in the grounds."

"Oh well, strike two," Yukawa said, giving his knees a slap and standing. "Unfortunately, it looks like we have to abandon this line of inquiry."

"It was a fantastic idea," Utsumi offered.

"Even if all it accomplished was wiping that smirk off Detective Kusanagi's face for a little while." Yukawa retrieved his lab coat from the back of the chair and put it on. "What's the good detective up to, incidentally?"

"Looking into Mr. Mashiba's past relationships."

"Ah, yes. Following through on his hunch, then. That might just turn out to be the best course to take, now that the kettle's proved to be a dead end."

"Do *you* think some ex-lover killed Mr. Mashiba?"

"Lover or fighter, the most logical explanation remaining is that our killer waited until Ms. Wakayama left on Sunday morning, entered the Mashiba residence by some means, and put poison in that kettle."

"So you're giving up."

"I wouldn't call it that. I would call it a consistent application of the process of elimination. Kusanagi may be smitten with Mrs. Mashiba, but that doesn't mean he's blind to the basic facts. The direction he's taking this investigation in makes a good deal of sense, if you ask me." Yukawa sat back down and crossed his legs. "The poison—arsenous acid, was it? Can't you identify the killer by tracing sales records?"

"That's proving difficult. Producing and selling arsenous acid as a pesticide was, for the most part, stopped about fifty years ago, but it is still being used elsewhere for some rather surprising things."

"Such as?"

Utsumi opened her notepad. "Well, there's pest control—that one's pretty obvious. Then there's wood treatments to prevent rotting, medicine used in dentistry, semiconductor manufacturing . . . that's about it."

"Dentistry! Now that *is* surprising."

"They use it to kill nerve endings in the teeth. But the chemical is in a paste form, which is then dissolved in water, leaving only about a forty percent concentration of arsenous acid. It's not likely the substance used in this case."

"So what is likely?"

"An exterminator would have access to arsenous acid in sufficient concentrations. They use it to control termites, mainly. You have to write down your address and name whenever you purchase it, so we're checking into that. Of course, merchants are only required to keep those records for five years, so if the poison was purchased before then, we're out of luck. We're equally out of luck if the killer obtained the arsenous acid illegally."

"I have a feeling our killer wouldn't slip up in such an obvious way. I think you'd better wait to see what Detective Kusanagi turns up."

"I just don't think our killer put the poison directly into the kettle."

"Why not?" Yukawa raised an eyebrow. "Because the wife couldn't have done it, then? You're right to suspect her, but you can't conduct your entire investigation based on an assumption like that."

"I'm not assuming anything. There's just no evidence anyone else visited the Mashiba residence that day—none at all. Say for instance an old lover came by, like Detective Kusanagi is suggesting. Don't you think that Mr. Mashiba would have at least offered her a cup of coffee?"

"Not everybody would. Especially if he didn't welcome the visit."

"How would an unwelcome person get poison into the kettle, then? Wouldn't Mr. Mashiba have seen?"

"They might've had a chance if, say, he had to go to the bathroom. If they hung around long enough that an opportunity presented itself."

"Not a very solid plan. What do you think they would have done if Mr. Mashiba didn't use the bathroom?"

"They might've had a backup plan, or they might have been prepared to call the whole thing off if the right moment didn't arise. There's no risk to the killer that way."

"Professor Yukawa," Utsumi said, staring the physicist in the eyes. "Whose side are you on, anyway?"

"If you must know, I'm on nobody's side. I simply want to analyze the data, perform the necessary experiments, and come up with the most logical answer I can find. Currently, your side's losing, that's all."

Utsumi bit her lip. "I'd like to amend my previous statement," she said. "In all honesty, I do suspect Mrs. Mashiba. Even if she didn't do it, at the very least, she was involved. Call me stubborn, but that's what I believe."

"So that's how it is, is it? I'm surprised." Yukawa chuckled. "What was the reason you suspect her, again? The champagne glasses? You thought it was odd that she hadn't replaced them in the cupboard, as I recall."

"There were other reasons, too. The night of the murder, our department left a message on her phone. I asked the officer who called her, and he said that he left a message saying he had urgent news concerning her husband, and wanted her to call back. When she called around twelve o'clock that night, he explained the general facts of the case. At the time he didn't mention there was a possibility Mr. Mashiba was murdered."

"Hmm. And?"

"The next day, Mrs. Mashiba took the first flight back to Tokyo. Detective Kusanagi and I picked her up at the airport, and in the car, she called Hiromi Wakayama and told her, 'I can't imagine what you've been through,'" Utsumi said, recalling the mood in the car. "That struck me as strange."

"Couldn't imagine what she'd been through, huh?" Yukawa muttered, tapping his knee lightly with one finger. "That would suggest the conversation in the car was the first she'd had with Ms. Wakayama after hearing about the death."

"That's what I thought. That's exactly what I thought," Utsumi said, a smile slowly spreading across her face. "Mrs. Mashiba left her house key with Hiromi Wakayama before leaving for Hokkaido. But she was already onto the relationship between her husband and Hiromi before leaving. If she'd heard that her husband died under unusual circumstances, don't you think she would have tried to call Hiromi right away? Not only that, but she didn't even call their friends, the Ikais. It just doesn't make sense."

"And what is your deduction from all this, Detective Utsumi?"

"I think she didn't call Hiromi or the Ikais because she didn't need to. She knew exactly why her husband had died, so why call to ask for details?"

Yukawa grinned and scratched his lip. "Have you shared this theory with anyone?"

"I told Chief Inspector Mamiya."

"And not Kusanagi."

"Detective Kusanagi would just tell me to stop basing everything on 'feelings.'"

Yukawa frowned and got up to walk over to the sink. "That kind of assumption will get you into trouble. I can't believe I'm the one saying this, but Kusanagi's quite a gifted detective. Even supposing he has feelings for a particular suspect, he's not the kind to abandon reason. What you just told me wouldn't necessarily change his mind on the spot, of course; he'd probably start off with a rebuttal, but he wouldn't ignore you. And he would think about it. Even if the conclusions he comes up with aren't the ones you want, he won't turn a blind eye to evidence."

"You seem to trust him quite a lot."

"If I didn't, I wouldn't have helped with so many of his cases," Yukawa said, his lips parting in a white-toothed smile. He scooped some coffee into the coffeemaker.

"What about you?" Utsumi asked. "What do you think about my idea?"

"It makes a lot of sense. I would expect someone who'd heard her husband had died to try to get all the information she could as soon as possible. It's extremely odd that the wife didn't try to contact anyone."

"I'm glad you agree."

"I am, however, a scientist," Yukawa continued. "If I'm presented with one theory that feels off for psychological reasons, and another theory that is physically impossible, though it might give me some pause, I'd have to choose the former. Of course, if there were some way to pull off a timed release of poison into the kettle other than the one I came up with, that would be a different matter." Yukawa poured tap water into the coffeemaker. "I wonder if coffee made with mineral water really tastes different."

"I understand it has less to do with taste than it does with health. Apparently, the wife occasionally used tap water when her husband wasn't looking. I might've mentioned this, but Hiromi also admitted to using tap water when she made coffee Sunday morning."

"So ultimately, the only one really using mineral water was the victim."

"Which is why we originally assumed the bottled water had been poisoned," Utsumi said.

"But you had to abandon that idea when the lab results came up negative."

"Just because they didn't find anything doesn't mean there's a zero percent chance the bottled water was poisoned. Some people wash out plastic bottles before recycling them. The lab admitted this could be the cause of the negative results."

"People wash out bottles of tea and juice, sure," Yukawa said. "But bottles of water?"

"Habits are hard to break."

"Well, that's true enough. But this would make our killer an extremely lucky person—to have the victim erase the evidence for them."

"Assuming the wife was the killer, that is," Utsumi said, glancing at Yukawa. "Unless you object to that kind of deductive reasoning?"

A wry smile came to Yukawa's lips. "I don't mind. We occasionally use hypotheses in my line of work . . . though most of them get thrown out pretty quickly. Is there some benefit to supposing that the wife was the killer?"

"It was the wife who told us that Mr. Mashiba only used bottled water. Detective Kusanagi thinks she wouldn't have told us that if she poisoned the water, but I think exactly the opposite. If she assumed we would eventually find poison in one of the bottles, she might have told us in advance to deflect suspicion. But in the end, we didn't find any poison. That left me confused, to be honest. If she was the killer and she did use some method to poison the water in the kettle, what reason could she possibly have for telling the police that Mr. Mashiba only used bottled water? It got me thinking. Maybe she expected us to find poison in the empties?"

While Utsumi was talking, a grim look came over Yukawa's face. He was staring at the steam coming from the coffeemaker. "Do you think she might not have expected her husband to wash the bottles after using them?" he asked.

"If I were she, I might not have. I would've expected them to find a bottle with poison in it on the scene. But Mr. Mashiba used all of the poisoned water in the bottle when he made his coffee. Then, while he was waiting for the water to boil, he washed the bottle clean. And because she didn't expect that, she tried to stay one step ahead of the police by suggesting that the killer had poisoned the bottled water. When you think of it that way, it all makes sense."

Yukawa nodded, pushing his glasses up with the tip of his finger. "There is a certain logic to it."

"I understand there are a lot of problems with the theory, but nothing that keeps it from being a real possibility."

"I agree. Still, I wonder if there's a way to prove your hypothesis."

"There isn't, unfortunately," Utsumi said, chewing her lip.

Yukawa removed the pot from the coffeemaker. He poured the coffee into two mugs and offered one to Utsumi.

She thanked him and accepted the mug.

"You two aren't in cahoots, are you?" Yukawa said abruptly.

"Huh?" Utsumi blinked.

"You and Kusanagi. You aren't working together to drag me into this, are you?"

"What makes you think that?"

"Because the two of you are doing such a good job at piquing my intellectual curiosity, even though I'd decided not to get involved in another police investigation. And you even threw in a tantalizing dash of spice to seal the deal: the prospect of seeing whether Kusanagi finds true love." Yukawa chuckled and sipped his coffee, savoring every drop.

FIFTEEN

The tea shop and café "Kuzay" was located on the first floor of an office building in Odenmacho, a corner of the Nihonbashi district in eastern Tokyo. Not far from Suitengu Avenue and its rows of bustling financial institutions, it was the perfect spot for an office lady's lunchtime outing.

Kusanagi walked in through the glass doors and up to the sales counter. He had heard that the store stocked over fifty varieties of tea, and sure enough, there they were, all individually labeled and sorted into neat rows. Behind the counter was a little tea room. Even at the relatively quiet hour of four in the afternoon, he saw a few customers scattered around the café, sipping tea and reading newspapers. One or two were dressed in company uniforms. Male customers were definitely in the minority.

A diminutive waitress in white approached. "Just one of you?" she asked with a plainly artificial smile. Kusanagi guessed he didn't have the look of the regular clientele.

He nodded and the waitress showed him to a table against the wall, her smile still intact.

The menu was a long list of teas, none of which Kusanagi had even heard of before yesterday. He now had a passing familiarity with several of the varieties and had even sampled a few. This was his fourth tea shop so far.

He called over the waitress and ordered a chai. He knew from a conversation at one of the previous cafés that Assam tea was made by steeping the tea leaves in milk, and had decided that he rather liked this combination. He could stand having another cup.

"I was wondering," Kusanagi said to the waitress, pulling out his business card and showing it to her, "if it might be possible for me to speak with the manager briefly?"

One look at the card and the waitress's smile evaporated. Kusanagi hastily waved his hand. "Don't worry, it's nothing serious," he said. "I just need to ask about one of your customers."

"I'll go ask."

"Thanks." Kusanagi was about to ask whether it was all right for him to smoke when he spotted the no smoking sign on the opposite wall.

He took another look around the tea room. The atmosphere was quiet and pleasantly relaxed. There was enough space between the tables that two people on a date wouldn't have to worry about other patrons overhearing a conversation. He could picture Yoshitaka Mashiba coming to a place like this. Nonetheless, Kusanagi kept his expectations low. The other three tea rooms he'd already visited were practically cookie-cutter versions of this one.

Moments later, a woman wearing a black vest over a white shirt was standing by the detective's table, a nervous look on her face. She wasn't wearing much makeup, and her hair was tied in a knot a the back of her head. Kusanagi guessed she was in her mid-thirties.

"Can I help you?"

"Hi." Kusanagi smiled. "Detective Kusanagi with the Metropolitan Police. I'm sorry, your name was?"

"Hamada."

"Thanks for coming out to talk with me. I promise not to take up too much of your time. Please, sit down." Kusanagi indicated the chair across from him as he pulled out a photograph of Yoshitaka from inside his jacket. "I was wondering if you ever saw this man at your establishment? This pertains to an ongoing investigation, but if he came here, it would have been about two years ago."

Mrs. Hamada took the photo from him and looked at it for a while before shrugging. "He looks familiar, but I can't say for sure. We have a lot of customers here, and I don't make a habit of staring at them."

It was the same answer he had gotten at the other three places.

"Right. I'm guessing he came here with a woman . . ." Kusanagi added, on the off chance that it might help.

She smiled and shrugged again. "We have a lot of couples here," she said, laying the picture back down on the table.

Kusanagi nodded and smiled again, a little thinly. He wasn't exactly disappointed—he hadn't expected much more. But the constant dead ends were getting a little tiresome.

"Was that all you wanted to know?"

"Yes, thank you."

The manager stood and walked away just as the waitress arrived with Kusanagi's tea. She was about to set it down on the table when she noticed the photograph and her hand stopped.

"Oh, sorry." Kusanagi picked up the picture.

The waitress stood there, cup and saucer still in hand, looking at him. She blinked.

"Yes?" Kusanagi prompted her.

"Is that the customer you came to ask about?" she asked with apparent reluctance.

Kusanagi's eyes widened, and he turned the photograph toward her so she could get a better look. "You know him?"

"Yes—only as a customer, though."

Now the manager returned; she'd been hovering nearby, and she had overheard the conversation. "Really?" she asked the waitress. "You know him?"

"I'm pretty sure it's him," the waitress said. "He came in several times." Though there was still some hesitation in her voice, the girl seemed confident in her memory.

"Do you mind if I speak with her a moment?" Kusanagi asked Mrs. Hamada.

"Yes, of course," the manager quickly replied, turning to greet a newly arrived customer.

Kusanagi invited the waitress to sit down across from him. "When did you see this man?" he asked.

"I think the first time was about three years ago. I had just started working here, and I didn't know all the teas yet. He got impatient with me. That's why I remember him."

"Was he alone?"

"No, he always came with his wife."

"His wife? What did she look like?"

"Pretty, with long hair. I thought she might not be entirely Japanese—maybe Eurasian?"

Not Ayane Mashiba then, Kusanagi thought. Ayane was pretty, but there was no mistaking her for anything other than pure

Japanese. In any case, three years ago was well before Mashiba had met her.

"How old did she look?"

"Oh, early thirties. Maybe a little older."

"Did they say they were married?"

"Well . . ." The waitress frowned, thinking. "Maybe I just assumed they were. They certainly looked like a married couple. They were very close . . . they often came in after going shopping."

"Do you remember anything else about the woman? Any little detail would be helpful."

A worried look came into the girl's eyes. "Well, this might've just been another assumption of mine, but . . ." she began slowly. "I think she was a painter."

"A painter . . . Like an artist?"

She nodded, looking up at him. "She brought a sketchbook with her one time . . . or something like that, anyhow. It was in a case about this size." She spread her hands about sixty centimeters apart. "It was square and flat."

"But you never saw inside it?"

"No, I didn't," she replied, looking down.

Kusanagi recalled that Hiromi Wakayama had told him one of Yoshitaka's exes was involved in publishing. If she was a painter, maybe she published books of her artwork. But that didn't jibe with what Hiromi had said about Yoshitaka not wanting to give his opinion of her books. Looking over a collection of drawings or paintings couldn't have been that onerous a task.

"Anything else you noticed?" Kusanagi asked.

The waitress shook her head, then shot him a curious look. "Were they not married?"

"I don't think so, but why?"

"Well, I don't remember all the details," she said, putting a hand to her forehead, "but I have the feeling they talked about kids—not their own kids, but about wanting to have kids. At least, I *think* that was them. Or, I don't know . . . I might be getting them mixed up with another couple."

Bingo. She wasn't confused. The couple had definitely been Yoshitaka Mashiba and his girlfriend of the time. *A lead, finally.* Kusanagi let himself get a little excited.

He thanked the waitress and let her go, reaching out for his cup of chai. It had gone cold, but the blend of spice and sweet milk was sublime.

He drank half the cup, considering how he might track down Mashiba's painter. Then his cell phone rang. He checked the display and saw with some surprise that it was Yukawa. He kept his voice low as he answered, not wanting to bother any of the other customers. "Kusanagi speaking."

"It's me. You good to talk?"

"Yeah. I'll have to keep my voice down, but how could I refuse a rare call from you? What's up?"

"Got something I wanted to talk to you about. Any time today?"

"I can make time, if it's that important. What's this about?"

"I'll save the details for when we meet, but suffice it to say, it's about your current case."

Kusanagi sighed. "You and Utsumi got some secret plan brewing again?"

"If it were a secret, would I be calling you? So do you want to meet or not?"

Arrogant bastard, Kusanagi thought with a dry chuckle. "Fine. Where do you want me?"

"I'll leave that to you. Just someplace smoke-free, if you don't mind," Yukawa said, his tone suggesting that it was irrelevant whether Kusanagi minded or not.

They met in a coffee shop near Shinagawa station, close to the hotel where Ayane was staying. Kusanagi planned to wrap up the talk with Yukawa quickly so he could go ask her about the painter ex.

He found Yukawa already there, sitting in the back of the no-smoking section, reading a magazine. Despite the fact that winter was around the corner, the physicist was wearing a short-sleeved shirt. A black leather jacket rested on the chair next to him.

Kusanagi walked over to his table and stood beside it. Yukawa didn't look up.

"What are you reading so intently?" the detective asked, pulling out a chair.

Yukawa tapped his magazine with his finger. "It's an article about dinosaurs. They're talking about using CAT scan technology to analyze fossils."

"A science magazine, then," Kusanagi said, secretly disappointed that he hadn't managed to catch Yukawa unawares. "So what's so great about CAT scanning dinosaur bones?"

"Not bones. Fossils," Yukawa said, finally looking up. He adjusted his glasses with one finger.

"What's the difference? Aren't all dinosaur fossils bones?"

Yukawa's eyes narrowed with mirth. "That's what I like about you. You never defy expectations. You always say exactly what I think you're going to say."

"Your point being that I'm an idiot."

A waiter approached, and the detective ordered a tomato juice.

"An unusual choice," Yukawa said. "Watching your health?"

"So what if I don't feel like tea or coffee right now? Cut to the chase. What's this all about?"

"I would've been happy to talk about fossils a bit more, but fine." Yukawa lifted his coffee cup. "Did you hear what Forensics had to say about my poisoning idea?"

"I did. Doing anything with gelatin would've left traces, meaning the possibility such a trick was used in this case is zero. I guess even the great Galileo makes mistakes sometimes."

"It's not very scientific to say things like 'absolutely' and 'zero possibility.' It's also rather unorthodox to say someone made a mistake when they've only presented a hypothesis that proved to be incorrect. But I'll forgive you on the grounds that you're not a scientist."

"If you want to be a sore loser, you could at least be a little more straightforward about it."

"I don't see how I've lost anything. Disproving a hypothesis is progress. It narrows our options by closing off a possible path of entry for the poison into the coffee."

Kusanagi's tomato juice arrived, complete with straw. He left the straw on the table and gulped it down. The sharp taste of the juice stung his tongue after all that tea.

"But there's only one path of entry," Kusanagi said. "Someone put the poison in the kettle. Either Hiromi Wakayama, or if it wasn't she, someone else Yoshitaka Mashiba invited in on Sunday."

"So you deny the possibility that the poison was mixed in with the water?"

Kusanagi's mouth curled upward at the corners. "I make it a policy to believe what Forensics and the labs tell me. They found no poison in any of the bottles. That means it wasn't in the water."

"Utsumi thinks the bottles might've been washed out."

"Yeah, I heard about that. She thinks the victim washed the bottle out himself. Problem is, people don't wash out bottles of water. I'd be willing to put money on that."

"But you have to agree there's a possibility he did?"

Kusanagi snorted. "Not a bet I'd like to make. But if that's the way you like to play, by all means. I'm more of a sure-thing kind of guy myself."

"I'll admit your current path of investigation is more of a sure thing. But remember, there are always exceptions. In science, it's important to cover everything." Yukawa shot the detective a serious look. "I have a request."

"Yeah?"

"I'd like to see the Mashiba house again. Think you can get me inside? I know you have a key."

Kusanagi raised an eyebrow at the eccentric physicist. "What are you going to look at? Didn't Utsumi show you everything the other day?"

"Yes, but my viewpoint's changed since then."

"How's that?"

"Call it a shift in my thinking. Maybe I did make a mistake, after all. I'd like to know for sure."

Kusanagi tapped a finger on the table. "You mind being more specific?"

"I'll tell you once we're there, if I find that I did, indeed, make an error. It's better for both of us that way."

Kusanagi leaned back in his chair and sighed deeply. "What are you up to, Yukawa? This is some deal you've made with Utsumi, isn't it?"

Yukawa chuckled. "Don't start jumping at shadows yet. Like I said, I'm only interested in this because it's piqued my scientific curiosity. Which means, by the way, that should I lose interest, I'm out. That's why I want you to let me into that house again. To make my final determination."

The detective looked his friend directly in the eye. Yukawa looked back, cool as ever.

Kusanagi hadn't the slightest idea what the physicist was thinking. This was nothing new. Kusanagi knew that there was a point when he just had to let go, and trust that Yukawa would come to the rescue as he had so many times before.

"I'll call Mrs. Mashiba. Give me a second," he said, standing and pulling out his phone.

Going to a quiet corner, he dialed Ayane's number, and when she answered he asked if it was all right for him to let himself in one more time. "I'm sorry to make this request yet again, but there was one last thing we really needed to check."

He could hear her give a little sigh on the other side of the line. "You don't need to check with me every time, you know," she said. "It's an investigation; I expect you to be going in and out frequently. I hope you find something."

"Thanks. I'll water the flowers while I'm there."

"Thank you so much. It's a big help."

Kusanagi went back to the table. Yukawa was looking up, observing him as he approached.

"You got something to say?"

"I was just wondering why you felt the need to get up in order to make the call?" Yukawa asked. "Was there something you didn't want me to hear?"

"Of course not. All I did was get permission to go inside her house."

"Huh."

"What is it now?" Kusanagi glared.

"Oh, nothing. It's just, when I watched you making the call, I couldn't help but think you looked less like a detective, and more like a salesman making a pitch to an important customer. Is there some reason you have to tread lightly around this Mrs. Mashiba?"

"I was asking if we could go into her house. It's a sensitive subject." Kusanagi picked up the bill from the table. "Let's get going. It's late already."

They hailed a cab by the station. Sliding into the seat, Yukawa pulled out the magazine he had been reading in the café.

"You were saying earlier that dinosaur fossils were all bones, but that assumption carries a considerable amount of risk. In fact, it's an assumption that led many paleontologists to discard a lot of extremely valuable material."

This again. "All of the dinosaur fossils I've seen at the museum were bones."

"That's right. That's because they threw out everything else."

"Everything else? Like what?"

"Say you're digging a hole and you find some dinosaur bones. Naturally, you get excited and dig them right up, brushing off all the dirt, so you can construct your big impressive dinosaur skeleton. Then you start making observations: "So that's what a tyrannosaurus jaw looks like," and "Look at those short forelimbs." But, it turns out, you've already made a terrible error. In

2000, a certain research group dug up a chunk of dirt with some fossils in it and ran the whole thing through a CAT scan without cleaning it all. And guess what? They found the heart. The dirt trapped inside the skeleton had preserved the shape of the creature's internal organs perfectly. These days, it's standard practice to run a CAT scan on all fossils."

Kusanagi grunted. "That's pretty interesting, actually," he admitted. "I'm just not sure what it has to do with anything. Or were you just making small talk?"

"When I first heard about the discovery, you know what I thought? I thought: here is a very clever trick, one that it took several millennia for Mother Nature to pull off. You can hardly blame the paleontologists who cleaned the dirt off the first dinosaur bones they discovered. But, as it turns out, the dirt they discarded as 'useless' turned out to be extremely important." Yukawa closed the magazine. "You may have heard me mention the process of elimination, by which we invalidate one hypothesis at a time, eliminating all the possibilities until we're left with a single truth. However, when there is a basic error in the way we form our hypotheses, that method can lead to extremely dangerous results. Sometimes, when we're too eager to get those bones, we end up missing the point."

So this conversation does have something to do with the investigation. "You think we made a mistake in our thinking about the route of entry for the poison?"

"That's what I'm going to go check now. It's just possible that our killer is quite the scientist," Yukawa added, half to himself.

The Mashiba residence was quiet and dark. Kusanagi retrieved the key from his pocket. He had already tried to return both copies of the key to Ayane, but she'd left him with one, saying that the investigators might still have need of it and as long as she didn't have any plans to go home, it was no use to her.

"The funeral's over, isn't it? No plans to do anything at the home?" Yukawa asked as he was taking off his shoes.

"She didn't mention anything. The husband wasn't a very religious man, so they did a flower ceremony in place of a formal funeral. There was a cremation, but none of the other usual observances."

"Sounds like a logical way to go about doing things. Maybe I should put in a request to receive the same treatment when I die."

"Fine by me," Kusanagi grunted. "I'd be happy to make the arrangements."

Inside, Yukawa walked swiftly down the hallway. Kusanagi watched him go, then made his way up the stairs, opening the door to the master bedroom. He opened the sliding door that opened onto the balcony and picked up the large watering can on the other side—a purchase he had made at the home repair center yesterday after Ayane asked him to water the flowers.

Can in hand, he went back downstairs. He found Yukawa in the kitchen, under the sink again.

"Didn't you check under there last time?" he called out.

"Aren't you police always talking about fine-toothed combs? That's all I'm doing," Yukawa countered. He was carefully examining the space by the light of a small penlight. "Oh well—no sign that anyone touched anything in here at all."

"Didn't you check that last time?"

"Yes, but I thought it might be prudent to go back to square one. We have the dinosaur fossil in front of us, all we have to do is avoid carelessly removing the dirt." Yukawa turned toward Kusanagi; a suspicious look came into his eyes as he caught sight of the object in the detective's hand. "What's that?"

"Never seen a watering can before?"

"Oh yeah, I seem to recall you sending Kishitani off to water the plants last time. Is this all part of a new PR campaign? 'The police—we're not just public servants, we're servants'?"

"Laugh it up," Kusanagi said, pushing past him to get to the sink. He placed the can under the faucet and opened the tap all the way.

"That's an awful big can," Yukawa noted. "Doesn't she have a hose in the garden?"

"This is for the flowers on the second floor. The balcony's covered with planters."

"A policeman's work is never done," Yukawa said, grinning, as Kusanagi headed out of the kitchen.

Back up on the second floor, Kusanagi began to water the flowers. Though he couldn't have named a single one of them to save his life, even he could tell that the plants weren't doing so well. *Better not let them wilt.* The watering complete, he shut the balcony door and hurried back through the bedroom. Even if he was here by permission, it didn't feel right to linger in someone else's sleeping quarters.

When Kusanagi got downstairs Yukawa was still in the kitchen. He was standing with his arms crossed, glaring at the sink.

"Why don't you just come out with it and explain to me what you're thinking? Because if you don't, there's no way I'm giving you special treatment like this again."

"Special treatment?" Yukawa asked, lifting an eyebrow. "Is that what you call it when one of your officers barges into my laboratory and involves me in yet another tangled, hopeless investigation?"

Kusanagi let his hands fall down to his hips and stared back at his friend. "I don't know what Utsumi said to you, but it has nothing to do with me. In fact, if you wanted to check the house, why didn't you just call her again? Why drag me into this?"

"Because a real debate can only happen between two people with opposing points of view."

"So you oppose the way I'm running this investigation? I thought you said I was on to a 'sure thing.'"

"I have nothing against you running a proper investigation. I just don't like it when people discard angles of attack just because they seem improper or unlikely. Even if only the slightest possibility remains that something might've occurred, one shouldn't disregard it too easily. Don't toss out the dirt."

Kusanagi shook his head in exasperation. "So what's the dirt, in this case?"

"Water," Yukawa replied. "The poison was mixed into the water. At least, I think so."

"Now we're back to the victim-washing-the-bottle theory." Kusanagi snorted.

"I'm not concerned with the bottle. There are other sources of water." Yukawa pointed at the sink. "That tap, for one. Plenty of water there."

Kusanagi stared back into Yukawa's cool eyes. "You're serious?"

"It's a possibility," Yukawa said with a shrug.

"But Forensics found nothing unusual about the water line at all."

"Yes, Forensics did analyze the tap water. But they only analyzed it in order to tell whether the water left in the kettle was from the tap or from a bottle. And I understand they couldn't tell the difference, because of all the tap water residue that had built up inside the kettle."

"But if there was poison in the tap water, wouldn't they have found it?"

"It's possible that by the time they checked, the poison had already washed out entirely."

"But the victim only used bottled water when making coffee."

"So I hear," Yukawa admitted. "But who told us that, exactly?"

"The wife." As soon as Kusanagi said it, he bit his lip and stared at Yukawa. "And of course you think she's lying, though you haven't even met her. What ideas has Utsumi been putting in your head?"

"She has her own opinion, and she's entitled to it. All I'm doing is formulating a hypothesis, based on objectively observable evidence."

"And does your hypothesis tell you the wife is the killer?"

Yukawa ignored him. "I gave some thought to the question of why the wife told you about the bottled water. There are two possibilities. One is that the statement 'Mr. Mashiba only uses bottled water' is false. The other is that it's true. If the statement is true, no problem. The wife is simply doing her best to aid the investigation. I think Utsumi would still say the wife is guilty, but I'm not half as stubborn. The real problem here is if the statement is false. Firstly, because lying would suggest that the wife was somehow involved with the crime—but it also means that there's some reason for her to tell that particular lie. So I considered the effect that her statement about the bottled water had on the course of the police investigation." Yukawa wet his lips and continued. "First, the police investigated the empties to make sure there was no poison in any of them. At the same time, they found poison in the kettle. This led to the assumption that it was likely that the killer put the poison in the kettle. Which naturally provides the wife with an ironclad alibi."

Kusanagi shook his head slowly from side to side. "That's where I don't follow you. Even if she hadn't given us that tip, Forensics would've checked the water line and the bottles. In fact, by telling us he only used bottled water, she actually *hurt* her alibi. For example, Utsumi still hasn't given up on the idea that the poison was in a bottle to start with."

"That's just it," Yukawa said. "Many people would think exactly the same thing as Detective Utsumi. It made me wonder if the whole bottled water testimony might be a trap laid to catch just that kind of person."

"Huh?"

"Anyone who suspected the wife wouldn't be able to let go of the idea that the poison was added to the bottled water, because they'd think there was no other way for her to have done it. But if she used an entirely different method to poison her husband, anyone still obsessed with the bottled water would be left spinning their wheels for an eternity, never reaching the truth. If that's not a trap, what is? That got me thinking. If the husband didn't use bottled water—" Yukawa stopped suddenly in midsentence. His face was frozen, his eyes looking over Kusanagi's shoulder.

Kusanagi turned around, then stood, as startled as Yukawa.

Standing there in the entrance to the living room was Ayane Mashiba.

SIXTEEN

"Er, hello . . . we let ourselves in," Kusanagi managed after a long pause. He realized it was an idiotic thing to say almost as soon as the words left his mouth. "Here to check up on things?"

"No," Ayane replied. "Just here for a change of clothes. Might I ask who that is?"

"Oh, this is Yukawa. He's a physics professor at Imperial University."

Yukawa remained silent.

"A university professor?" Ayane asked, clearly puzzled.

"And my friend, actually," Kusanagi explained. "He often helps our department with, er, scientific investigations . . . which is why he's here today."

"Oh, I see," Ayane replied. Though she was clearly still puzzled, she said no more about him. Instead she asked, "Is it all right for me to touch things?"

"Of course. You're free to do whatever you like. I'm sorry we've taken so long."

"No need to apologize." Ayane moved toward the hallway. But after two steps she stopped, once again turning to face Kusanagi and the physicist. "I'm not sure if I'm allowed to ask, but what are you looking for, exactly?"

"Oh, right," Kusanagi began, wetting his lips. "Well, we're still having trouble determining the route by which the poison got into the coffee, so were doing some follow-up tests. I hope you don't mind. We'll be done soon."

"No, I don't mind at all," she said. "It wasn't a complaint, just curiosity. Don't let me interrupt. I'll be upstairs if you need anything."

"Right, thanks."

Ayane gave Kusanagi a curt bow and turned to leave, but Yukawa spoke suddenly. "Might I ask a question?"

The widow stopped again. "Yes?" The expression on her face made it clear that she did not trust this newcomer.

"There's a water filtration system on your sink here in the kitchen. I'm assuming you regularly change the filter, but do you remember when you last did that?"

"Oh, that . . ." Ayane came around to peer into the kitchen. She frowned as her eyes fell on the sink. "Actually, I don't think I ever changed it once."

"Huh? Not even once?" the physicist said with evident surprise.

"I was thinking I should call the company and have them do it one of these days. The filter on there is the one they put in just after we moved in, so it's about a year old. Which, if I recall what the serviceman told me, is right about when you're supposed to change it."

"So the last time the filter was replaced was a year ago?"

"Did . . . I do something wrong?"

"No, no, of course not," Yukawa said. "I was just curious. And, you probably should go ahead and get it changed. There are data that show old filters can actually do more harm than good."

"Well, I'll do it right away," Ayane said. "But I suppose I should clean under the sink first. It's a mess under there."

"That's the same in every house," Yukawa said. "You should see the roach nest under the sink in our laboratory—but I shouldn't be comparing my lab to a proper residence. You know—" Yukawa glanced at Kusanagi before continuing. "If you had the number of the serviceman handy, I bet Kusanagi here could give him a call for you. No time like the present, after all."

Kusanagi shot a surprised look back at Yukawa, but the physicist ignored him, instead looking back toward Ayane. "Sound like a good idea?"

"You mean right now?"

"Yes, if it's all right. To be honest, it might help with the investigation, and the sooner the better."

"Well, if that's the case, I certainly don't mind."

Yukawa smiled and turned again to Kusanagi. "There you go. You have your orders."

Kusanagi glared back at the physicist, but he knew his friend well enough by now to know that he wasn't doing it on a lark. Whatever Detective Galileo was up to, he had a plan. "Could you get the number?" Kusanagi asked Ayane. "If you don't mind . . ."

"Sure, just a moment."

Kusanagi waited for the widow to leave the room before glaring again at Yukawa. "You could've at least given me a heads up first."

"There wasn't time. And besides, before you start complaining, I think there's something you need to be doing."

"What?"

"Call Forensics. You don't want the filtration system serviceman to destroy any evidence, do you? One of your Forensics guys should handle the actual removal of the filter."

"You mean you want Forensics to take the old filter back with them?"

"Yes, and the connection hose," Yukawa said in a low voice. In his eye was the cool gleam of a scientist who's caught sight of his quarry. Kusanagi swallowed as Ayane returned to the living room.

About an hour later, an officer from the Metropolitan Forensics Division had removed the filter and the filtration system hose from the sink under the watchful eyes of Kusanagi and Yukawa. The Forensics officer took great care in placing the two parts inside an acrylic case, making sure not to disturb the considerable amount of sediment that had built up inside them.

"I'll get right on these," he told the detective as he left.

The man from the filtration system company arrived a short time later, and Kusanagi watched him start replacing the filter and hose before returning to the living room. Ayane was sitting on the sofa, a glum look on her face. Beside her was a bag containing the clothes she had taken from her bedroom.

Still committed to not living here for a while, Kusanagi noted.

"Sorry about all the fuss," the detective apologized.

"No, it's fine," she said. "I'm happy that at least the filter's gotten changed."

"I'll talk to the chief about getting that paid for."

"Don't worry about it. I'm the one who's going to be using it, after all." Ayane smiled briefly before her expression turned serious again. "Was there something wrong with the filter? Was that where the poison was?"

"We're not sure. We're just looking into every possibility right now."

"Well, if it was the filter, how would someone have put poison in there?"

"Er, good question . . ." Kusanagi said, looking toward Yukawa, who was standing in the entrance to the kitchen, watching the serviceman work. "Hey, Yukawa," he called out.

Yukawa turned around, but to Ayane, not the detective. "Is it true that your husband only drank bottled water?" he asked.

Kusanagi blinked, and watched to see Ayane's reaction.

She nodded. "Yes. That's why we always have a supply in the fridge."

"I've heard he asked you to use bottled water when you made coffee, too?"

"He did."

"But ultimately, you didn't always use the bottled water. Is that correct?"

Kusanagi's eyes opened wider. He hadn't told Yukawa any of these details, which meant that Utsumi was feeding him privileged information. Kusanagi pictured her smiling face, and he scowled.

"Well, no. It's not very cost-effective," Ayane replied, her expression softening. "And honestly, I never thought tap water was as bad for you as he claimed. Besides, hot water boils faster. I doubt he ever noticed."

"I'd have to agree," the physicist said. "I don't think the choice of tap water versus mineral water would have much of an effect on the taste of the coffee at all."

Sage wisdom from a guy who used to drink only instant coffee. Kusanagi shot his friend a mocking look.

Yukawa either failed to notice or chose to pay the detective no mind. "The woman who made coffee on Sunday," he said. "What was her name again? Your assistant . . ."

"Hiromi Wakayama," Kusanagi reminded him.

"That's right, Ms. Wakayama. So . . . she also used tap water at your direction? And nothing happened when she did. Which leads one to think that the poison was probably in the bottled water. But there is another kind of water available here, filtered water, from the filtration system set up next to the regular sink faucet. It's possible that for some reason, perhaps to avoid wasting the bottled water in the fridge, your husband used water from that, which would lead me to suspect the water filter."

"Well, that's true . . . but is it even possible to poison a filtration system? I mean, wouldn't it filter the poison out?"

"Not necessarily. Either way, I'm sure we'll hear from Forensics soon."

"Well, if the poison was in the filtration system, then when was it put there?" Ayane asked, focusing on Kusanagi. "I know I've already told you this a hundred times, but we had that party here on Friday night, and the water filter was fine then."

"So it would seem," Yukawa said. "Which would mean that if it was poisoned, it happened afterward. And, if we assume the killer only wanted to poison your husband, then they would have set their sights on a time when he would be alone."

"Meaning after I left the house—assuming I'm not the killer, of course."

"Exactly," Yukawa said.

"Let's not get ahead of ourselves," Kusanagi cautioned. "We don't know whether or not the filtration system was poisoned yet." He excused himself and left the living room with a meaningful glance at Yukawa.

Kusanagi stood in the entrance hall until Yukawa joined him. "What are you doing?" he asked his friend, his voice low, but sharp.

"What do you mean, 'what am I doing'?"

"What do you mean, 'what do you mean'? You're basically *telling* her she's the suspect. Don't go taking Utsumi's side just because she was the one who asked for your help."

Yukawa's forehead crinkled between the eyebrows. He looked surprised. "Now, that's baseless conjecture if I ever heard it. Since when have I taken Utsumi's side? I'm just working through the facts in a completely rational manner. You might try it yourself. The bereaved widow in there seems to be a lot more collected than you are."

Kusanagi bit his lip, but just as he was about to respond, he heard a door open. The serviceman was walking toward them from the living room, with Ayane close behind.

"He's done replacing the filter," she told them.

"Thanks," Kusanagi told the serviceman. "About the bill . . ."

"I've already paid it," Ayane said.

"Oh," Kusanagi replied weakly.

Once the man had left, Yukawa began putting on his shoes, looking up at Kusanagi. "Well, I should be going," he announced. "You?"

"I'll be here bit longer," the detective replied. "I have a few more things to check with Mrs. Mashiba."

"I see. Well, thanks for your time," Yukawa said to Ayane, lowering his head.

"Not at all," she said to his back as he left. Kusanagi watched him walk out to the street, then sighed. "Sorry about all that. He's not a bad person, just not very thoughtful. A bit eccentric, you might say."

"Oh?" Ayane looked surprised. "There's no need for you to apologize. He seemed fine to me."

"Well, that's good."

"You said he was a professor at Imperial University? It's funny. When I think of the professorial type, I always picture someone quiet and reserved. But he wasn't like that at all, was he?"

"Even academics come in all types, and that guy in particular's a special case."

Ayane smiled. "You two seem close."

"Oh, well . . . I forgot to mention we were classmates back in college. Completely different majors, though."

The two returned to the living room, where Kusanagi told Ayane how he and Yukawa were in the same badminton club, and how the physicist had started helping with investigations during a particularly thorny case.

"I always think it's great when people are able to keep in touch with old friends through their work."

"Yeah, well, sometimes it can get a little stale."

"Oh, I doubt that. I'm envious."

Kusanagi smiled. "At least you have a friend to go to the hot springs with back home."

Ayane nodded, then her eyes widened as a realization came to her. "That's right, you visited my parents' home. My mother mentioned it."

"Yes, we had to cover the bases, and all that. I'm not sure we accomplished much on that trip, but that's always the chance you take," Kusanagi added hastily.

Ayane smiled at him. "Of course. It's very important to know if I really went home or not. I understand."

"I'm glad that you're so understanding. I wouldn't want you to feel like we were singling you out."

"My mother said you seemed like a very nice detective. So I told her maybe the investigation wouldn't be so bad after all."

Kusanagi chuckled and scratched his neck in embarrassment.

"And you met my friend, Ms. Motooka?" Ayane asked. Sakiko Motooka was the friend who had joined Ayane on her trip to the hot springs.

"Actually, Utsumi went to speak with her. She told me that Ms. Motooka mentioned she'd been worried about you from before the—the unfortunate incident. She said you seemed much more tired than you ever did before you got married."

A lonely smile came to Ayane's face, and she breathed a light sigh. "She said that, did she? I guess that's old friends for you. You do your best to hide it, and they see right through you."

"But you didn't talk to her about your husband asking for a divorce?"

She shook her head. "It didn't even occur to me to tell her. I guess I just wanted to forget about the situation for a while . . . And it's not really something I felt I needed to talk to anyone about. You know, we made a promise before he got married, that if we couldn't have a child we'd split up. Of course, I never told my parents."

"I heard from Mr. Ikai that your husband regarded marriage as a means to having children, and little else. I have to admit, I was surprised to learn that there are men like that."

"Oh, I wanted a child, too," Ayane explained. "I assumed we'd have one right away, so I admit I never thought too deeply about that promise. But after we'd gone a year with nothing . . . the gods can be cruel sometimes." Her eyes dropped to the table for a moment before she looked up again. "Do you have any children, Detective Kusanagi?"

Kusanagi smiled thinly and looked back at her. "I'm single."

"Oh," she said, her lips parting. "I'm sorry."

"No need to be. People tell me to hurry up now and then, but it's hard when you don't have somebody . . . My friend Yukawa's single, too."

"Yes, he struck me as a single man. Doesn't really give off a domestic vibe, does he?"

"Well, unlike your late husband, he hates children. Their 'lack of the capacity for reason' stresses him out. Can you believe it?"

"He's a very *interesting* individual."

"I'll let him know you said that.—Actually, not to change the subject, but I have a question about your husband."

"Yes?"

"Did he happen to have any friends who were painters?"

"Painters? You mean, like, artists?"

"Yes. It doesn't have to be somebody he'd seen recently. Maybe someone he mentioned having known in the past?"

Ayane thought for a bit, then looked at him curiously. "Is this person involved with the case?"

"That I don't know. I may have mentioned the other day that we're looking into your husband's previous relationships. And we found out that he might've been dating a painter of some kind."

"I see. Well, I'm sorry, but I never heard about any artists. Do you know around when this might have been?"

"Not exactly, but I'd say roughly two or three years ago."

"Sorry," Ayane said after a moment's thought. "If there was someone like that, he never told me."

"I see, no problem then." Kusanagi glanced at his watch and stood up from the sofa. "Sorry to take so much of your time. I should be leaving."

"I'm heading back to the hotel myself," Ayane said, collecting her bag as she stood.

The two left the Mashiba residence together. Ayane locked the door behind them.

"I can get that bag for you. Let's walk until we get to a place where we can find a taxi," Kusanagi said, extending his hand.

Ayane thanked him and handed him the bag. Then, turning to look back at the house, she said quietly, "I wonder if the day will ever come when I move back."

Unable to think of anything appropriate to say, Kusanagi strolled alongside her in silence.

SEVENTEEN

According to the chart on the door, Yukawa was alone inside the laboratory—exactly as Utsumi had expected. She knocked on the door.

"Come in," came the curt reply. She entered to find Yukawa in the middle of making coffee. He was using a dripper and a filter.

"Good timing," Yukawa said, pouring two cups.

"I'm surprised. You're not using your coffeemaker?"

"That's right. I thought I'd try being a coffee snob for a while. I even used mineral water," Yukawa said, holding out a cup.

"Thanks." Utsumi accepted the drink and took a sip. One taste told her that he hadn't upgraded his choice of grind.

"Well? How is it?" Yukawa asked.

"Delicious."

"More delicious than usual?"

Utsumi hesitated a moment before saying, "Can I be frank?"

A despondent look came over Yukawa's face and he turned

back to his chair. "No need. I'm guessing your reaction is exactly the same as mine." He peered inside his coffee cup. "You know, a little bit ago, I used tap water to make the coffee. The results were exactly the same. Or at least, so similar I couldn't tell the difference."

"I don't think anyone could tell the difference, really."

"And yet it's commonly agreed upon in culinary circles that water does make a difference to taste," Yukawa said, picking up a sheet of paper from his desk. "Water has a hardness, which is calculated by comparing total calcium ions and magnesium ions to the water's calcium carbonate content. If the ratio's low, the water is soft. A little higher means medium hardness. A lot higher and it's hard water."

"I've heard of that."

"Apparently, soft water is best for most cooking. The point is the calcium content. If, for example, you use water that's high in calcium when you cook rice, the calcium fuses with the rice fibers, and you end up with drier rice."

Utsumi quirked an eyebrow. "Not good for making sushi."

"Conversely, if you're trying to make a beef stock, hard water is preferable. The calcium fuses with the excess fluid in the meat and bones, making it rise to the surface so you can scoop it out. Something to remember the next time I do a consommé."

"You cook?"

"Sometimes," Yukawa replied, setting the paper down.

Utsumi tried to picture the professor standing in his kitchen. An image popped into her mind—Yukawa with a wrinkled brow, hovering over a pot of soup, adjusting the water content and the strength of the flame as if it were some kind of science experiment.

"So, any word?" Yukawa asked.

"Forensics got back to us. I have a report," Utsumi said, pulling a file out of her shoulder bag.

"Let's hear it." Yukawa sipped his coffee.

"No arsenous acid was found in either the filter or the hose. However, they go on to note that even if there had been any poison in there, running a sufficient quantity of water through the filter would be enough to make any traces undetectable. The next part gets sticky," Utsumi said, taking a breath before continuing. "The filter and hose both showed a considerable buildup of undisturbed grime from long years of use, making it unlikely that either had been tampered with. Any recent removal of the filter or hose would have left some indication. There was some additional material: apparently, Forensics also checked beneath the sink for poison on the day of Mr. Mashiba's death. At the time, they moved the old detergent and containers that were sitting in front of the filter, and were able to confirm that only where those objects had been sitting was the dust beneath the sink disturbed."

"So not only the filter, but the entire area under the sink hadn't been touched for some time?"

"That's what Forensics thinks, at least."

"Well, I agree with them. That was certainly the impression I got when I first looked under there. But, there is one other thing they should have checked on."

"I know what you're going to say. Could poison have been inserted into the filter from the other direction—via the tap, right?"

"That's what inquiring minds want to know. Their answer?"

"Though theoretically possible," Utsumi said, "realistically, it's impossible."

Yukawa took another sip of his coffee and frowned—not because the coffee was bitter, Utsumi guessed.

"They tried your idea about using a long tube, like a stomach camera, inserting it into the faucet end all the way up to the filter, then introducing the poison up through the tube, but they couldn't get it to work. The problem was that the joint where the faucet connects to the filter is practically a right angle, and they couldn't get the tube to go around it. It might be possible if one were to use a specialized tool with a manipulable tip—"

"That's okay, you don't have to go on," Yukawa said, scratching his head. "I don't think our killer went to such technical extremes. Looks like I have to give up on the filter theory. Too bad; I had high hopes for that one. What we need now is another shift in approach. There has to be a blind spot somewhere."

He poured the remaining coffee in the server into his own cup. A little spilled, and Utsumi heard the professor grind his teeth.

So he does get irritated, she thought. *Such a simple question: where did the killer put that poison? And yet he can't figure it out. None of us can.*

"What is our famous detective friend up to?" Yukawa asked.

"He's gone to Mr. Mashiba's office to ask some more questions."

"Hmph."

"Did you hear something from him?"

Yukawa shook his head and took another sip. "I was with him the other day and we ran into Mrs. Mashiba."

"So I heard."

"We talked a bit. She is a beautiful woman—enchanting, even."

"Were you helpless before her charms, Professor?"

"I was merely reporting an objective observation. That, and I was a little worried about Kusanagi."

"Really? Did something happen?"

"Not something happening, per se, just another observation—one that requires the telling of a tale to be understood.

"Once, back when we were in college, Kusanagi picked up these stray cats—kittens, actually, just born. They were both really weak, and anyone could see they weren't long for this world. But he brought them up to his room anyway, and he skipped class to take care of them. He was using an eye-dropper to feed them milk. One of his friends asked him, 'What's the point? They're just going to die anyway.' I remember his answer: 'So what?' That's all he said." Yukawa gazed off into the distance. "Kusanagi's eyes when he looked at that woman were just like his eyes when he was taking care of those kittens. He knows something's not quite right. And at the same time he's saying to himself, 'So what?'"

EIGHTEEN

Kusanagi sat on the sofa in the reception area, peering up at a painting of a single rose floating in darkness. The design seemed somehow familiar. Maybe he'd seen it on a bottle of wine once.

"What are you staring at so intently?" Kishitani asked. "That painting has nothing to do with her. Look. The signature's a foreign name."

"I'm not a complete idiot," Kusanagi said, turning away from the painting. The truth was that he hadn't noticed the signature until Kishitani pointed it out.

The junior detective twisted his head around to look at it again. "It's hard to imagine him hanging onto the work of an ex-girlfriend. If it was me, I'd throw all that crap out."

"If it was you. Maybe not if it was Yoshitaka Mashiba."

"You think? We're not just talking about keeping something at home, in private. This is the company, a public space. I dunno. It would bug me, seeing it up there all the time."

"Maybe he didn't display it."

"Who would bring a painting to their office if they weren't going to display it? That seems a little strange to me, too. How would he explain it to an employee who found it?"

"I don't know . . . He could just say he got it from someone."

"That's even stranger. If someone gives you a present as a gift, it's customary to hang the thing up. Who knows when they might visit?"

"Will you button it, Kishitani? Look, I don't think Yoshitaka Mashiba was the type to worry about that kind of thing."

Just then a woman wearing a white suit emerged from a door next to the reception desk. She wore thin-rimmed glasses beneath short-cropped hair. "Thank you for waiting," she said. "Detective Kusanagi . . . ?" Her gaze flickered between the two men.

"I'm Kusanagi," the senior detective said as he rose to his feet. "Thanks for meeting us."

"Not at all." She offered her card, which introduced her as Eiko Yamamoto, head of PR. "I understand you wanted to go through some of the former CEO's private effects?"

"Yes, if that's possible."

"Certainly. This way, please."

She led them to a room with a plate on the door that read "meeting room."

"You're not keeping them in the CEO's office?" Kusanagi asked.

"The new CEO has already moved in. I'm sorry he's out today, or he'd want to greet you personally."

"No worries. Glad to hear you've got a new CEO."

"Yes. We got the office ready right after the funeral. Everything work-related we left in place, but all of Mr. Mashiba's personal effects we moved here. We were planning on sending them to his home, and we haven't thrown anything out. That was the advice of Mr. Ikai, our legal counsel."

Ms. Yamamoto spoke without a hint of a smile. Her tone was guarded, as if she was choosing each word with care. The message was clear: *Our CEO's death had nothing to do with the company, so why should you suspect us of destroying evidence?*

Tan cardboard boxes of varying sizes had been stacked inside the meeting room. In addition, Kusanagi spotted some golf clubs, a trophy, and a mechanical foot massager. *No paintings in sight.*

"Can we take a look through this?" Kusanagi asked.

"Of course, take your time. I can bring you something to drink, if you'd like. Any preferences?"

"No, that's fine. I appreciate it."

"Very well," Ms. Yamamoto said. She left the room with a steely look on her face.

Kishitani watched the door close and shrugged. "Not a very warm welcome, was it?"

"Do you get a lot of warm welcomes usually, Detective? Just be thankful she's letting us in here."

"You'd think she'd be a little more eager to help resolve this case as quickly as possible, for the company's sake if nothing else. Or, I don't know, she could at least smile a little. She was like a robot."

"As far as the company's concerned, as long as the newsworthiness of the investigation erodes quickly, they don't care whether it's solved or not. Our very presence in the building is the problem. Just picture trying to rally behind your new CEO, only to have to deal with the police again. Would you be smiling if you were her? Anyway, enough chitchat." Kusanagi slipped on a pair of latex gloves. "Let's get going."

Kusanagi was actually looking forward to the day's task. Any semblance of progress was enough to distract him from his main concern: that all they had to go on was a suggestion that one of Yoshitaka's exes might have been a painter. They didn't even know what kind of paintings she might have done.

"I don't think we can say she was an artist just because she carried around a sketchbook," Kishitani opined, opening the nearest box. "She could be a fashion designer, or even a comic book artist."

"True enough," Kusanagi admitted. "Just keep all the possibilities in your head while we go through this stuff. Maybe she's in furniture or architecture. You think of those?"

"Right," Kishitani muttered.

"I've got to say, you don't sound very enthusiastic."

The junior detective gave Kusanagi a sorrowful look. "It's not about enthusiasm. It's just, I don't get it. We haven't found a single shred of evidence suggesting that anyone other than Hiromi Wakayama came to the Mashiba house on the day of the murder."

"I know that. But can we say for sure that no one else was there?"

"Well . . ."

"If no one did come, how did the killer get the poison into the kettle? Tell me that."

Kishitani glared at Kusanagi in silence.

"You can't, right?" Kusanagi continued. "Of course you can't. Not even Yukawa, the great Detective Galileo, has a clue. That's because the answer is too simple. There wasn't any trick. The killer got into the house, poisoned the kettle, and left. That's all. And I think I've already explained why we can't find any evidence of who it might have been."

"Because it was someone Mr. Mashiba didn't want anyone else to know about, so the visit was a secret."

"You *have* been paying attention. And when a man wants to conceal who he's been meeting with, our first step is to check for women. That's Investigation 101. Anything wrong with what I'm saying?"

"Nope." Kishitani shook his head.

"Then if you're down with the program, let's get back to work. We're not made of time here."

Kishitani nodded and turned back to his cardboard box in silence.

Kusanagi sighed inwardly. *What are you so worked up about?* he asked himself. He knew he shouldn't let something like a simple question from his partner get under his skin, but somehow it had released a wave of irritation.

The problem, he realized, was that he'd begun to wonder whether there was any point at all to what they were doing. He was growing increasingly uncertain that checking into Yoshitaka Mashiba's past relationships would turn up anything useful.

This kind of uncertainty was typical of most investigations. A detective who worried about hitting dead ends should consider a change of profession. But at the same time, he knew that his present unease stemmed from a different concern altogether.

He was afraid that if they didn't find anything, they would be forced to turn to Ayane Mashiba as the last suspect. He didn't care what Utsumi and Kishitani thought. Kusanagi was worried about what would happen when *he* started suspecting her.

He was acutely aware of the sensation he felt whenever he was in her presence—a kind of high-strung tension, like a knife pointed at his own throat. It was a challenge, an insistence to focus on that moment alone. It was also a feeling of immediacy that made the blood rise to his face, and tugged at his heart. But when he wondered what it meant, a picture came into his mind that made him even more uneasy.

Kusanagi had met plenty of good, admirable people who'd been turned into murderers by circumstance. There was something about them he always seemed to sense, an aura that they shared. Somehow, their transgression freed them from the confines of a mortal existence, allowing them to perceive the great truths of the universe. At the same time, it meant they had one foot in forbidden territory. They straddled the line between sanity and madness.

This was what Kusanagi felt when he was near Ayane. He could try to deny it, but his sixth sense as a detective knew better. *So I'm investigating dead ends in order to silence my own doubts.* Kusanagi shook his head. It was his knowledge of his own willful stupidity that had brought on his irritation.

An hour passed. They had found nothing suggesting any painters—or anyone in a profession requiring a sketchbook, for that matter. Nearly all the things inside the boxes were gifts or commemorative knickknacks of one kind or another.

"What do you think this is?" Kishitani held up a small stuffed toy. At first glance, it resembled a beet, complete with green leaves on top.

"It's a beet."

"Yes! But it's also an alien."

"How so?"

"Look at this," Kishitani said, placing the beet leaf-side down on the table. Kusanagi noticed there was something like a face on the upper white tip, and if you thought of the leaves as legs, it did resemble one of those jellyfishlike aliens from the cartoons.

"Incredible," Kusanagi deadpanned.

"There's an instruction card," the junior detective went on. "Our friend here is Beetron from the Planet Beetilex. Look at the copyright—it was made by Mashiba's company."

"Okay, I'll bite. Why are you showing me this?"

"Wouldn't the person who designed this have used a sketchbook?"

Kusanagi blinked and looked at the toy more closely. "Huh. Definitely a possibility."

"Let's ask the friendly Ms. Yamamoto," Kishitani said, standing.

The PR director arrived shortly after and nodded when she looked at the toy. "Yes, we did have that made a while ago. It's the mascot for an online anime we produced."

"Online anime?" Kusanagi prompted.

"Something we had up on our home page until about three years ago. Would you like to see it?"

"Very much," Kusanagi said, not entirely facetiously.

They went into an office where Ms. Yamamoto began opening files on the computer until the screen was filled with the opening titles to the Internet anime *Beetron, Go!* She pressed play, and the anime ran for about a minute. The show featured the Beetron character stepping through the paces of a largely forgettable story.

"So this isn't online anymore?" Kishitani asked.

"It was popular for a bit—thus that stuffed toy—but sales weren't so good, and eventually it was canceled."

"Did one of your employees design the character?" Kusanagi asked.

"No, actually. The designer posted some illustrations of Beetron on a blog and developed a small following, so we comissioned the anime."

"Was the designer a professional illustrator?"

"No, a schoolteacher, actually. Not even an art teacher."

"Huh."

This was starting to sound like a definite possibility to Kusanagi. Tatsuhiko Ikai had insisted that Mashiba would never have let work relationships develop into romance, but he could see it working the other way around.

"Ah," Kishitani said, as he typed on the computer. "Looks like another dead end, Detective. This isn't her."

"How do you know?"

"Because it's a him. Look at the artist's profile."

Kusanagi stared at the screen and frowned.

"Guess we should've asked ahead of time," Kishitani said. "I guess guys draw cute designs, too."

"Yeah, I assumed it was a girl myself," Kusanagi said, scratching his head.

"Excuse me," Ms. Yamamoto said, inserting herself into the conversation. "Is there some problem with the artist being a man?"

"No, it has to do with our investigation," Kusanagi explained. "We're looking for someone who might provide us with the lead we need to close the case—and that someone had to be a woman."

"By 'case,' you *are* talking about Mr. Mashiba's murder, yes?"

"Of course."

"And the Internet anime has something to do with that?"

"I can't go into the details, but suffice it to say that if the creator of the anime were a woman, it might have had something to do with Mr. Mashiba's death . . . but since this gentleman is clearly not a woman . . ." Kusanagi sighed and looked over at his partner. "I think we're done here for today."

"Yep," Kishitani agreed, his shoulders sagging.

Ms. Yamamoto saw them to the front door, where Kusanagi turned and thanked her. "Sorry to interrupt your day—and apologies in advance if we need to come back for anything."

"Not at all. You're welcome anytime," she said, a curious look on her face, one markedly different from her cold demeanor when they first arrived.

The detectives started to walk away; but they had only taken a couple steps when Ms. Yamamoto called after them. "Detective?"

Kusanagi looked around. "Yes?"

She trotted over to them and whispered, "There's a lounge on the first floor of the building—could you wait there for just a moment? There is something I wanted to talk to you about, but not here."

"Does this concern the case?"

"I'm not sure. It has to do with the beet alien, actually. About the creator."

Kusanagi and Kishitani exchanged glances. "Of course."

"I'll be down as soon as I can," she told them, then disappeared back inside the office.

The lounge on the first floor was spacious. Kusanagi drank coffee and glared at the no smoking sign on the wall.

"What do you think she wants to talk to us about?" Kishitani asked.

"Who knows? I can't imagine some amateur illustrator—a guy—having anything to do with anything, but we'll see."

Ms. Yamamoto arrived quickly. She glanced around before

holding up an envelope about half the size of a standard sheet of paper.

"Sorry to keep you waiting," she said, sitting down across from them. The waitress came over but Ms. Yamamoto waved her off.

Clearly not planning on staying long, Kusanagi thought. "What did you want to talk to us about?"

She looked around again, then leaned forward. "You have to understand, I really can't have this released to the public. If for some reason you have to let it out . . . please don't tell anyone you heard it from me."

Kusanagi peered at her intently. He wanted to tell her that whether or not it became public knowledge depended on the nature of the information, but he also didn't want to jeopardize their chances of hearing about a possible lead. So he kept quiet. It wouldn't be his first time breaking a promise, and he would cross that bridge when he came to it.

He nodded. "Okay, the word stays here."

Ms. Yamamoto wet her lips. "That beet alien you were looking at before? Well, the designer *was* a woman."

"Huh?" Kusanagi said, his eyes widening. "Really?" He straightened in his chair. This might actually be something worth hearing.

"Yes. For various reasons, we had to lie on the Web page."

Kishitani nodded, beginning to take notes. "That's not so unusual. People's names, ages, and genders are often falsified online."

"Was the bit about him being a teacher also not true?" Kusanagi asked.

"No—or rather, the teacher we have featured on our site

does actually exist. He was the one writing the blog. But some- one else designed the character. She had nothing to do with him at all."

Wrinkles formed between Kusanagi's eyebrows, and he rested his elbows on the table. "So why all the subterfuge?"

Ms. Yamamoto hesitated before saying, "Actually, everything was prearranged."

"Can you elaborate?"

"The story I gave you before, about the alien becoming popu- lar on the teacher's blog, and us making an anime—in fact, it happened the other way around. We planned on producing a character-driven Internet anime first, and as part of our PR strat- egy, we decided to start the character out on a private blog. Then we started doing things online, search engine optimization and the like, to make sure people saw the blog. Once the character started gaining popularity, we published the story that we had contracted with the blogger to make our show."

Kusanagi crossed his arms and grunted. "Sounds like an aw- ful lot of trouble to go through, if you ask me."

"People online respond better to things that seem organic. It was our CEO's idea."

Kishitani looked over toward Kusanagi and nodded. "She's right. Everyone likes it when something created by a nobody goes viral like that."

"So ultimately," Kusanagi said, "the designer was one of your employees?"

"No. We started with a search of relatively unknown manga artists and illustrators. Then we had them submit ideas for char- acter designs, and we picked one we liked: the beet alien you saw. We wrote up a nondisclosure agreement with the designer, to keep it a secret, and we had her draw some illustrations to put on our teacher's blog. She did all the initial work, though we switched to another artist about halfway through. I'm sure it's obvious by now, but we were also paying the teacher to write his blog."

"Quite the show," Kusanagi muttered. "You weren't kidding when you said everything had been prearranged."

"It takes a real strategy to introduce a new character these days," Ms. Yamamoto said with a light laugh. "Not that ours worked very well."

"So who was this illustrator you ended up using?"

"A children's book illustrator, originally. She's had a few books published," Ms. Yamamoto said, producing a slim volume from the envelope on her lap.

Kusanagi took the book and examined it. It was titled *It Can Rain Tomorrow*, and it apparently chronicled the adventures of a teruterubozu—a diminutive tissue-paper ghost created by children wishing for good weather. The illustrator's name was listed as Sumire Ucho—*Violet Butterfly*, Kusanagi thought. *If that's not a pen name, I don't know what is.*

"Is this illustrator still connected with your company?"

"No, not since she made those first illustrations. The company holds all the rights to the character."

"Did you ever meet her personally?"

"I didn't, I'm afraid. Like I said, we had to keep her existence a secret. Only the CEO and a few other people ever saw her. The contract talks and everything were handled directly by the CEO."

"By Mr. Mashiba?"

"Yes. I think he was the beet alien's biggest fan," Ms. Yamamoto said, staring at the detective.

Kusanagi let his eyes drop back down to the book. There was a little "About the Author" section, but no mention of her real name or age.

Still, it was clear that this woman fit the bill. Kusanagi lifted the book in one hand. "Do you mind if I borrow this?"

"Not at all," the receptionist replied, glancing at her watch. "I should be getting back. I've told you everything I know. I hope it helps."

"Tremendously. Thank you," Kusanagi said, inclining his head.

Once she had left, Kusanagi handed the book to his partner. "Give the publisher a ring, would you?"

"Think she's the one?"

"There's a chance. At the very least, we know there was something between this illustrator and Yoshitaka Mashiba."

"You sound confident."

"It was the look on Ms. Yamamoto's face that sold me. She suspected before today that something was up between those two."

"Then why do you think she didn't say anything before now? The officers we sent to the company earlier asked everybody for information about Mr. Mashiba's female friends."

"Maybe she was too unsure to say anything at the time. We didn't exactly ask her to tell us about the ex-CEO's lovers, either. We just asked about the illustrator, and she put two and two together, and realized there was something to her hunch."

"Interesting. I'm sorry I called her a robot."

"You can make up for it by getting on the phone with that publisher now."

Kishitani pulled out his cell phone and stepped out of the lounge, book tucked under his arm. Kusanagi watched him make the call in the building lobby. He drank his coffee. It had gone completely cold.

Kishitani returned, a glum look on his face.

"Couldn't get ahold of anybody?"

"No, I did."

"But they'd never heard of Ms. Ucho?"

"No, they had."

"So what's with the long face?"

Kishitani opened his notebook. "Her real name is Junko Tsukui. This book here was published four years ago. It's out of print now."

"You get a number for her?"

"She doesn't have a number." Kishitani looked up from his notebook. "She's dead."

"What? When?"

"Two years ago, at her home. She committed suicide."

NINETEEN

Utsumi was at the Meguro Police Station writing a report when Kusanagi and Kishitani marched into the room, familiar scowls on their faces.

"The old man go home already?" Kusanagi asked when he saw her.

"No, I think the chief's over in Investigations."

Kusanagi left without another word, leaving Kishitani behind.

"Looks like he's in a bad mood," Utsumi said.

Kishitani shrugged. "We finally managed to track down Yoshitaka Mashiba's old flame."

"Really? Isn't that a good thing?"

"Well, we hit a little snag when we went to follow up." He dropped into a folding chair and related the story of the beet alien and its illustrator to a surprised Utsumi. "We ended up going to the publisher," he concluded, "and we got a photograph of her to show to that waitress at the tea café, who confirmed her as Yoshitaka's ex-girlfriend. Which nicely wraps up that chapter, and leaves Kusanagi's former-lover theory dead in the water."

"No wonder he's grumpy."

"I'm a little disappointed myself," Kishitani said. "We do the run-around all day only to end up with this. Talk about exhausting." He yawned and stretched.

Just then Utsumi's phone rang. It was Yukawa.

"Hello again," she said into the receiver. "Didn't I just talk to you earlier today?"

"Where are you now?" Yukawa asked.

"Meguro Station, why?"

"I've been thinking about things, and realized I need you. Can you meet?"

"Again? Sure, no problem. But what's up?"

"I'll tell you when I see you. You pick the place," Yukawa said. He sounded uncharacteristically excited.

"Okay, well, I could just go to the university—"

"No, I already left. I'm headed toward you, actually. Just pick a place somewhere in between."

She gave him the name of a nearby twenty-four-hour restaurant, and he hung up. Utsumi placed her half-written report in her bag and grabbed her jacket.

"Was that Galileo?" Kishitani asked.

"Yes. He said he needed to talk to me about something."

"I hope he figures out the poisoning trick so we can solve this case and go home. Take notes, if you don't mind. Sometimes his explanations can be a little dense."

"I know," Utsumi said as she headed out of the room.

She was drinking tea when Yukawa hurried into the restaurant. He sat down across from her and ordered a hot chocolate.

"No coffee?"

"No, the two cups earlier were enough," Yukawa said, with a slight frown. "Sorry for dragging you out like this."

"It's not a problem. So what's this about?"

"Right—" He glanced down at the table once before looking back up at her. "First, I need to know if you still suspect Mrs. Mashiba."

"Huh? Well, yes, I do. I suspect her."

"Right," Yukawa said again, reaching inside his jacket to pull out a folded piece of paper. He placed it on the table. "Read this."

Utsumi picked up the paper, unfolded it, and began to read, her eyes narrowing. "What is this?"

"Something I want you to look into. In detail."

"And this will solve the mystery?"

Yukawa blinked and gave a little sigh. "No, probably not. But this will at least prove it's unsolvable. Think of it as a kind of way to cover the bases."

"What do you mean?"

"After you left my laboratory today, I started thinking. If we hypothesize that Mrs. Mashiba poisoned the coffee, then the question is: How did she do it? The answer is: I have no idea. My conclusion was that this is a problem without a solution— save one."

"Save one? So there *is* a solution."

"Yes, but it's an imaginary solution."

"You lost me."

"An imaginary solution is one that, while theoretically possible, is *practically* impossible. There appears to be only one method by which a wife in Hokkaido can poison her husband in Tokyo.

However, the chances that she pulled it off are infinitely close to zero. You see? The trick *is* doable, but pulling it off isn't."

Utsumi shook her head. "I'm not sure I do see, actually. So this homework you've given me is to prove that the trick is impossible? Why?"

"Sometimes it's as important to prove there is no answer to a question as it is to answer it."

"Except I'm looking for answers, Professor. I'd much rather be getting to the truth of what happened than engaging in theoretical exercises, if you don't mind. That's my job."

Yukawa fell silent. His hot chocolate arrived. After a moment he lifted the cup and took a sip. "Of course," he muttered at last. "You're right."

"Professor . . ."

The physicist reached out and retrieved the piece of paper off the table. "It's a habit we scientists get into," he said. "Even if the solution to a problem is imaginary, we can't rest until we look into it. But, of course, you're a detective, not a scientist. You can't be wasting your valuable time proving something's impossible."

He neatly refolded the paper and placed it in his jacket pocket. The edges of his mouth curled upward into a smile. "Forget I said anything."

"Why don't you tell me what this impossible trick was?" Utsumi said. "Then I can decide for myself whether or not it's really impossible. Based on that, I can look into whatever you wanted me to check."

"I can't do that," Yukawa replied.

"Why not?"

"If you knew what the trick was, it would color your opinion, rendering you unable to conduct your research objectively. And, if you're not going to look into it anyway, there's no need for you to know the trick. Either way, I can't tell you."

Yukawa reached for the bill, but Utsumi grabbed it before he could pick it up. "It's on me," she said.

"Unthinkable," Yukawa said. "I made you come out here."

Utsumi held out her other hand. "Give me that paper. I'll look into it for you."

"But it's an imaginary solution."

"I don't care. If it's the only solution we've got, I want to know what it is."

Yukawa sighed and produced the paper. Utsumi peered at it briefly before putting it in her bag. "So . . . if it turns out that the answer isn't 'imaginary,' as you call it, after all, we have a chance at solving the mystery."

"Maybe," Yukawa muttered noncommittally as he pushed up his glasses with one finger.

"We don't have a chance?"

"If it's not imaginary," the physicist said, a keen glimmer in his eye, "then you still won't be able to solve it. Neither will I. It's the perfect crime."

TWENTY

Hiromi Wakayama stared at the tapestry on the wall. Linked filaments of gray and navy blue formed an irregular belt that ran through the design. Bending and twisting, the belt curved under and over itself, ultimately returning to its point of origin to complete an elaborate loop. Though it was a fairly complicated design, when seen from a distance it appeared to be a simple geometrical pattern. Yoshitaka had called it an "ugly DNA spiral," but Hiromi was rather fond of it. When Ayane did her show in Ginza, the piece had been displayed right next to the entrance. It was her design, but Hiromi's work.

It wasn't all that unusual in the art world for many of the works in an artist's individual show to have actually been executed by their apprentices. In the case of patchwork particularly, where a single large piece could take several months to make, some division of labor was necessary, or an artist would be hard-pressed to make enough pieces to hold a show.

Nonetheless, Ayane had done most of the work in the Ginza show herself. At least eighty percent of the tapestries there had been entirely her own product. And yet she had chosen to show the one that her apprentice made up front. Hiromi remembered the thrill she had felt when she saw it there—a thrill that came from knowing her talent was being recognized by her teacher.

At the time, she had thought she wanted to work for Ayane Mashiba forever . . .

Ayane's coffee mug made a loud *clink* as she set it down on the worktable. The two women were sitting across from each other at Anne's House Patchwork School. Ordinarily at this time of day a class would be in session, and several students would be there, cutting and sewing cloth. But Ayane had yet to reopen the school to students. Today there were only the two of them, and the bomb that Hiromi had dropped between them—

"Oh?" Ayane said, holding her mug in both hands. "Well, if that's your decision . . ."

"I'm sorry to spring this on you," Hiromi said, lowering her head.

"There's no need to apologize. I was a little worried about how things might go myself. Maybe this is really for the best."

"It's all my fault," Hiromi said. "I . . . I just don't know what to say."

"Then don't say anything. I don't really want to sit here watching you apologize anymore."

"Oh, right. Sorry . . ." Hiromi hung her head. She felt tears stinging her eyes, but she held them back. She didn't want to make Ayane any more uncomfortable than she already had.

Hiromi had been the one who called, saying she needed to talk. Ayane had invited her to come to Anne's House without even asking what she wanted to talk about.

She really has no idea I'm going to quit, Hiromi had thought.

She'd broken the news while Ayane was making tea.

And now Ayane was somehow managing to be solicitous. "Hiromi, are you sure you'll be okay?" she asked.

Swallowing a sob, Hiromi looked up.

"I mean financially," the widow went on. "I'm worried you might not be able to find work so easily. Unless your family is in a position to help?"

"Honestly, I haven't figured any of that out yet. I'd like to leave my parents out of it if possible, but I might not have a choice. Still, I have a bit of savings, so I'm going to try to do things on my own as much as possible."

"Well," Ayane said, "that doesn't sound so reassuring." She brushed her hair back across her ear several times—a sure sign she was irritated. "But maybe it's not my place to worry about that."

"I don't deserve it."

"Can we please lay off the self-pity?" Ayane said, the sudden harshness in her voice sending shivers through Hiromi's body. Her head drooped again.

"Sorry," Ayane added quietly. "That wasn't very nice of me. But I really don't want you acting like this. Maybe it's impossible for us to work together, but I *do* want you to be happy. That's the truth."

With some trepidation, Hiromi raised her head. Ayane was smiling—a thin, lonely smile; but it seemed genuine.

"And the person responsible for making both of us feel like this isn't around anymore." The widow's voice was soft and distant. "It's time we started looking forward, not back."

Hiromi nodded, though the suggestion sounded all but impossible. Her love for Yoshitaka, her sadness at losing him, and her guilt for betraying her mentor all weighed too heavily on her heart.

"How many years is it since you started working for me?" Ayane asked, abruptly and deliberately cheerful.

"About . . . three years, maybe a little more."

"Three years already? If you were in high school, you'd have already graduated. Maybe that's how we should think of it: your graduation!"

Hiromi almost shook her head. *I'm not so much of a fool that that would cheer me up.*

"You had a key for the classroom, didn't you?"

"Oh, right, I'll give it back," Hiromi said, reaching into her bag.

"No, you hold onto it."

"But—"

"I know you've left lots of stuff here. It will take you a while before everything is cleaned out. And if there's anything else you need, go ahead and take it. How about that tapestry? I know you like it." Ayane indicated the tapestry Hiromi had been admiring before.

"That one—really?"

"You're the one who made it, after all. And people loved it at the show. I didn't sell it because I wanted to give it to you, you know."

Hiromi recalled with a pang of guilt that even though most of the works on display in the Ginza show had sported price tags, this tapestry had been marked "not for sale."

Now Ayane turned more brisk. "How many days do you think it will take to gather all your stuff?"

"Only today and tomorrow, I think."

"Okay, well, then, how about you give me a call when you're

finished? The key . . . You can leave the key in the mail slot in the door. Be careful not to forget anything—I'm going to call a professional and have them come in to clean this place out when you're done."

Hiromi blinked, not understanding.

"Well, it's not like I can go on living at that hotel forever. It's not very frugal, or convenient. I thought I would live here until I figure out where I'm going next."

"So you're not going back home?"

Ayane sighed, her shoulders dropping. "I thought about it, but I've decided not to. So many happy memories . . . But they're all bitter now. Twisted up. And anyhow, it's far too large for me to live in by myself. I'm amazed he lived there alone for so long before meeting me."

"Are you going to sell it?"

"I'll try, though it might be hard with word getting out about what happened there. I thought I would talk to Mr. Ikai first. I'm sure he has some connections who could help."

Hiromi sat looking down at the mug on the worktable, unable to think of anything more to say. The tea Ayane had made for her was probably cold by now.

"Well, I'm going to leave now," the older woman said, picking up her now empty mug.

"Just leave that, I'll wash it before I leave," Hiromi offered.

"Oh? Well, thanks," Ayane said, returning the mug to the table. "You brought in these mugs, didn't you—something from a friend's wedding, wasn't it?"

"Yes, the pair of them."

Now they were sitting side by side on the worktable. Hiromi and Ayane had often drunk from them when they held their monthly curriculum meetings.

"You should definitely remember to take them when you're packing."

"Right," Hiromi said in a small voice. She hadn't been planning to take the mugs at all; but it occurred to her now that leaving them might give Ayane yet another reason to remember what had happened. One more weight settled on her heart.

Ayane hoisted her shoulder bag and made for the door. Hiromi followed.

When she was done putting on her shoes, Ayane looked up at her assistant. "It's strange, isn't it? Me leaving first, even though it's you who's quitting."

"I'll clean up as fast as I can. Maybe I can even finish today."

"No, there's no need to hurry. I didn't mean it like that," Ayane said, looking directly at her. "Be well, Hiromi."

"You, too."

Ayane nodded and opened the door, smiling as she stepped out. The door closed behind her.

Hiromi sat on the floor and breathed a deep sigh.

It was painful to quit her job, and she was worried about what she would do for money, but she was certain that this was her only option. It had been a mistake to try to carry on as though everything was the same, even after she had admitted to her relationship with Yoshitaka. No matter how understanding Ayane might seem, Hiromi knew she hadn't forgiven her, not deep in her heart.

And then there was the baby. Hiromi was terrified Ayane might ask what she was planning to do. She still hadn't been able to come to a decision.

Maybe Ayane hadn't asked because she assumed the obvious:

that Hiromi would terminate the pregnancy. The more she thought about it, the more it seemed obvious that it never occurred to Ayane that Hiromi might actually *want* the child . . .

Hiromi paused, realizing with a shock that when she looked deep down inside herself, all she could think of was keeping it.

But what sort of life would she lead as a single mother? She couldn't go back to her parents. They were both still in good health, but they weren't exactly on easy street, and she could only imagine how they would react when they heard that their daughter had become an unwed mother, and destroyed a marriage in the process.

Maybe I have to have an abortion—the more she thought about it, the more she kept coming back to the same obvious choice. Yet it was a conclusion she wanted desperately to avoid. How many times since Yoshitaka's death had she wished for an easy way out? *There is no easy way.*

She was shaking her head at her own stupidity when her phone rang. Hiromi stood slowly and walked back to the worktable. She pulled the phone out of her bag. Recognizing the number on the display, she hesitated a long moment before she pushed the call button. *Ignoring them now won't make them go away.*

"Yes?" she said, her voice unintentionally dark.

"Hello, this is Detective Utsumi from the Metropolitan police. I was wondering if you had a moment?"

"Sure."

"I'm sorry to bother you again, but there were a few more things I wanted to ask. Maybe we could meet up?"

"When?"

"As soon as possible."

Hiromi breathed a long sigh, not really caring if the detective heard. "Then, could you come here? I'm at the patchwork school."

"In Daikanyama, right? Is Mrs. Mashiba there as well?"

"No, she's gone for the day. It's just me."

"Okay, I'll be right over."

Hiromi returned her phone to her bag and rubbed her forehead with one hand.

It occurred to her for the first time that quitting the patchwork school didn't mean it was all over. The police would never let her go until they'd solved the case—*if* they solved the case. She would never be allowed to have her child in peace.

She gulped the remaining tea from her mug—lukewarm, as expected.

The events of the past three years floated in her mind. When she first came to Anne's House, her budding patchwork skills had been inconsistent, her lack of experience evident; but she'd made tremendous progress in the first three months—so much so that she'd even surprised herself. When Ayane asked her to become her assistant, she'd said yes on the spot. She had long since grown tired of the pointless, mechanical work the temp agency occasionally sent her.

Hiromi glanced at the computer sitting in the corner of the room. She and Ayane relied heavily on drafting software when making their designs. Sometimes it took a whole night just to decide on colors; but not once had she ever found the work onerous. Once they had decided on a design, they would go buy the cloth. And then, after spending all that time meticulously deciding on colors, once at the store they would inevitably be swept away by some new fabric in stock, often changing their minds on the spot, ruefully laughing together at their own lack of restraint.

I was satisfied, Hiromi realized. *I had a good job, and a good life.* And now it had all come to an end. She shook her head. It was all her fault. She had stolen the husband of another woman— and not just any woman, the very person who had helped her become who she was today.

Hiromi clearly remembered the first time she met Yoshitaka Mashiba. It was in this very room. She'd been getting ready for class when Ayane called to tell her a man would be showing up, and she was to ask him to wait there for her. She never mentioned who the man was.

Yoshitaka arrived shortly after. She let him in and offered him tea. He looked around the room with interest, asking about this and that. Her first impression was that he had the curiosity of a little boy, combined with the relaxed poise of a man. It was clear from just a few moments' conversation that he was very smart, as well.

Ayane arrived afterward and introduced him. Hiromi was surprised to hear they had met at a singles party. She had no idea Ayane attended that kind of event.

Looking back on it now, she realized that her interest in Yoshitaka began that day. She remembered clearly feeling a pang of something remarkably like jealousy when Ayane told her they were dating.

If their meeting had happened some other way—if Ayane had shown up with him—Hiromi was sure she would've felt differently. It was that time they had spent together, just the two of them, before she knew who he was, that had planted the seed of her later feelings.

Once love began to grow, even though it might remain a fragile thing, it was hard to quench entirely. Once Ayane married, Hiromi began visiting the house, feeling even closer than before to Yoshitaka. The times when they were alone together became more frequent.

Of course, Hiromi had never confessed her feelings. That would only cause trouble, she'd thought; and she had never really considered a relationship, not even as a remote possibility. It was enough for her at that time to feel like part of the Mashiba family.

But somehow, she thought, *somehow he knew*. Her feelings must've shown through, despite her attempts to hide them. Gradually, the way he acted around her began to change. Where he used to look at her like a younger sister, now there was something else in his eyes. And it would have been a lie to say she wasn't elated when she saw it.

She gazed around the room. She'd been working right here one night about three months ago when Yoshitaka called. "Ayane was telling me that you've been eating late these days. It must be pretty busy at the school."

He was late getting off work himself, and there was a ramen place he'd been meaning to check out. He invited her along.

She was hungry, so she said yes, and Yoshitaka came to pick her up.

She didn't remember the taste of the ramen. Maybe it wasn't so good—or maybe it was because they'd sat side-by-side at the counter, and every time he took a bite, his elbow would brush against her shoulder. That touch was all she remembered.

Yoshitaka drove her to her apartment afterward. He stopped the car out front and smiled at her. "Maybe we can go get ramen again sometime soon?"

"Sure thing, anytime," she told him.

"Thanks. You're a pleasure to be with."

"Really?"

"Yeah," he said. "I guess I've just been tired a lot here and here," he said, pointing at his head and his chest in turn. "Being with you is a relief from that." Then a serious look came over his face. "Thanks for joining me tonight. I had fun."

"Me, too," she said; and he reached his arm around her shoulders and pulled her gently toward him. She let herself be drawn in. Their kiss felt completely natural, completely right.

"Good night," he said.

"Good night," she replied.

Her heart was soaring so high that night she had trouble getting to sleep. But not once did she feel like she had made a mistake. All they had done was create a little secret for them to share—that was how she thought of it.

Soon, Yoshitaka was all she could think about. His presence loomed large in her mind, accompanying her throughout her day. Maybe if they hadn't met again her fever would've passed in time. But he kept calling her, with increasing frequency. And she kept staying later at the school, even when she had nothing to do, just to wait for his calls.

Like a balloon cut from its string, her heart was lofting out of reach. It was not until they crossed that final line in a relationship between a man and a woman that she thought for the first time she was doing something wrong. But the words Yoshitaka told her that night were strong enough to whisk away her unease.

"I'm asking Ayane for a divorce," he said. "We made a promise that if, after a year, we were still without a child, then we would dissolve our marriage. We still have three months left, but my hopes aren't very high. I can tell it's not going to work."

His words were cold, but nothing could have lifted Hiromi's spirits higher. *That's how far I'd fallen*, she thought now. *That's how thoughtless I'd become.*

In retrospect, it was obvious they'd committed a monumental betrayal. How could Ayane not hate her? *Maybe Ayane killed him after all. Maybe she wants to kill me, too.* Hiromi wouldn't have been all that surprised if Ayane's kindness toward her was just an act, a kind of camouflage to conceal her murderous intent.

But Ayane had an alibi, and it didn't sound like the police suspected her; so maybe it really wasn't she.

Hiromi wondered if there was anyone else who hated Yoshitaka enough to kill him. The thought gave her yet another reason to be depressed: here she was, pregnant with the man's baby, and she knew so little about him.

Utsumi's arrival roused her from her bleak reverie. The detective was wearing a dark suit, and she sat in the chair where Ayane had been sitting only thirty minutes before, apologizing again for the trouble.

"I just don't think asking me questions is going to get you anywhere in your investigation," Hiromi told her. "The truth is, I don't really know that much about Mr. Mashiba."

"And yet you had a relationship?"

Hiromi's mouth tightened. "I knew what kind of person he was, but that's not what you need now, is it? You need to know about his past, or his troubles at work, and I don't know any of that."

"Actually, knowing what kind of person Mr. Mashiba was is very important for our investigation. But I didn't come here to talk about anything difficult like that today. I wanted to ask you about things that are more everyday."

"What do you mean, everyday?"

"Like, about Mr. and Mrs. Mashiba's daily lives. You are the one who knew both of them best."

"Actually, I would think Mrs. Mashiba would know better than I. Shouldn't you be talking to her?"

Utsumi smiled. "It's hard to get an objective view of someone's life by asking them directly."

Hiromi sighed. "So what is it you want to know?"

"I understand that you began visiting the Mashibas' house soon after they were married. Can you tell me how often you were there?"

"Well, it varied, but if I had to guess, I'd say it was about once or twice a month on average."

"Any particular days?"

"No, nothing as formal as that. Though I guess I was there on Sundays more than any other day. That's when the school was closed."

"So Mr. Mashiba was usually home on the Sundays you visited?"

"Usually, yes."

"Did you two talk much then?"

"Sometimes, but usually, Mr. Mashiba would be in his study. Apparently he worked from home on the weekends. Besides," Hiromi said, a bit defensively, "I usually only visited the house because I had something to go over with Ayane. It wasn't just a social call." She didn't want the detective to think that she had been going to see Yoshitaka.

"Where would you meet with Mrs. Mashiba when you visited?"

"The living room."

"Always?"

"Yes, pretty much. Does it matter?"

"Did you ever drink tea or coffee while you were together?"

"There was always something."

"Was it ever you who made it on those occasions?"

"Sometimes. Like when Ayane was busy making something else."

"You told us that she taught you how to make coffee at their house, which is why you followed her directions on the morning of Mr. Mashiba's death."

"Yes." Hiromi took a sharp breath. "I can't believe we're talking about the coffee again. How many times have we gone over this?"

Maybe she was used to her interviewees getting upset, but the young detective's expression didn't even register Hiromi's comment.

"When you came over with the Ikais for that party, did you open the refrigerator at all?" Utsumi asked.

"Excuse me, the refrigerator?"

"Yes. There should have been some bottles of mineral water inside. Did you notice them at the time?"

"Well, yes, I did. I actually went to get a bottle that night."

"Do you remember how many bottles were inside?"

"How could I remember a thing like that? There were a couple, I guess."

"One or two bottles, then? More?"

"I just told you I don't remember. They were in a row, though, so maybe four or five?" Hiromi said, her voice getting louder.

"Right," the detective replied, her face as expressionless as a Noh mask. "You told us that just before his death, Mr. Mashiba invited you over. Was that a frequent occurrence?"

"No, that was the first time ever."

"Why do you think he did that? On that day in particular?"

"Well, because Ayane had gone back to her parents' home in Sapporo, I guess."

"So that was the first time an opportunity like that had presented itself?"

"Yes, that's part of it. He probably also wanted to tell me in person, as quickly as possible, that Ayane had agreed to the divorce."

"I see," Utsumi said, nodding. "Do you know anything about their hobbies?"

"Hobbies?" Hiromi echoed, raising an eyebrow at the sudden shift in topic.

"Mr. and Mrs. Mashiba's hobbies. Did they play any sports? Did they like to travel, or go for drives?"

Hiromi shrugged. "I know Mr. Mashiba played tennis and golf, but I don't think Ayane had any hobbies per se. Just patchwork and cooking."

"How did they spend their time off together?"

"Sorry," Hiromi replied, "I don't know much about that."

"Anything is fine," the detective told her.

"Well, I know that Ayane was usually working on her patchwork. And I guess Mr. Mashiba watched DVDs sometimes."

"Which room did Ayane use to work on her patchwork when she was at home?"

"The living room, I think," Hiromi said, starting to wonder where all this was leading. The questions seemed entirely random.

"Did they ever go on trips together?"

"I know that right after their wedding they went to Europe—Paris and London. I don't think they went on any trips after that, except when Mr. Mashiba went somewhere on business."

"What about shopping? Did you ever go out shopping with Mrs. Mashiba?"

"Sure. We bought cloth for the patchwork school together all the time."

"Was that on Sundays, too?"

"No. We went on weekdays, before class started. There was usually a lot, so we would bring it to the classroom right from the store."

Utsumi nodded and scribbled something in her notebook. "Thanks for your time. That's all the questions I have for now."

"Sorry, I have to ask," Hiromi said, "Why were you asking me all those things? I couldn't tell at all what you were getting at."

"Which question in particular were you wondering about?"

"All of them. What do hobbies and going shopping have to do with the case?"

After a moment's hesitation, Utsumi smiled. "It's okay if you don't understand. It has to do with a theory we're working on."

"Can you tell me what it is?"

"Sorry," she replied, standing quickly. "That's against the rules."

Utsumi apologized again for the intrusion and showed herself out.

TWENTY-ONE

"When she asked me why I was asking those questions, I had no idea what to tell her. What could I say when even I didn't understand them?" Utsumi picked up her coffee cup. "You know, they tell us to always have a clear goal in mind when questioning someone." She had brought the results from her latest round of questioning to share with Yukawa in his laboratory.

"Well, that's an excellent policy, most of the time," Yukawa said, looking up from her report. "But what we're trying to do here is to determine whether or not an extremely unusual, unprecedented crime has taken place. Determining the existence or nonexistence of something extraordinary is never a straightforward task, and those who set themselves to do it are often overly swayed by their preconceived notions. You've heard of the physicist René-Prosper Blondlot—wait, no, of course you haven't heard of him."

"I haven't."

"He was a French researcher active in the latter half of the nineteenth century. Blondlot announced the discovery of a new kind of radiation late in his career. These 'N-rays,' as he termed them, had the effect of making electrical sparks appear brighter. It was hailed as an epoch-making discovery, and sent the whole physics world into a tizzy. However, in the end, N-rays were shown not to exist after all. No matter how much researchers from other countries tried, no one could duplicate the results or increase the sparks' brightness."

"So it was a sham?"

"Not a sham, exactly. Because Blondlot himself believed in the N-rays' existence until the day he died."

"How does that work?"

"Well, for one thing, Blondlot was judging the brightness of the electrical sparks by his own eyes alone. That was the origin of his error. The increase in brightness due to the supposed application of N-rays wasn't an actual effect, but nonetheless he saw it—simply because he desired to see it."

"That seems like a pretty blatant mistake for a respected physicist to make."

"I told you that story to illustrate the inherent danger of preconceptions. Which is why I sent you to that interview without any background information. As a result, you were able to give me extremely objective information." Yukawa returned his eyes to the report.

"So, what's the verdict? Are we still dealing with an imaginary solution?"

Yukawa just stared at the paper in his hand. A deep wrinkle formed between his eyebrows. "Several bottles in the fridge, huh?" he said, half to himself.

"I thought that was strange, too," Utsumi said. "Mrs. Mashiba told us that she never let their stock of bottles run out. But on the day after she went to her parents' house, they were down to one bottle. What do you think it means?"

Yukawa crossed his arms and closed his eyes.

"Professor?" she said, half afraid he'd fallen asleep.

"Impossible," came the physist's reply.

"What's impossible?"

"It just couldn't be, and yet—" Yukawa took off his glasses, pressed his fingertips to his eyelids, and said nothing more.

TWENTY-TWO

Kusanagi made his way up Kagurazaka-dori Avenue from Iida-bashi Station, taking a left immediately after the Bishamonten temple. At the top of the steep slope was his destination, an office building on the right-hand side of the road.

Plates with the names of the resident businesses hung on the wall just inside the front entrance. Kunugi Publishing was on the second floor.

There was an elevator, but Kusanagi took the stairs. This turned out to be extremely awkward due to the large number of cardboard boxes stacked in the stairwell. It was a flagrant violation of fire codes, but he decided not to mention it—at least, not today.

He peeked in through the wide-open door at the top of the stairs and saw several employees sitting at their desks. The woman closest to the door noticed Kusanagi and came over.

"Can I help you?"

"Yes, is Mr. Sasaoka here? I spoke with him on the phone."

"Oh, yes, hello." A slightly pudgy man's face appeared from behind a cabinet.

"Mr. Sasaoka?"

"Yes! Er . . ." The man turned to the desk beside to him, opened a drawer, and pulled out his card, which he offered to the detective. "Pleasure to meet you!"

They exchanged cards. Kusanagi glanced down at the one he had received, which read:

Kunio Sasaoka
CEO, Kunugi Publishing

Mr. Sasaoka beamed. "This is my first time ever getting a card from a police officer. This'll make an excellent keepsake." He reversed the card and huffed with surprise. "It says, 'To Mr. Sasaoka'! And you've written the date here—I see. This is to prevent inappropriate use, am I right?"

"Don't take it personally."

"No, no, I completely understand," the editor said. "So, would you like to talk here, or maybe we should go to a café?"

"Here is fine."

He led Kusanagi to a simple meeting area in a corner of the office.

"Sorry to bother you during business hours." Kusanagi sat down on a black Naugahyde sofa.

"No worries. Things are pretty laid-back here. Not like at the major publishers!" Sasaoka guffawed loudly.

"Like I said on the phone, I wanted to ask you a bit about a Ms. Junko Tsukui."

The smile faded from Sasaoka's amiable face. "Yes . . . I was her editor, in fact. She had real talent. What a loss."

"Did you know her for long?"

"I wouldn't say long, maybe two years and a bit. She did two books for us . . ." Sasaoka stood and retrieved two books from his own desk. "Here they are."

The first was titled *The Snowman Tumbles* and the other *The Adventures of Taro the Temple Dog*.

"She liked writing about characters that already have a certain place in the kid-lit tradition. She even did one about a teruter-ubozu," Sasaoka explained.

"Actually, I know that one," Kusanagi told him, remembering the book that had launched the illustrator's brief career as a character designer for Yoshitaka's online anime.

Sasaoka nodded, his eyes crinkling at the corners. "Ms. Tsukui could take the most familiar characters and make them sparkle. We all miss her."

"Do you remember anything about her death?"

"All too well. She left a letter addressed to me, after all."

"Yes . . . according to her family, she sent a few notes to people she knew."

Junko Tsukui's family home had been in Hiroshima. Kusanagi had spoken with her mother over the phone. When the young woman died of a sleeping pill overdose, she had left three letters behind, each addressed to someone she knew professionally.

"She apologized for abandoning her work," Sasaoka said, shaking his head. "I had just asked her to start her next book. I guess she was concerned that it was never going to get finished."

"Nothing about why she committed suicide?"

"Nothing. Just an apology. As if I wouldn't forgive her!"

Tsukui also mailed a letter to her mother just before killing herself. When her mother read it, she immediately phoned her daughter, and when she couldn't reach her, she told the police. A local squad rushed to the apartment, where they found the body.

Junko hadn't written about her reasons for committing suicide in her letter to her mother. Instead, she had thanked her mother for giving birth to and raising her, and she apologized for throwing away the life she had received.

"We still don't know why," the mother had told Kusanagi over the phone, breaking into tears, the pain in her voice still fresh even after two years.

"Do you have any idea why she might've done it?" Kusanagi asked Sasaoka.

The editor frowned. "The police asked me that back then, too, but I still don't know. I saw her about two weeks before she died, and maybe I'm just dense, but I didn't notice anything out of the ordinary at all."

It wasn't just you, Kusanagi thought. He had already met with the other two recipients of Junko's letters, and both of them had said the same thing. No one understood why she had taken her own life.

"Did you know she was seeing someone?" he asked, changing the topic.

"I heard something like that. But I never knew who it was. You have to watch what you say about those things these days, what with the sexual harassment suits and all," Sasaoka said with evident sincerity.

"Boyfriends aside, then, do you know anyone else she might've been close to? A female associate or friend?"

Sasaoka crossed his thick arms and shrugged. "They asked me

that, too, but I couldn't think of anyone. I think she liked being alone, honestly. She was one of those people who are happy sitting in their room, drawing, not going out of their way to be around other people much. I was kind of surprised when I heard there was a man, to tell you the truth."

Sounds a lot like Ayane, Kusanagi thought. With the exception of her assistant and one old friend back home, she was basically alone, sitting on the sofa in her big living room, working on her patchwork all day long.

Maybe the "lonely woman" was Yoshitaka's type? Kusanagi recalled his conversation with Tatsuhiko Ikai. Yoshitaka Mashiba chose women who led lonely lives because it was only their function as childbearers that interested him. If that was how he thought of them, then friends and the obligations of society would be needless accessories for a machine with only one purpose.

"Detective?" Sasaoka broke the silence. "Can I ask why you're looking into her suicide now? I know there was no motive, but at the time they said it was a clear-cut case of suicide. There was no investigation back then."

Kusanagi shook his head. "It actually has nothing to do with her suicide itself. Her name came up in the course of a different investigation."

"Oh. Right." Sasaoka was clearly curious but lacked the temerity to press for more information.

Kusanagi took the opportunity to leave before Sasaoka asked more questions. "I should be going," he said. "Sorry for taking you away from your work."

"Are you sure that's all you need? Gee, I didn't even remember to offer you some tea."

"It's okay, I'm fine. Though I was wondering if I could borrow these books for a bit?" He held up the two picture books in his hand.

"Those? Please, you can have them."

"Are you sure?"

"Yeah. They're just going to be shredded at some point anyway."

"Well, then, all right. Thanks." Kusanagi stood and headed for the door with the editor close behind him.

"I have to say it was a real surprise when I heard she was gone. When I got the word that she'd died, suicide was the last thing I expected. Even when we heard what had actually happened, we debated it for a long time, me and my friends. Some even thought she was killed. I mean, who would have the guts to actually drink that stuff? It had to be painful."

Kusanagi stopped and fixed his gaze on Sasaoka's round face. "Excuse me? Drink what stuff?"

"The poison."

"Poison? Not sleeping pills?"

The editor's mouth formed the shape of an O and he waved his hands. "No way, I thought you knew! It was arsenic."

Kusanagi froze. "Arsenic?"

"Yeah, the same stuff they found in that poisoned curry down in Wakayama."

"You mean arsenous acid?"

"Right. Yeah. They did call it that."

Kusanagi's heart nearly leapt out of his chest. He quickly excused himself and left the offices. He dashed down the stairs to the street, ringing Kishitani on his cell phone as soon as he was clear of the building. He instructed the junior detective to call the local Police Station who handled Junko Tsukui's suicide and get everything they had on it.

"Still chasing after that picture-book illustrator?" Kishitani asked. "What's up this time?"

"I've already got the chief's okay on this, so stop whining and get on the phone," Kusanagi growled. He disconnected and hailed a cab. "Meguro Police Station!" he told the driver.

As the taxi sped down the road, Kusanagi contemplated the situation. They had spent far too many days on the Mashiba case already. Their inability to determine the entry point of the poison was one reason, and the lack of suspects with a convincing motive was another. The only person with a real motive was Ayane, and she had the perfect alibi.

So, two days ago, Kusanagi had told the chief he was convinced that someone else must have come to the Mashiba residence the day he died. It was then Kusanagi had asked for permission to investigate further into the dead executive's most recent ex-girlfriend.

"But isn't she already dead?" Mamiya asked.

"Yeah, that's why I want to know more," Kusanagi told him. "If Yoshitaka Mashiba was the cause of her suicide, it would give anyone close to Junko Tsukui a motive."

"You're talking about revenge? I dunno, it's been two years since she killed herself. If this was revenge, what took them so long?"

"I can't say. Maybe they waited until everyone forgot about the suicide, so no one would make the connection?"

"If that's true, then our killer is awfully patient, Kusanagi. It's not everyone that can, for two years, hold onto enough hatred to kill a man."

Though Mamiya didn't look very convinced, he gave his permission to look into the suicide case, and Kusanagi had wasted no time. The editor of *It Can Rain Tomorrow* had given him the home phone number of Junko's family, which led to a string of phone calls to them and to every associate who had received one of her suicide letters.

Yet no one he talked to had said so much as a word connecting Yoshitaka Mashiba to her suicide. In fact, hardly anyone even knew she'd been dating anyone. According to her mother, there were no signs that a man had ever visited Junko's apartment, and she didn't think a romantic entanglement had anything to do with her daughter's suicide. It had been three years since Mashiba and Junko were spotted at the tearoom. If they had broken up soon after, then maybe Junko's suicide a year later really didn't have anything to do with him.

Even if it did, however, if no one knew that, then no one would have reason to seek revenge against the businessman. Despite getting the go-ahead from Mamiya, Kusanagi felt like his investigation had fallen flat just out of the gate.

Until he heard about the poison.

If he'd requested case file from the officers who handled the Tsukiu death in the first place, he might have discovered the connection before now; but after calling and hearing her mother's tearful story, Kusanagi had cut corners. After all, if the officers on the case had been comfortable calling it a suicide, what else was there to know?

But arsenous acid—

There was always the possibility it was sheer coincidence. After the news story about the curry poisoning incident, the effectiveness of the poison became public knowledge, which would, of course, lead people considering suicide or murder to try it.

But for a man to die by the same poison his ex-girlfriend used to commit suicide—that was a little too much coincidence for Kusanagi.

While the detective was pondering the possibilities, his phone rang. It was Yukawa.

"You again? You must be going toe to toe with every high school girl in the country in terms of your phone bill this month."

"When you have something you want to say, it can't be helped," Yukawa noted sagely. "Can you meet today?"

"I can, but what's this about? You finally figure out how the poison got into the coffee?"

"Not exactly 'figured out.' Let's say I found a possible method, instead."

Even while he rolled his eyes at the professor's painstaking way of talking, Kusanagi's grip tightened on his phone. When Yukawa started talking possibilities, it usually meant a solution was just around the corner.

"Did you tell Utsumi?"

"No, not yet. And, to be honest, I'm not ready to tell you either. So don't get all excited about meeting me, because you'll only be disappointed."

"What's that supposed to mean? Why *do* you want to meet, then?"

"I have a request concerning the investigation. I need to see if all of the conditions were in place for our killer to pull off the particular trick I have in mind."

"So you won't tell me what this latest trick is, but you want me to share information with you? I shouldn't have to tell you this, but you do know that talking about the details of an investigation with civilians is officially taboo."

After several seconds of silence, Yukawa replied. "I'm surprised to hear you, of all people, saying that. But no matter. There's a reason why I can't tell you about the trick. I'll explain in person."

"See, when you put it like that, I think you're just leading me on. Anyway, I have to go to the Meguro station right now. I'll stop by the university afterward. Should be about eight o'clock."

"Then give me a ring when you get here. I might not be in the lab."

"Right." Kusanagi hung up, suddenly feeling tension mounting in the pit of his stomach.

He wanted to know what trick Yukawa had discovered, though he knew that guessing it was likely impossible. What worried him most was how the explanation might affect where Ayane stood on their roster of suspects.

If Yukawa's trick breaks her ironclad alibi . . .

There will be no way out, the detective thought—meaning not Ayane, but rather, no way out for himself. Kusanagi would be forced to suspect her. Usually, the prospect of an elucidating lecture from Yukawa was reason for excitement. Today, however, it just brought Kusanagi more distress.

Kishitani was standing in the Meguro Police Station, a fax in his hand—details on Junko Tsukui's suicide. Mamiya was standing next to him.

"Now I know why you wanted more info," Kishitani said, holding up paper.

Kusanagi ran his eyes down the report. Tsukui had been found in her bed at her apartment. On the table next to her was a glass half full of water and a small plastic bag of white powder. The powder was oxidized arsenic, a.k.a. arsenous acid.

"Nothing here about how she got the poison. They didn't figure it out?" Kusanagi muttered.

"They probably didn't look into it," Mamiya said. "There was no reason to suspect murder. And arsenous acid isn't all that hard to come by. They probably thought it would be a waste of time."

"Still, it's pretty significant that Mashiba's ex killed herself with the same kind of poison that killed him. Not bad, Kusanagi," Kishitani said, his excitement palpable.

"Did they keep the poison as evidence, by any chance?" Kusanagi asked.

"We checked into it, but no luck. It was two years ago, after all," Mamiya said with a frown. There was no chance to compare the poison used in each case to see if both samples came from the same source.

"And they told the family about the poison?" Kusanagi asked no one in particular.

"What do you mean?" Mamiya asked.

"Tsukui's mother told me she had died from a sleeping pill overdose. I was wondering why she thought that."

"Maybe she just got the wrong idea somehow?"

"It's possible . . ." Kusanagi said. But he doubted that a mother would forget how her own daughter killed herself.

"Well, with this and what Utsumi was talking about, it's nice that we're finally making a little progress," Kishitani said.

Kusanagi looked up. "What was Utsumi talking about?"

"Some tidbit she got from Detective Galileo," Mamiya put in. "He's having her reexamine the filter on the water line at the Mashiba house. They sent it to—what was that place?"

"Spring-8," Kishitani said.

"Right, that place. Yukawa specifically requested we get it tested there. I'd imagine Utsumi is running around Metropolitan right now putting that request together."

Spring-8 was the name of a radiology facility in Hyogo Prefecture, the largest in the world. Its ability to detect even the most minute traces of material had made it a popular choice for delicate Forensics work; their role in the poisoned curry case had put it on the map.

"So Yukawa thinks the poison was in the filter?"

"According to what Utsumi was saying, yes."

"But I thought he was saying there was no way to—" Kusanagi stopped himself short.

"What?" Mamiya raised an eyebrow.

"Nothing. Just, I was supposed to meet with him later on. He said he'd hit upon a trick—maybe he meant a trick for getting poison into the filtration system?"

"That seemed to be what Utsumi was indicating—that Yukawa had figured it out. But apparently, he wouldn't tell her exactly what the trick was. He's as stubborn as he is brilliant," Mamiya added, shaking his head.

"He wouldn't tell me how the trick works, either," Kusanagi said.

A wry smile spread across the chief's face. "Well, since he's helping us for free, I suppose we can't complain. And if he's going through all the trouble of calling you over there, he's probably got some good advice for us. Go hear him out."

It was already past eight when Kusanagi arrived at the university. He called Yukawa as he stepped out of the taxi, but there was no answer. As he made his way across the campus he called again; after he'd let it ring several times, Yukawa finally picked up.

"Sorry, I couldn't hear the phone."

"You in the lab?"

"No, the gym. You remember the place?"

"How could I forget?"

Kusanagi turned off the phone and headed for the gym. Just inside the main gate of the university, a little off to the left, stood a gray building with an arched roof. Kusanagi had spent more time there than in his dorm back when he was in college. This was where he had met Yukawa. Then they both were fit and trim, but now the only one with an athletic figure was the professor.

When he made it to the athletic facility, a young man in a training suit came out the front door, badminton racket in hand. He nodded to Kusanagi as he passed. Inside, the detective found Yukawa sitting on a bench, putting on a windbreaker. Kusanagi glanced at the court and saw that the nets were up.

"Now I finally understand why there are so many old professors. They get to use the university facilities as a free personal gym their whole lives."

Yukawa looked up, unperturbed. "There's nothing personal about it," he said. "I have to reserve my time on the courts just like everybody else. And I take issue with your basic premise that university professors live long lives. First of all, it takes a considerable amount of time and effort even to become a professor, which would suggest that one needs to meet a certain standard of health just to get the job. You're confusing causes with results."

Kusanagi gave a dry cough, and looked down at Yukawa over folded arms. "What did you want to talk about?"

"Don't be in such a rush. How about it?" Yukawa said, offering a racquet to Kusanagi.

"I didn't come here to play games—badminton included."

"I applaud your dedication to your work," Yukawa said, "but I can't help but notice that your waist size has grown by at least nine centimeters over the last several years—and that's being generous. I'd have to theorize that walking around questioning people isn't quite enough to keep you in shape."

"Well, when you put it that way . . ." Kusanagi took off his jacket and grabbed the racquet.

The two took to the court, facing each other across the net for the first time in at least twenty years. Yet despite the time lapse everything was instantly familiar to Kusanagi: the feel of the racquet, the look of the nets, the squeak of the floor. But the flow of the game, the angles of racquet and shuttlecock didn't come back so readily; and it was painfully clear to him that his stamina was sadly lacking. In less than ten minutes he was hunched over, breathing hard.

Kusanagi watched as Yukawa smashed the shuttlecock into the empty half of the court. He sat down on the floor. "Guess I'm getting old," he said. "Though I can still arm wrestle our young recruits to the floor, I'll have you know."

"The kind of fast-twitch muscles you use in arm wrestling can grow weak with age and still spring back with a little training. But the slow muscles responsible for maintaining stamina aren't so elastic. That includes the heart. I highly recommend regular training," Yukawa said matter-of-factly. His breathing was calm and even compared to Kusanagi's ragged gasps.

Bastard, Kusanagi thought. Still sitting, Kusanagi leaned back against the wall. Yukawa pulled out a water bottle and poured some into the lid, which he offered to his friend. Kusanagi took a sip. It was a sports drink of some kind, and very cold.

"It's just like being back in school, huh? Except I'm completely out of shape."

"If you don't keep at it, strength and technique will both weaken. I kept at it, you didn't. That's all."

"Is that supposed to make me feel better?"

"No," Yukawa said, a curious look on his face. "Am I supposed to be trying to make you feel better?"

Kusanagi chuckled, picked himself off the floor, and then returned the bottle lid to the physicist. His face grew serious. "So you think the poison was in the filter?"

Yukawa nodded. "As I said on the phone, I can't prove anything yet. But I'm pretty sure it was."

"You did some follow-up tests?"

"I actually tried a test here at the university. We acquired four copies of the exact same filter, laced each with arsenous acid, rinsed them several times, and then tried to see if we could find any traces. Of course, with our lab here, we were restricted to induction-coupled plasma analysis."

"Induction-coupled what?"

"It doesn't matter. Just think of it as an extremely sensitive analytical method. We tested the four filters, and found clear traces in two of them, while the other two gave us insubstantial findings. A very special coating was used on that particular make of filter, making it extremely difficult for minute particles to adhere to the surface. According to Utsumi, Forensics used atomic absorption analysis on the Mashiba filter, which is an even less accurate method than the one I used. Thus, Spring-8."

"You must be pretty sure about this to go that far."

"I wouldn't say I am absolutely sure, but it's really the only option remaining."

"So how did the killer get the poison in there? I thought you said it was impossible."

Yukawa fell silent. He was gripping his towel in both hands.

"You think it is this trick of yours," Kusanagi said after a moment. "But you won't tell me what it is."

"Like I told Utsumi, I don't want to give either of you pre-conceived notions."

"Why would my preconceived notions have anything to do with the trick used to poison the filter?"

"It has everything to do with it," Yukawa said, staring directly at the detective. "If the trick I'm thinking of *was* used, it's highly likely that there will be some telltale trace remaining. That's why I had the filter sent on to Spring-8, to find that trace. But even if they find no trace, it doesn't prove that the trick wasn't used. That's the kind of problem we're dealing with here."

"So why can't you tell me?"

"Let's say, for argument's sake, that I explained the trick to you now. If, later on, we found some trace that proved the trick had been used, no problem. But what if we don't? Would you be able to reset your thinking at that point? Would you still be able to allow the possibility the trick had been used?"

"Well, sure, if there was no proof the trick *hadn't* been used."

"That's what I have a problem with," Yukawa said.

"Explain."

"I didn't want anyone to suspect a particular person in the absence of proof. And there's only one person in the world who could have used this trick."

Kusanagi glanced at the professor's eyes behind his glasses. "Ayane Mashiba?"

Yukawa gave a slow blink, which Kusanagi took for a yes. He gave a deep sigh. "Fine, then. I'll just keep on with my investigation and hope for a breakthrough. I finally got something like a lead, you know."

"Do tell."

"I found one of Yoshitaka Mashiba's ex-girlfriends. And

there's a connection to the case." Kusanagi explained how Junko Tsukui had committed suicide using arsenous acid.

"And this was two years ago?" Yukawa asked, his gaze wandering off into the distance.

"Yes, which is why, trick or no trick, I'm happy investigating my own way. This case isn't as simple as a wife taking revenge for her husband's infidelity. I think it's a lot more complicated than that."

Yukawa looked up at Kusanagi and a smile spread across his face.

"What's that for?" the detective asked. "You think I'm barking up the wrong tree, don't you?"

"Not at all. I was just thinking that I really didn't need to bring you all the way over here today after all."

Kusanagi frowned, not understanding.

"You see," Yukawa continued, "what I wanted to tell you was exactly that: the roots of this case are deep. We can't afford to look only at the events around Mashiba's death, we need to go as far into the past as we're able, and to look at everything from every angle. What you just told me about this ex-girlfriend is particularly interesting—especially the part about the arsenous acid."

"Now you've lost me," Kusanagi grunted. "Don't you suspect Mrs. Mashiba? Why should the past matter?"

"It *does* matter, very much," Yukawa said, picking up his racquet and his sports bag. "My muscles are getting cold. Let's get going."

They left the gymnasium together. As they neared the front gate, Yukawa stopped. "I'm heading back to the lab. Want some coffee?"

"Was there something else you had to tell me?"

"Nothing right now."

"Then I'll take a rain check. I've got some stuff to do back at the station."

"Right," Yukawa said, turning to leave.

"Hey," Kusanagi called out. "Ayane made a patchwork vest for her father once. She sewed a pillow in at the waist, to cushion him if he slipped on the ice and fell."

Yukawa turned. "And?"

"She doesn't act irrationally. She's the kind of person who can consider her own actions in advance. I don't think someone like that would commit murder just because her husband betrayed her."

"Your detective's intuition tell you that?"

"I'm just giving you my impression. Regardless of whether you and Utsumi think I have special feelings for Mrs. Mashiba."

Yukawa's eyes dropped to the ground for moment before he looked back up and said, "I don't care if you have special feelings for her or not. I don't think you're so weak a person as to let your feelings influence your detective work. And another thing," he said, lifting his index finger. "What you say is certainly correct. Ayane is no fool."

"So you don't suspect her?"

Yukawa lifted his hand and waved, then turned his back and walked away.

TWENTY-THREE

Kusanagi took a deep breath before pressing the intercom button. He stared at the small placard on the door that read "Anne's House," bemusedly wondering why he felt so tense.

There was no response from the intercom, but after a moment Ayane opened the door. She gave him an oddly gentle look, as if she were a mother looking at her son. "Right on time, I see," she said.

"Huh? Oh, right," Kusanagi murmered with a glance at his watch. It was exactly 2 P.M.—the time he had set when he called.

She opened the door wider and invited him inside.

The last time Kusanagi had visited the school was when he had brought Hiromi Wakayama down to the station for questioning. Though he hadn't really looked around the place then, something felt different about it today. The workstations and the furniture were all still there, but the place seemed somehow less alive.

He took the seat offered to him and gazed around the big room while Ayane poured tea, a wry smile on her face. "It looks barren in here, I know. I never realized how many things Hiromi had brought in until they were gone."

Kusanagi wasn't surprised to hear that Hiromi had quit. Most women would have hit the road the moment the secret was out.

Ayane had left her hotel yesterday to take up residence here at the school. She wasn't planning to move back into the house—which made sense to Kusanagi. It was the scene of a murder, after all.

The widow placed a teacup in front of the detective. He thanked her.

"I went there this morning," Ayane said, sitting across from him.

"To your house?"

She put a finger on the edge of her cup, nodding. "Yes, to water the flowers. They were all wilted."

Kusanagi frowned. "I'm sorry. I have the key and everything, but I've been so busy—"

She waved off his apology. "No, don't worry about it, please. I never should've asked for that sort of favor in the first place. Honestly, I didn't say it out of spite."

"I really meant to water them, I just forgot. I'll be more careful going forward."

Ayane shook her head. "Please, it's quite all right. I'm going to make a point of going there every day to take care of them myself."

"I see . . . well, then, I'm sorry I couldn't be of more help. Maybe I should return your key?"

Ayane thought for a moment, then stared at the detective.

"Are you finished with that part of your investigation, or will you need to go back in?"

"Well, that's difficult to say," Kusanagi admitted.

"Then please hold onto it. That way you don't have to come and ask me every time someone needs access."

"Right. I'll be sure to keep it safe," Kusanagi said, patting his left breast pocket.

"That reminds me—were you the one who brought that big watering can?"

Kusanagi paused, teacup raised to his mouth, and waved his free hand. "Oh, that," he said. "Well, I liked the empty coffee can you had before, but, ah, I thought a proper watering can might be more convenient. I'm sorry if it was an imposition."

"No, not at all. I had no idea they even made such large watering cans. It was very convenient, so much so that I wish I'd bought one earlier. Thank you."

"That's a relief, then," Kusanagi said. "I was afraid you might have been attached to that can of yours."

"Why would anyone be attached to a can? I take it you threw it out?"

"Yes . . . I hope that's not a problem?"

"No, not at all. You did me a favor."

Ayane lowered her head, smiling. Just then the school's phone—sitting on a nearby shelf—began to ring. She stood up to answer it.

"Anne's House, can I help you? Ms. Ota? Hello! . . . What? Oh, I see."

Though she was still smiling, Kusanagi could see the corners of Ayane's mouth tense. By the time she hung up the phone, she was frowning.

"Sorry about that," she said, sitting back down.

"Is something wrong?" Kusanagi asked.

A lonely look came into her eyes as she spoke. "It was one of my students. Something came up with her family and she's had to quit. She's been coming here for more than three years."

"I guess it's tough running a family and keeping up a hobby like this."

Ayane smiled. "Actually, people have been quitting right and left since yesterday. She's the fifth one to leave."

"Because of the case?"

"A bit, maybe. But I think Hiromi leaving has had a larger effect. She's been teaching full-time for the last year, and I think many of the students thought of themselves as *her* students."

"So when she left, they left?"

"Nothing so organized as that, but I think they're noticing a shift in the mood at school. Women are sensitive to these things, you know."

"Right . . ." Kusanagi said, not really understanding. He had been under the impression that people came to the school in order to learn techniques from the master herself. Shouldn't they be happy that Ayane would now be teaching them directly, instead of through an apprentice?

Utsumi would probably understand, he thought glumly, a vision of the smiling junior detective appearing in his mind.

"I'm sure more will quit in the coming days. These things tend to be a chain reaction. Maybe I should close the school altogether. At least for a while." Ayane sat for a moment with her head bowed, resting her chin on one hand. Then abruptly she straightened in her seat. "I'm sorry. This has nothing to do with why you're here, does it, Detective Kusanagi?"

She looked at him directly, and Kusanagi reflexively averted his eyes. "I know a lot of things are up in the air right now, and

I apologize," he said hurriedly. "Believe me when I say that we are doing everything in our power to resolve this case as quickly as possible. In the meantime, maybe it would be a good idea for you to take a break."

"I think you're right," she said. "A little trip might be just the thing. I haven't traveled for quite some time. Certainly nothing like I used to. Once I even went overseas by myself."

"That's right—England, wasn't it?"

"Did my parents mention that? It was quite a while ago." Ayane's eyes drifted downward, then she lifted her head. "That's right, there was something I wanted you to help me with, if it's all right?"

"Sure thing," Kusanagi said, setting his teacup down on the table.

"It's this wall," Ayane said, looking up at the wall closest to them. "It's a little bare."

Indeed, the wall was completely empty, save for the faint outline showing where, until recently, something had hung.

"The tapestry there was one of the ones that Hiromi made, so I gave it to her when she left. Now that it's gone, everything feels a little empty, don't you think?"

"I see. Have you decided what you're going to put up there?"

"Yes. Actually, I brought it from home today."

Ayane stood and went to fetch a large paper bag, bulging at the sides, that was resting in the corner.

"What's that?" Kusanagi asked.

"The tapestry that was hanging in my bedroom. I didn't think I would need it there."

"Right," Kusanagi said, standing. "Let's put it up then."

Ayane reached into the bag, but then she stopped. "Wait,"

she said laughing. "I should probably let you ask your questions first. That is why you're here, isn't it?"

"Oh," Kusanagi replied, "I'm happy to get to that afterward."

Ayane shook her head, a serious look on her face. "No, that won't do. You came here for your work, and work should always come first."

Kusanagi chuckled and pulled out his notepad. When he looked back up, her mouth was closed, lips tight.

"Right, some questions then. I'm afraid these won't be entirely pleasant, but I beg your cooperation."

Ayane nodded.

"We've uncovered the name of a woman your husband was seeing before he met you. Junko Tsukui. Ever heard that name?"

"Tsukui . . . ?"

"Yes, written like this," Kusanagi said. He jotted down the characters for the name on his notepad and showed it to her.

Ayane stared directly at him. "That's the first time I've heard the name."

"Did your husband ever tell you anything about a children's book writer? Any little thing at all?"

"A children's book writer?" Ayane frowned.

"Yes, Junko Tsukui was a writer and an artist who did children's picture books. Maybe your husband mentioned something about knowing an illustrator, something like that?"

Ayane glanced down at the table and took a sip of her tea. "I'm sorry," she said at last, "but I don't remember him saying anything about children's books or a children's book illustrator. And I think I would remember if he had—illustrators weren't exactly in his social circle."

"Right," Kusanagi said with a frown.

"Does this ex-girlfriend have something to do with the case?" Ayane asked.

"That's what we're looking into."

"I see," she said, lowering her eyes. She blinked, her long eyelashes fluttering.

"Do you mind if I ask another question?" Kusanagi said. "This isn't something I would normally ask someone in your position, but given that those directly involved are no longer with us—"

"Excuse me?" She looked up. "Those?"

"Yes. The woman I mentioned, Junko Tsukui, also passed away. Two years ago."

Ayane's eyes widened.

"As you might've guessed from the difficulty we've been experiencing with our investigation, we found some evidence that your husband had concealed his relationship with Ms. Tsukui. I was wondering, why do you think he did that? Did your husband ever make any attempt to conceal your relationship?"

Ayane held her teacup in both hands and thought for a moment. She was still thinking when she said, "My husband didn't hide our relationship from people around us—Mr. Ikai, his closest friend, was there when we met."

"Right, of course."

"That said," Ayane continued, "if Mr. Ikai hadn't been there when we met, it wouldn't have surprised me if my husband had tried to keep our relationship secret."

"Why's that?"

"Because then he wouldn't have to explain anything when we broke up."

"So you believe he was considering the possibility of breaking up from the start?"

"I think he was considering the possibility that I couldn't bear children. He would have far preferred that I get pregnant before we married."

"But you did end up marrying before trying to conceive."

Ayane smiled knowingly, a certain coyness in her eyes that Kusanagi hadn't seen before. "There's a simple reason for that," she said. "I didn't let him. I insisted on contraception until we were legally married."

"I see. I wonder if there was no contraception involved in Tsukui's case, then," the detective said, aware that he was crossing a line.

"I'm guessing there wasn't. Which is why he cut her off."

"Cut her off?"

"Because she didn't get pregnant according to his schedule," Ayane said, smiling as if they were chatting about the weather.

Kusanagi closed his notebook. "I see. Thank you."

"Is that all?"

"That's more than enough. I'm sorry if any of my questions seemed inappropriate."

"Nothing of the sort. I saw other men before meeting my husband, you know."

"I'm sure you did," he said, wincing almost as soon as he had said it, but Ayane only smiled.

"Er, let me help you with that tapestry now," Kusanagi offered.

"Right," Ayane said, once again going to the bag; but then she stopped. "Actually, maybe I'll wait on this one after all. I haven't washed the wall yet. I'll put it on myself once that's done."

"Really? I think it would make a nice addition to the room. Let me know if you need any help when you do get around to it."

Ayane thanked him, her head bowed.

After leaving Anne's House, Kusanagi mulled over the questions he'd asked, Ayane's responses, and his reaction to her responses. As he did so, he became aware of another voice in his head: Yukawa's.

I don't think you're so weak a person as to let your feelings influence your detective work.

Kusanagi hoped his friend was right.

TWENTY-FOUR

"Next stop: Hiroshima . . ."

Utsumi heard the announcement over her music and pulled out her earbuds, stashing her iPod in her travel bag. As the train began to slow she stood and made her way to the doors.

She checked the address in her notepad. Junko Tsukui's family home was in Takayacho, a part of East Hiroshima. The nearest station was Nishi-Takaya. She had already called ahead to let Junko's mother know she would be paying her a visit. The mother, Yoko Tsukui, had seemed a little flustered on the phone. *No doubt she's wondering about all the sudden interest in a two-year-old suicide.*

At Hiroshima station, Utsumi picked up a bottle of mineral water at a kiosk, then hopped on the local train. Nishi-Takaya was nine stations down the San'yo Main Line, about a forty-minute ride, so she took her iPod back out and plugged in. She sat restlessly, listening to a Masaharu Fukuyama album, drinking her water—soft water, according to the label. Yukawa had told her what cuisine that was best for, but she had already forgotten.

Thinking of water reminded her of Yukawa's idea that the filtration system had been poisoned, and she began to wonder exactly what this trick was that the physicist was so reluctant to reveal. The trick was something theoretically possible, but extremely improbable—that was the first thing he had said. Then, after Utsumi had asked the questions he put her up to, his only comment had been, "Impossible."

If she took his words at face value, this trick Yukawa had dreamed up must be pretty extraordinary, almost ridiculously so. Yet he seemed almost convinced that it had actually been used.

Still unwilling to disclose any details, the physicist gave Utsumi further instructions: first, they had to reexamine the water filtration system thoroughly, looking for anything out of the ordinary. In order to detect any trace amounts of poison, she sent the filter on to Spring-8. Yukawa even wanted to know the part number of the filter used.

Though results were still forthcoming from Spring-8, they had already learned some things. For one, Forensics assured them there was nothing unusual about the filtration system. The filter had an appropriate amount of crud in it for a year of use, and there was no sign that any adjustments or modifications had been made to any of the pieces. The part number of the filter checked out as well.

When she told all this to Yukawa, his only response had been, "Right, thanks." And he'd hung up the phone.

Utsumi was hoping for at least a little something more—a

hint, maybe—but that was too much to expect when dealing with this particular physicist.

What bothered her most, however, was what Yukawa told Kusanagi about looking into the past. In particular, Junko Tsukui's suicide by arsenous acid interested him.

She wondered what it meant. If Yukawa thought that Ayane Mashiba was the killer, wasn't it enough to look at what happened right around the time of her husband's death? Even if the seeds of murder had been planted in the past, it wasn't like Yukawa to be interested in the backstory.

At some point the album playing on her iPod ended, and another song, by a different artist, began. She was trying to remember the title when her train arrived at the station.

It was about a five-minute walk to the Tsukui residence, a two-story Western-style house on a hillside at the edge of a wood. Utsumi thought the house seemed rather large for an older woman all by herself. She'd been told that Junko Tsukui's father had passed away, and that her older brother moved to downtown Hiroshima after getting married.

Utsumi pressed the intercom button, and a familiar voice answered.

Yoko Tsukui was a thin, gray-haired woman; Utsumi guessed she was in her mid-sixties. She seemed relieved that the detective had come alone. *She was probably expecting some muscle-bound patrolman sidekick.*

Though the exterior of the Tsukui residence was fairly modern, the inside was traditional Japanese. Mrs. Tsukui led Utsumi into a tatami mat room with a large, low table in the middle and a family altar off to the side.

"You've come quite a long way. You must be tired," Yoko said as she poured hot water into a teapot.

"Not at all," Utsumi replied. "On the contrary, I'm sorry to be so inquisitive about your daughter at this late date."

"Yes, well, I did think it a bit odd. It was some time ago, and I'd already started putting it behind me."

She offered a steaming cup of tea.

"At the time of your daughter's death, you told the police you had no idea why she would commit suicide. Is that still the case?"

Yoko smiled a thin smile. "There wasn't much to go on. None of the people she knew in Tokyo had any clue, either. But I think that maybe she was just lonely."

"Lonely?"

"She always loved drawing, and she went to Tokyo to try to make a career of it—the children's books, you know. But she was always a quiet girl, even at home. It must have been tough for her out there all by herself, in a strange place, without much progress in her career. She was thirty-four, so I don't doubt she was a little worried about her future. If only there had been someone for her to talk to . . ."

Apparently Yoko didn't know her daughter had been seeing someone, either.

"She made a visit home shortly before her death, is that correct?" Utsumi asked.

"That's right. I remember her seeming a bit out of sorts, but I had no idea she was contemplating . . . dying," Yoko said, blinking back tears.

"So your conversation at the time was fairly normal?"

"Yes. She said she was doing well."

Utsumi pictured herself going home, having already decided to take her own life, and wondered how she would talk to her mother. She could imagine not being able to meet her mother's eyes, but she could also imagine pretending that nothing was wrong at all.

"Detective?" Yoko looked up. "Why is Junko's suicide of interest to anyone now?"

"It's come to our attention that her death might have some connection to another case. Nothing is certain yet, so I'm afraid we're just gathering information at this stage. I would tell you more if I could."

"I see." Yoko sighed.

"In particular, we're interested in the poison she used."

Yoko's eyebrows twitched at the mention of the word. "Poison, did you say?"

"Yes. Your daughter killed herself with poison. Do you happen to remember the kind she used, by any chance?"

For a moment, the woman seemed unsure of what to say. *Maybe she's really forgotten?*

"It was a poison called arsenous acid," Utsumi offered. "The other day, when a colleague of mine, Detective Kusanagi, called, you told him your daughter died of a sleeping pill overdose, but according to our records, it was arsenous acid poisoning. Were you unaware of this?"

"Right . . . well . . . I . . ." Again, the woman seemed bewildered. After a moment, she asked hesitantly, "Is the kind of poison important? I mean, was it a problem that I told him she died from sleeping pills?"

That's odd, Utsumi thought. "Do you mean you knew it wasn't an overdose of sleeping pills, but you told him that anyway?"

"I'm sorry," Yoko whispered, her face suddenly rigid with pain. "I thought it didn't matter anymore how she had died, it was so long ago now—"

"Was there some reason you didn't want to tell us about the arsenous acid?"

Yoko was silent.

"Mrs. Tsukui?"

"I'm sorry," Yoko said again. She shuffled backward, placed both hands on the tatami, and bent into a deep bow. "I'm truly sorry. I just couldn't bring myself to say it—"

This time, it was Utsumi's turn to be bewildered. "You don't need to apologize. Please, just explain what this is all about. Is there something you haven't told us?"

Yoko looked up slowly. She blinked several times. "The arsenic was from our house."

Utsumi gasped. "But the report said the source was unknown?"

"I couldn't bring myself to say it. I told the detective back then that I didn't know where the arsenic—I mean the acid—came from. I just couldn't bear to tell them that she had gotten it from here. I might've said something if they had asked again, but they seemed to be satisfied . . . I'm really sorry."

"So you're telling me that the arsenous acid she used was taken from your house?"

"Yes, I'm fairly sure it was. My husband got some from a friend to use as rat poison. We kept it in our storage shed."

"And you're sure Junko took it?"

Yoko nodded. "As soon as I heard how she had died, I went to check. The bag that used to be in the shed was gone. That's when I realized why she had come home. She came back to get the poison."

Utsumi realized that, in her shock, she'd forgotten to take notes. She quickly began to write in her notepad.

"How could I say that my own daughter had come home to

kill herself, and I had no idea? That she got the poison from us! I know it was wrong to lie . . . I'm truly sorry if it's caused you any problems. I'd be more than happy to go make a formal apology," Yoko said, bowing her head repeatedly.

"Could I see this storage shed?" Utsumi asked.

"Certainly."

Utsumi stood.

The shed, a simple steel affair, sat in a corner of the back-yard. It was large enough to hold some old furniture, electrical appliances, and a collection of cardboard boxes. Utsumi stepped inside, the smell of dust and mold filling her nostrils.

"Where was the poison?" Utsumi asked.

"Right there," Yoko said, pointing to an empty can sitting on a dusty shelf. "The bag was in that can."

"How much did Junko take with her?"

"Well, the whole bag was gone when I checked. About this much," Yoko said, putting her hands together to form a scoop.

"That's quite a lot," Utsumi said.

"Yes. At least enough to fill a rice bowl."

"She wouldn't need that much to kill herself. And the report indicates that they didn't find such a large amount at the scene."

Yoko shrugged. "I know. It bothered me, too . . . At first, I'm ashamed to say, I was worried that they'd blame me for being so careless. Then I just assumed that Junko had thrown out the rest."

It seemed unlikely to Utsumi that someone committing suicide would go to the trouble of getting rid of excess poison.

"Do you use this storage shed frequently?" she asked.

"No, hardly at all. I haven't even opened it for some time."

"Can it be locked?"

"Locked? Yes, there's a key somewhere."

"Then, could you lock it for me today? We might have to come back here and examine it."

Yoko's eyes widened slightly. "Examine the storage shed?"

"Yes. I promise we won't impose more than is absolutely necessary."

Utsumi felt a hint of excitement. The department hadn't been able to find out where the poison used to kill Yoshitaka Mashiba had come from. If it turned out that the poison from Junko's home was a match, it would change the course of the entire investigation.

I'll just have to hope that some trace amount of the acid was left in that shed. Utsumi resolved to speak to Mamiya as soon as she was back in Tokyo.

"By the way," she asked Yoko, "I heard that Junko sent you a letter by post?"

"Yes . . . yes she did."

"Might I see it?"

Yoko thought for a moment before she said, "All right."

They went back inside, where she showed Utsumi to her daughter's old room. It was a Western-style room, with a desk and a bed.

"I've kept all of her things in here. I keep planning on cleaning it out someday, but I never seem to get around to it." Yoko opened the drawer in the desk to reveal a stack of letters. She lifted out the topmost envelope. "Here you are."

Utsumi thanked her and took the envelope.

The contents of the letter were pretty much as she had heard from Kusanagi. There was no suggestion of a reason why she might have committed suicide. The only concrete impression Utsumi got from it was that Junko felt she had no pressing reasons to stay in this world.

"I can't help but feel like there was something we could've done," Yoko said, her voice trembling. "If I had been a bit more attentive, maybe I would've noticed she was in so much pain."

At a loss for something appropriate to say, Utsumi returned the letter to the drawer, noticing the other letters as she did so. "What are these?" she asked.

"More letters from her. I don't use e-mail, so she would write me now and then to tell me how she was doing."

"Do you mind if I look at these as well?"

"Certainly, go ahead. I'll bring tea," Yoko said, leaving the room.

Utsumi sat down at the desk and began looking through the letters. Most of them were simple reports about the picture books Junko was working on or future projects she was planning. There was hardly anything suggesting relationships, or even friends.

She was on the verge of giving up when she saw a postcard. The front showed a red double-decker bus. The back held a note written in blue ink. Utsumi held her breath as she read the tightly spaced letters.

How are you? I'm finally in London. I met another Japanese girl here! She's an exchange student from Hokkaido, and she's offered to show me around town tomorrow.

TWENTY-FIVE

"According to Mrs. Tsukui, Junko got a job right out of college, but quit after three years because she wanted to study art in Paris. She sent that postcard during her two years over there."

Kusanagi listened to the junior detective rattle off the facts, growing steadily gloomier as she grew more animated. A part of him didn't want to acknowledge the importance of her discovery.

Mamiya leaned back in his chair, thick arms crossed across his chest. "So what you're trying to say is that Junko Tsukui and Ayane Mashiba were friends?"

"Well—it's very likely. The postmark on the postcard coincides with the time that Mrs. Mashiba was studying in London, and she's from Hokkaido. I don't think it's a coincidence."

"Come on," Kusanagi said. "It *could* be a coincidence. How many exchange students do you think there are in London at any given time? At least one hundred, maybe two."

"Take it easy." Mamiya hushed the older detective with a wave of one hand. "So, Utsumi—say the two of them *were* friends. How do you think that relates to the current case?"

"This is still just conjecture," she told him, "but there's a chance that the arsenous acid Junko used to commit suicide passed into Mrs. Mashiba's possession."

"Forensics will be on that shortly, though there's no telling whether they'll be able to give us a definitive answer. So: if what you're suggesting is true, then Mrs. Mashiba essentially married her friend's ex-boyfriend."

"That's what it would mean, yes."

"Doesn't strike you as odd?"

"Not really."

"Why not?"

"Plenty of women date their friends' exes. I know at least one personally. Some people make a habit of it—that way they know a fair bit about a potential mate before getting involved with them."

"Even when it's the ex of a friend who committed suicide?" Kusanagi butted in. "What if this ex-boyfriend was the cause?"

"What if he wasn't?"

"You're forgetting something really important," Kusanagi said. "Ayane met her husband at a party. Does your theory assume that she just happened to run into her friend's ex-boyfriend?"

"It's not impossible. They were both single."

"And then they just happened to fall in love? Sorry if I'm not overly convinced here."

"Maybe it was more than a coincidence, then?"

"What's that supposed to mean?" Kusanagi asked.

Utsumi fixed him with a stare. "Maybe Ayane set her sights on Mr. Mashiba right from the start. She was interested in him when he was dating Junko—her death might have even brought the two of them closer. Their meeting at the party might not have been their first encounter. And maybe it wasn't a coincidence, either."

"Ridiculous!" Kusanagi spat under his breath. "She's not that kind of woman."

"Then what kind of woman is she? Exactly how much do you know about Mrs. Mashiba, Detective Kusanagi?"

"That's about enough of that," Mamiya said, standing. "Utsumi, you've got a good nose, but an overly active imagination. Save the conjecture for when we have a little more proof. And Kusanagi, try listening to what someone says without nitpicking every little detail. Sometimes you have to toss around a few ideas before you find something that sticks. I was under the impression you were a good listener."

Kusanagi nodded silently, and Utsumi lowered her head.

"Sorry," she said.

Mamiya sat back down. "Right. This is all very interesting, Utsumi, but a little too tenuous to do much with. And really the only thing it might explain is how Mrs. Mashiba got her hands on the poison. I don't see how it relates to the rest of the case. Unless. . . ." He rested his elbows on the desk, looking directly at the junior detective. "Are you thinking Ayane got close to Yoshitaka Mashiba in order to avenge her friend's death?"

"I wouldn't go that far . . . I can't imagine anyone who would get married solely for the purpose of revenge."

"Then I recommend we lay off the hypothesizing for now. We can pick it up again once Forensics has taken a look at that storage shed in Hiroshima."

It was past midnight by the time Kusanagi made it home. He wanted to take a shower, but in the end the best he could manage was to take off his jacket and crawl into bed. He wasn't entirely sure whether his exhaustion was physical or mental or some combination of the two.

"Then what kind of woman is she?"

Utsumi's words ringing in his ears.

"Exactly how much do you know about Mrs. Mashiba, Detective Kusanagi?"

Nothing, he thought. He had only talked to her a little, just grazed the surface. Yet he felt like he knew what was inside.

It was hard to picture her marrying the former lover of a friend who had committed suicide. *She would feel guilty—even if Yoshitaka Mashiba had nothing to do with the reason her friend took her own life.*

He sat up and loosened his tie, his eyes falling on the two picture books he had tossed on the table. He went over and got them, then padded back over to his bed.

Lying back down, he flipped through the pages of *The Snowman Tumbles*. The story involved a snowman who, after living his life in the wintry north, decides to go on a trip to a warmer country. He starts heading south, but realizes that if he goes any farther he'll melt. Giving up, the snowman returns north. On his way back he passes by a house. Looking into the window, he sees a happy family sitting around the fireplace, talking and laughing. The subject of their conversation was how nice it is to be warm inside when it's so cold outside.

When Kusanagi's eyes fell on the picture Junko Tsukui had drawn for that page, he leapt out of bed.

Something familiar was hanging on the wall of the room the snowman was looking into—a tapestry with intricate flower designs that spread out in a regular pattern like a kaleidoscope image against a background of brown.

Kusanagi remembered his impression upon first seeing that pattern with vivid clarity. And he knew exactly where he had seen it: the Mashibas' master bedroom.

It was the very same tapestry that Ayane had been talking about hanging in her classroom with his help earlier that day.

Maybe she thought better of it because I mentioned Junko Tsukui's name? Maybe she knew Junko had used the tapestry in one of her books?

Kusanagi put his head in his hands. His ears were ringing in time with his pulse.

The next morning, Detective Kusanagi awoke to the sound of an incoming phone call. He checked the time and saw that it was already past eight in the morning. He was on the sofa. A whiskey bottle and a glass were sitting on the table in front of him. The glass was half full.

Only then did he recall being unable to sleep the night before, though he didn't care to be reminded of why.

He reached out a leaden arm to answer the phone, still ringing loudly on the tabletop. It was Utsumi.

"Yeah?"

"Sorry to call you so early, but I thought you'd like to know as soon as possible."

"Know what?"

"The results came back from Spring-8. They found arsenous acid in the filter."

TWENTY-SIX

The Ikai Law Offices, a five-minute walk from Ebisu station, oc-cupied the entire fourth floor of a six-story building. A recep-tionist in her early twenties wearing a gray suit greeted Kusanagi when he arrived. She showed him into a meeting room—a small side office, with a little table and some folding chairs. Kusanagi spotted several other similar offices along the same hall. Presum-ably Ikai employed several lawyers at his firm.

Which is how he was able to spend so much time helping run Yoshi-taka Mashiba's company, Kusanagi mused.

More than fifteen minutes passed before Ikai showed up. He said hello without bothering to offer an apology.

He probably thinks I should be the one apologizing for bothering him at work, Kusanagi thought.

"Any developments?" Ikai asked, sitting down. "I haven't heard anything from Ayane."

"I'm not sure whether you would call them developments,

but several pieces of new information have come to our attention. Though, I must apologize for not being able to share them with you at this time."

Ikai chuckled dryly. "I'm not here to needle you for information. I haven't got the time. Now that Mashiba's place seems to have settled down finally, all I'm interested in is getting the case closed as quickly as possible. So why did you want to see me? As is no doubt quite clear to you by now, I'm not an expert on Mashiba's private life." He glanced at his watch.

"Actually, I've come to talk about something you know very well," Kusanagi said. "Maybe it would be better to say something about which *only* you know."

Ikai raised an eyebrow. "Something only I know about? I wonder what that might be."

"I wanted to ask a bit more about Mr. and Mrs. Mashiba's meeting. You were there, correct?"

"That again?" Ikai gave a disappointed sigh.

"I was hoping you could describe in detail how the two of them acted around each other at the party. How exactly did they meet each other there?"

Ikai furrowed his brow with suspicion. "This has something to do with the case?"

Kusanagi only smiled a thin smile. Ikai sighed again.

"Another secret, then? Still, we're talking about something that happened quite a while ago. I can't see how it *could* have anything to do with the case."

"We're not sure that it does yet. We're just trying to get all the details. Leave no stone unturned, as it were."

"You don't seem like the detail type to me but, whatever. What exactly did you want to know?"

"Well, what you told me before was that the event where they met was essentially a dating party. As I understand it, these parties are intended to bring together men and women who have never met before, and give them an opportunity to talk and get to know each other. Was it that sort of party? Were there some kind of introductions?"

Ikai shook his head. "No, nothing like that. Think of it more as a semiformal cocktail party. If it was one of those ridiculous meet-your-future-wife things, I never would've gone along with him."

Kusanagi nodded. "Speaking of which, did Ayane come to the party alone?"

"I'm pretty sure she did. I remember seeing her at the bar, drinking a cocktail. She wasn't talking to anyone."

"Who spoke first?"

"Mashiba," Ikai said quickly.

"So Mr. Mashiba went up to her?"

"We were having a drink at the bar, too. She was about two seats down. Then, out of the blue, Mashiba commented on her cell phone case."

Kusanagi stopped writing in his notepad and looked up. "Her cell phone case?"

"Yes, she'd put it up on the bar. It was made out of patchwork, with a little window to read the display. He said something like, 'That's pretty,' or, 'That's unusual,' I forget which. But it was definitely Mashiba who spoke first. Then she told him she made it herself, and smiled. That got them started."

"So that was how they met?"

"Yep. Of course, I didn't imagine at the time that they'd be getting married."

Kusanagi leaned forward. "Was that the only time you'd gone with Mr. Mashiba to a party like that?"

"Once was enough."

"Was Mr. Mashiba the type, in your opinion, to make comments like that to complete strangers?"

Ikai frowned. "That's hard to say. He wasn't nervous talking to women he doesn't know, but he wasn't exactly the type to hit on girls at bars, either. Not even in college. He used to say that content mattered more than looks, and I think he actually meant it."

"So would it be safe to say that talking to Ayane at that party was exceptional behavior for him?"

"A little, sure. I was surprised, but I chalked it up to being a spur-of-the-moment thing. Maybe she inspired him in some way. And that in turn led to the two of them getting together. That was my interpretation, at any rate."

"Did you notice anything unusual about them at that time? Anything at all?"

Ikai thought for a moment, then shook his head again. "I don't remember much. Once they got to talking, I kind of faded into the background. But why would you ask me that, Detective?"

Kusanagi smiled and stuck his notepad into his pocket.

"Not even a little hint?" Ikai asked.

"I'll be happy to talk to you about it when the time is right. Thanks for seeing me today." He stood, but stopped on his way to the door. "If you wouldn't mind, I'd appreciate it if you don't mention the details of our conversation to Mrs. Mashiba."

Ikai's eyes narrowed. "So she's a suspect?"

"That's not what I'm saying. Just . . . it would be helpful if you could keep it secret for now." Kusanagi hurried from the room before Ikai could ask him more.

———

Outside the building, the detective paused on the sidewalk. He breathed a deep sigh.

If what Ikai had just told him was true, Ayane hadn't been the one who initiated the encounter with Yoshitaka Mashiba. Their meeting at the party was a coincidence.

Or was it?

When Kusanagi asked Ayane if she knew Junko Tsukui, she had told him she didn't. That bothered him. *She must have known her.*

How else could he explain the tapestry on the wall in Junko's book? It was an Ayane Mita original—Ayane didn't spend months making copies of other people's designs. Which meant that Junko Tsukui had seen her work somewhere.

However, as far as Kusanagi was aware, that particular tapestry wasn't featured in any of Ayane's published collections. Tsukui had to have seen the piece at a gallery show—and taking photos at such a show was strictly prohibited. Tsukui's art wasn't bad, but Kusanagi didn't peg her for someone with a photographic memory. That would suggest that Ayane had shown the tapestry to Junko personally, which in turn meant the two women knew each other.

So why did Ayane lie? Why did she tell him that she didn't know Junko Tsukui? Did she just want to hide the fact that her deceased husband was also her friend's ex?

Kusanagi glanced at his watch. *Just past four. I better get going.* He was supposed to be at Yukawa's by four thirty; but something slowed his pace. The truth was that he didn't want to see his old friend. It was pretty clear that the physicist would be waiting for him with exactly the kind of answers Kusanagi didn't want to hear. And yet, there was no way he could send someone else to stand in for him. As the detective in charge, it was his responsibility to get all the information he could, like it or not. And increasingly he found himself longing for an end to his own confusion.

TWENTY-SEVEN

Yukawa used a spoon to scoop coffee into the paper filter.

"I see you've gotten used to your coffeemaker," Utsumi commented from behind him.

"Gotten used to it, yes—but at the same time I've become aware of a shortcoming."

"Oh? What's that?"

"You have to decide how many cups you want to make up front. Of course, once you realize that two or three won't be enough, you can always make more. But it's obnoxious to go to all that trouble for just one extra cup. Which means I find myself making enough for an extra cup but then I risk making too much. I hate to throw out perfectly good coffee, and if I leave it on the burner too long, the flavor changes. You see?"

"Well, you won't have to worry about that today. I'll drink whatever's left over."

"Oh, we're fine today. I've only made four cups. One for you, one for me, and one for Kusanagi. The final cup I'll drink at my leisure after you've left."

Clearly, the physicist wasn't planning on keeping them long. Utsumi had her doubts that things would go so smoothly. *Unless Yukawa's going to stop being coy and solve the puzzle once and for all.*

"You know, the entire department is grateful to you, Professor," she said. "If you hadn't insisted on it, we never would have taken the extra step of sending the filtration system on to Spring-8's lab."

"There's no particular need to thank me. I merely gave the advice that any scientist would in that situation." Yukawa sat down across from the detective. There was a chessboard on the workstation between them; he picked up the white knight and began toying with it. "So they found the arsenous acid."

"We had them run a full analysis. The acid in the filtration system was almost certainly that used to kill Yoshitaka Mashiba."

Yukawa nodded, returning the piece to the chessboard. "Did they say in which part of the system they found the poison?"

"It was near the water outlet, not in the filter itself. Forensics thinks the killer inserted the poison into the joint that connects the filtration system with the water hose running up from the main line."

"I see."

"The only problem," Utsumi continued, "is that they can't figure out how the killer did it. So how *was* it done? We've got the results from Spring-8 you wanted. Surely you can reveal the trick now."

Yukawa rolled up the sleeves of his white lab coat and crossed his arms. "Forensics couldn't figure it out?"

"They say there's only one possible method: you would have to remove the hose from the filtration system, put the poison in, then reattach it. But that would leave certain telltale signs—marks on the hose or whatever—which they didn't find."

"And you have to know exactly how it was done?"

"Of course. If we can't prove how the crime was committed, it doesn't matter if we have a suspect."

"Even though you found the poison?"

"We won't have a chance in court if we don't know how the crime was committed. The defense will claim police error."

"Oh?"

"They'll say that there's a possibility that some of the arsenous acid in the coffee made its way to the filtration system after the fact. We are talking about trace molecules here."

Yukawa sat back in his chair, nodding his head slowly. "They might make that argument, it's true. And if prosecution couldn't provide a means of insertion, the court would have to listen to the defense."

"Which is why we really need you to explain how it was done. Please. Forensics wants to know, too. Some of them even wanted to come with me to hear it from you firsthand."

"Well, that won't do. I can't have police tromping through my lab."

"Which is why I came by myself. Well, and Detective Kusanagi's coming later on."

"Speaking of which, shouldn't we wait for him to get here? I don't want to have to repeat my explanation. Also, there's one last thing I need to check first." Yukawa lifted an index finger. "In your department's opinion—no, actually, your personal opinion is fine—what was the motive for the murder of Yoshitaka Mashiba?"

"Well, I think romantic troubles would pretty much sum it up."

Yukawa frowned. "Isn't that a rather abstract motive on which to rest your case? Try telling me who loved whom, who hated the victim enough to kill him, and why."

"Well, it's all conjecture at this point . . ."

"Fine. Like I said, all I'm looking for is your personal opinion."

Utsumi nodded; she lowered her eyes, collecting her thoughts.

Steam bubbled from the coffeemaker. Yukawa stood and retrieved two coffee mugs from the sink.

"Well," Utsumi said as he began to pour the coffee, "I think Ayane Mashiba did it. Her motive was that she felt her husband had betrayed her—not just because he asked her for a divorce when he decided she couldn't bear him children, but also because he had started seeing another woman. That's what pushed her to murder."

"Do you think she made up her mind the night of the party at the Mashiba house?" Yukawa asked.

"She probably made her final decision that night, yes. But I think it's likely she had started harboring murderous intentions a little earlier than that. She knew about Yoshitaka and Hiromi Wakayama. She also had intimations of Hiromi's pregnancy. Yoshitaka's declaration was the final straw."

Yukawa returned to the table, holding a coffee cup in each hand. He placed one in front of Utsumi. "What about this woman, Junko Tsukui? Did she have nothing to do with the murder, then? Isn't Kusanagi out there right now questioning people about that?"

The likelihood of a personal connection between Junko Tsukui and Ayane Mashiba was the first thing Utsumi had mentioned to Yukawa when she got to the lab.

"I wouldn't say there's *no* connection. It's likely that the arsenous acid used in this murder was the same that Ms. Tsukui used to kill herself. If Ayane was close to her, she would've had an opportunity to get the poison from her."

Yukawa raised his cup and his eyebrow at Utsumi. "And then?"

"Excuse me?"

"Is that all Junko Tsukui had to do with it? She just provided the poison? Her death doesn't factor into the motive at all?"

"Well, it's hard to say . . ."

Yukawa smiled thinly and sipped his coffee. "Then it's hard for me to tell you the trick."

"What?! Why?"

"Because telling you would be far too dangerous. You haven't yet figured out what this case is really about."

"And you have?"

"More precisely than you."

Utsumi was glaring at Yukawa, both hands clenched around her mug, when they heard a knock at the door.

"Good timing! Maybe Kusanagi can shed a little light on the subject," the professor said, rising to his feet.

TWENTY-EIGHT

As soon as Kusanagi walked into the room, Yukawa asked how the latest questioning had gone. After a moment's hesitation, the senior detective told them what he'd heard from Ikai.

"Yoshitaka Mashiba talked to her first. Which pretty much dismantles your theory, Utsumi," Kusanagi said, with a sidelong glance at the junior detective. "I mean, the idea that Ayane used the party as a way to get close to him."

"It was less a theory than it was a possibility."

"Okay. Well then, it's no longer a possibility. So what do you think happened now?" He turned to look at her directly.

Yukawa offered Kusanagi a mug of coffee. The detective nodded in thanks.

"What do *you* think?" Yukawa asked his friend. "If we accept what Mr. Ikai told you at face value, then the couple first met at that party. Which would make the fact that Mr. Mashiba's ex was Ayane's friend a simple coincidence. How does that sit with you?"

Kusanagi sipped his coffee, sorting out his thoughts. He opened his mouth to speak, then hesitated, tapping his fingers on the tabletop.

Yukawa grinned. "So you don't believe the lawyer?"

"Ikai's not lying," Kusanagi said at last. "But there's no proof that what he saw was the truth."

"Go on."

Kusanagi took a breath before saying, "It could have been an act."

"A performance?"

"Yes. Intended to give the impression that it was their first meeting . . . in order to hide the fact that they had a relationship before the party. Ikai was brought along so that there would be a witness. A cell phone case on a bar leading to true love is a little too perfect."

"Perfect indeed," Yukawa said, a spark in his eye. "And I happen to agree with you. Let's see what the lady thinks." He turned to Utsumi.

She nodded. "It makes sense. But why go through all that trouble?"

"That's the rub, isn't it? Why put on an act?" Yukawa looked at Kusanagi. "What do you think they were up to?"

"It's simple. They were trying to hide the truth."

"And what truth is that?"

"The truth of how they actually met. Which would have been through Junko Tsukui. A fact which they didn't want getting out, what with her being Mashiba's former girlfriend, and dead besides. They needed to create a situation where they could meet again, for the first time, under different circumstances: the party."

Yukawa snapped his fingers. "An excellent theory. Unassailable, really. So let's talk about how they really met. More to the point, when they fell in love. Was it before or after Tsukui committed suicide?"

Utsumi took a deep breath, straightening in her chair before she looked toward Yukawa. "Do you think Ms. Tsukui committed suicide after Mr. Mashiba started seeing Ayane?"

"It makes sense. Imagine her, betrayed by both her lover and her friend. That would be quite a shock."

Kusanagi felt his heart sinking into darker depths. What Yukawa was suggesting did indeed make sense. That scenario had occurred to him as well while he was in the middle of his chat with Ikai.

"That certainly clears up the point of that party," Utsumi said. "With Mr. Ikai there to testify that the two had met for the first time while he was watching, they would be able to deny any connection between their relationship and Junko Tsukui's suicide."

"See? Now we're getting somewhere," Yukawa said, a satisfied look on his face.

"Should we confront Mrs. Mashiba about it?" Utsumi wondered out loud, looking toward Kusanagi.

"Confront her how?"

"What if we showed her the picture book, the one with the tapestry in it? Doesn't that prove they knew each other?"

Kusanagi shook his head. "All she'd have to say is, 'Sorry, no idea.'"

"But . . ."

"She's been hiding her friendship with Yoshitaka's ex—even

the fact that she knew he had an ex at all. If all we do is bring her some picture books, we won't get anywhere. We'd simply be tipping our hand."

"I have to agree with Kusanagi," Yukawa said, stepping over to the chessboard and picking up a black pawn. "If you're going for checkmate, better do it in one move, or you'll have a stale-mate on your hands."

Kusanagi looked at the physicist. "So—she did it."

Yukawa remained at the chessboard. "This next part is the most important. Now that we know a little more about Mrs. Mashiba's past, how does that knowledge relate to the case at hand? Is the arsenous acid really the only connection?"

"Maybe," Utsumi said thoughtfully, "Mrs. Mashiba couldn't forgive her husband for leaving her *especially* because of what their relationship had done to her friend?"

"I could see that," Yukawa said, nodding.

"No," Kusanagi said, "that's not how she would think about it. She betrayed her friend and stole her man—just as her assis-tant betrayed her and stole her husband."

"Karma, then? So she would just resign herself to her fate?" Yukawa said. "No hatred toward her husband or his lover—is that what you're trying to say?"

"Not exactly . . ."

"I think there's a question both of you need to ask." The physicist turned away from the chess set, catching both detec-tives with his stare. "Why do you think Yoshitaka Mashiba switched from Junko Tsukui to Ayane?"

"I don't know," Utsumi said, "probably just a change of heart—" She put her hand to her mouth. "Oh. No, that's not it, is it?"

"It's not," Kusanagi said. "He left her because she didn't give him a child. Remember, Mashiba was ready to marry any woman who'd get pregnant for him. If it looked like she couldn't, he would switch."

"That fits with everything we've heard thus far," Yukawa agreed. "So the question is, did Ayane know his reason at the time? Did she think Yoshitaka left Junko and chose her because he thought she would bear him children?"

"Well . . ." Kusanagi fell silent.

"I doubt it," Utsumi said crisply. "What woman would want to be chosen like that? If she realized it at all, it was just before they got married—when they arranged to split up if she couldn't get pregnant within a year."

"That's what I think, too," Yukawa said. "So let's talk about motive again. You mentioned that Mr. Mashiba's betrayal was the motive, Utsumi, but was what he did really a betrayal? After one year, there was no pregnancy, so he asked for divorce and hooked up with another woman—wasn't he just living up to the agreement they made?"

"That's true; but emotionally speaking, how could she accept that?"

Yukawa smiled. "So let's phrase it a different way: if we assume that Ayane was the killer, then her motive was that she didn't want to honor her own promise. Correct?"

"I guess you could say that."

"What are you driving at?" Kusanagi asked his friend.

"Try to imagine how Ayane was feeling just before she got married. What were her intentions when she made that agreement with Yoshitaka? Was she optimistic that she could get pregnant within the year? Or had she decided that, even if she didn't get pregnant, her husband wouldn't follow through on his end of the deal?"

"Both, I'd say," Utsumi answered.

"Okay. Let me ask you this, then: if she thought there was a chance she might get pregnant, wouldn't she have gone to the hospital?"

"Hospital?" Utsumi furrowed her brow.

"According to what you've told me, not once during the year did Ayane undergo infertility treatment. With a promise like the one this couple had made, I would have expected her to start visiting a gynecologist within a few months of the wedding."

"According to what Mrs. Mashiba told Hiromi Wakayama, they hadn't tried infertility treatments because those take too long."

"That would be *Mr.* Mashiba's thinking. Why bother with all that time and money when it would be quicker to simply find a new wife? But what about Ayane's perspective? Wouldn't she want to try anything, even if it meant grasping at straws?"

"Yeah, sure," Kusanagi muttered.

"So why didn't she go to the hospital? Therein lies the key to this case." Yukawa adjusted his glasses with one finger. "Think about it. She had time, she had money. So why wouldn't she go?"

Kusanagi thought. He tried to put himself in Ayane's shoes, but no answer was forthcoming.

Suddenly, Utsumi stood. "Maybe she didn't go because she knew there was no point."

"No point? What do you mean?" Kusanagi asked.

"What if she knew any treatments would be pointless?"

"Exactly," Yukawa said. "She knew going to the hospital would do nothing for her. That's why she didn't go. It's the most logical explanation."

"So . . . she knew she was completely infertile," Utsumi said.

"She was over thirty. Surely she'd had at least one gynecologic exam by that age. Maybe she had been told earlier that she couldn't have children. If so, not only would there be no point in going to the hospital, there would also be the danger that if she did go, her husband might learn the results."

"Wait a second. You're saying that she made that bargain with her future husband even though she knew she *couldn't* have children?" Kusanagi asked.

"That's what I'm saying. Her only hope was that her husband wouldn't follow through on his threat. Of course, he did, with flying colors. So, she decided to kill him. Now, let me ask you—when did she first contemplate killing Yoshitaka Mashiba?"

"When she found out about him and Hiromi—"

"No, that's not it." Utsumi cut Kusanagi off. "If she had planned on killing her husband *if he kept the promise*, then she made up her mind when she made the promise."

"That's the answer I was waiting for," Yukawa said, his face taking on a sudden sober intensity. "Essentially, Ayane predicted that, within a year's time, she would have reason to kill her husband. Which meant it was possible for her to prepare the means to kill him in advance."

"Excuse me? Prepare?" Kusanagi's eyes widened.

Yukawa looked over at Utsumi. "You told me what Forensics thought when they examined the filtration system—that there was only one way to get the poison in there, which was to remove the hose, insert the poison, then reconnect it. Correct? Well, Forensics was absolutely right. That's exactly what happened . . . one year ago."

"No way," Kusanagi spluttered, then fell silent.

Utsumi shook her head. "But—if she did that, she couldn't have used the water filter!"

"That's right. She didn't use the water filter for an entire year."

"But that just doesn't make sense. Wasn't there evidence that the water filter had been used?"

"The crud in the filter wasn't from the past year. It was from the year before." Yukawa opened his desk drawer and produced a piece of paper. "Remember when I had you check on the filter part number? Well, I called up the maker and asked when that particular part was on the market. It turns out that number range was used two years ago. They went so far as to say it was highly unlikely a part with that number had been used to change a filter only one year ago. In other words, when they changed the water filter a year ago, our killer immediately replaced the new filter with the old one, thinking that if the filter was found to be unused after the poisoning, she'd be discovered. That's when she put in the poison."

"Impossible," Kusanagi whispered, his voice hoarse. "That's simply impossible. You're saying she put the poison in, then didn't use the filter for a whole year, not even once? It doesn't make sense. What if someone else had used the water from the filter? How dangerous is that?"

"Very," Yukawa agreed coolly. "But she pulled it off. For an entire year, whenever her husband was home, she never went outside, and she never let anyone else near the kitchen water system. Whenever they held a party at their house, she did all the cooking. And she always had bottled water in good supply, making sure they never ran out. Everything to ensure that her plan worked."

Kusanagi shook his head several times. "I don't believe it. It's impossible, Yukawa. Show me one person capable of pulling that off."

"Actually, it *is* possible," Utsumi said. "Yukawa had me ask all kinds of questions about the couple's life after they got married. I talked at length with Hiromi Wakayama. Even though I didn't know why I was asking the questions at the time, I get it now. You were checking whether anyone other than Mrs. Mashiba had a chance to touch that water filtration system, weren't you?"

"Correct. The most compelling piece of evidence by far was how the Mashibas spent their days off. Ayane would sit on the living room sofa, working on a patchwork all day long. Why did she choose that room? So she could keep an eye on the kitchen."

"You're delusional," Kusanagi said, his voice almost a groan.

"Logically speaking, it's the only possible answer. Our killer was extraordinarily tenacious, and extraordinarily strong-willed, you have to admit."

Kusanagi shook his head, muttering, "no way," over and over. But as the argument sank in, his denials gradually lost their strength.

He remembered something Ikai had said about Ayane's peculiar devotion to her husband.

"She was the perfect wife, you know. Utterly dedicated to him. Whenever he was home, she would sit there on the living room sofa, doing her patchwork, ready to serve if he needed anything."

His thoughts traveled back to his visit with Ayane's parents at their home in Hokkaido. Hadn't they told him that she had never been a good cook, until those classes she took right before getting married?

In both cases, she was just making sure that no one else would ever enter the kitchen.

"So when she finally wanted to kill him . . . she didn't have to do anything," Utsumi said.

"That's right. Nothing at all. All she had to do was leave

her husband alone in the house. Actually, that's not quite true; there was one thing. She emptied a few of the bottles of mineral water first, leaving only one or two behind. As long as Yoshitaka was drinking those, nothing would happen. He probably used the bottled water the first time he made coffee. But when he made it for himself the second time, he was down to one bottle, and since he wanted to save that for later, he used water from the filter. After sitting in place for a whole year, the poison finally had its chance to do its job."

Yukawa picked up his coffee mug from the table. "She could have killed him at any point over the last year, but she didn't. Instead she watched carefully over her trap to make sure he never poisoned himself by accident. Most killers worry about how they'll do the deed, but in this case, it was the complete opposite. All of her efforts went toward not killing him. It was a very unusual kind of murder, you have to admit. While it is theoretically possible, it's entirely unrealistic. An imaginary solution, if you will."

Utsumi took a step toward Kusanagi. "We have to go confront Mrs. Mashiba and get her to turn herself in."

Kusanagi took one look at the victorious expression on the junior detective's face before turning his gaze to Yukawa. "Is there proof? Is there any way to show what she did in court?"

The physicist took off his glasses, resting them on the table beside him. "Of course there's no proof," he said.

Utsumi looked at him in surprise. "Really?"

"Give it a moment's thought and you'll see. If she had *done* something, she might've left a trace. But she killed him by doing nothing. Look all you want for some trace of what she did, and you won't find a thing. About the only thing you have to go on is the poison they found in the filter, but you told me yourself that evidence is inconclusive. And the detail about the part number on the filter is circumstantial at best. In other words, there's no way at all to prove she killed her husband."

"I don't—" Utsumi's protest trailed away into silence.

"Didn't I tell you before?" Yukawa's face was grim. "It's the perfect crime."

TWENTY-NINE

Utsumi was going through paperwork at the Meguro station when Mamiya came in from outside and shot her a look. She stood and went over to his desk.

"I was just talking to the section chief about that case," Mamiya said, sitting down. He had a glum look on his face.

"Did we get a warrant?"

Mamiya gave her a shake of his head. "No, we didn't, and we won't unless there's some significant development. We don't have enough material to identify our killer. I'm impressed as always with Galileo's detective work, but without proof, we can't go to trial."

"That's what I was afraid of," Utsumi said, her head hanging. This was playing out just as Yukawa said it would.

"Everyone in administration is pulling their hair out. Who the hell arranges everything for someone to poison themselves, then watches carefully for a year to keep them from doing it?

No one believed me at first. Not even I believed me at first. It's clearly the only answer here, but that doesn't make it any easier to swallow. It just sounds so . . . impossible."

"I didn't believe it myself when Professor Yukawa first laid it out."

"There's no accounting for what some people are capable of, clearly. That goes for this woman, Ayane, as well as the professor. You have to wonder what's going on in those heads of theirs, sometimes," Mamiya said, a bitter look on his face. "We still don't even know if he was actually right. And as long as we can't say for sure, we can't touch Ayane Mashiba."

"What about the Junko Tsukui angle? I hear Forensics checked out her mother's house in Hiroshima?"

Mamiya nodded. "They sent that can that had the arsenous acid in it down to Spring-8. The problem is, even if they do find traces, and those happen to match the arsenous acid used in this case, it's still not conclusive evidence. It may not even be circumstantial evidence. After all, if Junko Tsukui was Yoshitaka Mashiba's former lover, it could've been him carting around the poison all that time."

Utsumi breathed a deep sigh. "So how *do* we get proof? Tell me what we need and I'll find it. I don't care what it takes! I can't believe that Yukawa's right and that this is the perfect crime!"

Mamiya's face twisted into a scowl. "Don't start barking at me," he said. "Believe me, if I knew how to get proof, we wouldn't be in this mess. About the only evidence we have worth anything right now is that water filter with the traces of arsenous acid in it. Section thinks we need to focus on that and get everything out of it we can."

Utsumi bit her lip. What the chief was saying sounded suspiciously like an admission of defeat.

"Don't give me that face, I haven't given up yet. We'll find something. It's not easy to pull off the perfect crime."

Utsumi nodded in silence, bowed, and left. *You're right*, she thought, *it's not easy*. But what Ayane Mashiba did would have been nearly impossible for an average person. *What if that's all it takes? What if she pulled it off?*

Back at her desk, Utsumi pulled out her cell phone and checked her voice mail, hoping that Kusanagi had found something, but the only message was from her mom.

THIRTY

Hiromi Wakayama was already there when Kusanagi arrived at the café. He hurried over to the table.

"Sorry to keep you waiting."

"I just got here myself," she told him.

"Well, thanks for coming out. I'll keep this as short as possible."

"Don't worry on my account," Hiromi told him with soft chuckle. "I'm not working right now, so I have plenty of time."

Her complexion seems to have improved, Kusanagi thought. *Back up on her emotional feet, maybe.*

A waitress came to hover by their table, so Kusanagi ordered coffee. "Milk for you?" he asked Hiromi.

"Lemon tea, please," she said.

The waitress left and Kusanagi smiled. "Sorry. I just remembered you ordering milk last time . . ."

"Actually, I'm not really a big fan of milk. And I'm trying to avoid it right now."

"Really? Why is that?"

Hiromi lifted an eyebrow. "Do I need to answer *every* question?"

"No." Kusanagi waved his hand. "Of course not. Sorry, I was just making small talk. I'll get down to business. The real question I have for you is about the Mashibas' kitchen, actually. Do you remember that they had a water filter attachment on their sink?"

"Sure."

"Did you ever use it?"

"Never," Hiromi said without a moment's hesitation.

"That was quick," Kusanagi observed. "I mean, that's the sort of question people usually have to think about a bit."

She shook her head. "I barely even went into their kitchen. I never helped cook. Why would I touch the sink? I think I told detective Utsumi this, too, but the only time I ever went into the kitchen was to put on coffee or tea when Ayane asked me to, and that was only when she was in the middle of preparing something else and didn't have time."

"So, is it true then that you were never in the kitchen alone?"

Hiromi frowned. "I'm not really sure what you're getting at."

"I just need to know if you were ever in the kitchen by yourself. Don't worry about why. Try to remember for me."

Hiromi thought about it until wrinkles formed across her brow. Eventually she looked back up at Kusanagi. "Maybe not. I always had the feeling I wasn't welcome in there without Ayane's permission."

"Did she specifically tell you not to go in without permission?"

"Not in so many words, no. It was just a feeling I had. And—you know, the whole thing about a housewife's kitchen being her castle."

"So they say."

The drinks arrived. Hiromi squeezed her lemon wedge over her tea and sipped at it, a smile on her face. She looked more alive than Kusanagi had ever seen her.

Certainly more alive than I feel. Everything she was telling him backed up Yukawa's story.

He took a sip of his coffee and rose from the table. "Thanks again for your help."

Hiromi's eyes went wide. "That's all?"

"I've heard what I needed to. Take your time," he said, picking up the bill and heading for the door.

He was out on the street, looking for a taxi, when his phone rang. It was Yukawa. The physicist said he had something to tell Kusanagi about the poisoner's trick.

"I need to check something, urgently. Can you meet?"

"Sure, I'll come right over. But what do you need to check at this point? I thought you were pretty confident about your theory."

"I am confident. That's why I need you to come as quickly as you can," Yukawa said, and hung up.

About thirty minutes later, Kusanagi was walking through the front gate of Imperial University.

"When I started reflecting back on the case, with the assumption that Ayane Mashiba used the trick I described, something kept bothering me—and I thought it might be useful to your investigation," Yukawa said as soon as the detective entered the room.

"Sounds important."

"Very. What I need to ask you is this: what did Ayane do first when she returned home after the murder? You were with her at the time, correct?"

"That's right. Utsumi and I gave her a ride home."

"What was the first thing she did when she walked in the door?" Yukawa asked.

"The first thing? Well, she took a look at the scene—"

Yukawa shook his head. "No. She went into the kitchen. She went into the kitchen to get water. Am I right?"

Kusanagi gaped. The moment played out again in his memory. "Actually, you're right. She did go to get water."

"What did she get water for? She would need a particularly large amount, if my theory is correct," Yukawa added, a twinkle in his eye.

"She watered her flowers. Said something about how it bothered her that they were all wilted. She put water in a bucket, and took it upstairs to water the plants on the second floor balcony."

"That's it!" Yukawa said, pointing at Kusanagi. "That completes the trick."

Kusanagi frowned. "I think I know what you're getting at, but explain it to me anyway."

"You see," Yukawa began, "I tried thinking as the killer would think. She knew there was poison in the filter when she left the house. And, as she had hoped, her target drank the water and died. But that's not enough. There could still be poison left over in the filter."

Kusanagi straightened his back. "That's true."

"It would be dangerous to leave it like that. If someone happened to drink it, she might have another body on her hands. Not to mention it would tip the police off to her trick. So she would have to find a way to destroy the evidence as quickly as possible."

"So she watered her flowers . . ."

"With water from the filter, no doubt. A bucketful would be enough to nearly completely wash the poison out of the system. So much so that, without a lab as precise as Spring-8, we never would've been able to detect it. She was going on about her flowers, and destroying the evidence right in front of your noses."

"So that water—" Kusanagi began.

"—is your evidence, if there's any left," Yukawa finished. "Even if finding trace particles of arsenous acid in the water filter isn't enough to prove how she did it, proving that a deadly amount of arsenous acid had come out of that water filter on the day of Mr. Mashiba's death would probably be enough to prove my theory."

"I just told you, she used the water on her flowers."

"Then check the soil in the planters. I'm sure Spring-8 wouldn't have any trouble finding arsenous acid if it's in there. Though it might be difficult to prove that it came from the water she used at that time, at least it's another piece of evidence."

While he listened to Yukawa talk, something was tugging at the back of Kusanagi's mind—something he couldn't remember, something he'd forgotten that he even knew.

Suddenly it dislodged itself from the depths of his brain. Kusanagi gasped. He looked intently at Yukawa.

Yukawa stared back at him. "What? Is there something on my face?"

Kusanagi shook his head. "I need a favor. Actually, consider it a formal request from the Metropolitan Police Department's Criminal Investigation Section to Imperial University's Professor Manabu Yukawa."

A hard look came over Yukawa's face. He adjusted his glasses with the tip of a finger. "Go on."

THIRTY-ONE

Utsumi stood in front of the door, looking at the now-familiar nameplate. Anne's House. According to what Kusanagi had told her, it might as well have read "Ayane's House." After moving in, the widow had almost entirely canceled classes.

Kusanagi, standing beside her, nodded. Utsumi pressed the doorbell.

A long interval passed without an answer. She was about to press the button again when a voice came over the intercom.

"Yes?"

It was Ayane.

"Hello, it's Detective Utsumi from the Metropolitan Police." Utsumi leaned in close to the speaker, talking quietly so the neighbors would not overhear.

After a moment of silence, Ayane said, "Oh, Detective Utsumi. How can I help you?"

"There's something I need to ask, if it's all right?"

Another pause. Utsumi could picture Ayane standing by the intercom inside, thinking.

"I'll be right there," she said at last.

Utsumi and Kusanagi exchanged glances. He swallowed.

They heard the sound of the door being unlocked. Ayane seemed surprised to see Kusanagi there as well.

Kusanagi lowered his head. "Sorry to drop in on you unexpectedly."

"I didn't know you were here too, Detective Kusanagi," Ayane said with a smile. "Please, come in."

"Actually," Kusanagi said, "can you come with us to Meguro?"

The smile evaporated from Ayane's face. "The Police Station?"

"Yes. There are a number of things we'd like to go over with you. I'm afraid some of them are a bit delicate—"

Ayane stared at the detective. Utsumi followed her eyes, looking up at Kusanagi in profile. There was a look of sadness, even regret, in his face.

If she didn't know why we were here before, she knows now, Utsumi thought.

"I see," she said. A strangely gentle light came into her eyes. "I'd be happy to go along with you. But I need to get some things. Won't you wait inside? It's against my nature to leave guests lingering in the hallway."

"Certainly, if you don't mind," Kusanagi replied.

She opened the door wider and invited them in.

The inside of the classroom was neat and tidy. She had obviously packed away some of the furniture she'd set up for her classes. Only the large table in the middle of the room remained exactly as it had been.

"I see you haven't hung up that tapestry yet," Kusanagi said, with a glance at the wall.

"Surprisingly, I haven't had the time."

"Really? You should definitely put it up. It's such a nice pattern, like something from a picture book."

She looked around at him, still smiling. "Thank you."

Kusanagi's eyes went out to the balcony. "I see you brought over your flowers."

Utsumi glanced out at the balcony, too. She could see flowers in a variety of colors on the other side of the glass doors.

"Just a couple of them, yes," Ayane answered. "I had a moving company help me bring over some stuff."

"That's good. They look well watered." Kusanagi's gaze lingered for a moment on the large watering can just inside the doors.

"That watering can has really come in handy," Ayane said. "Thank you again."

"Glad it could be of service," Kusanagi said, looking back at her. "Please, don't mind us. Do what you need to get ready."

Ayane nodded and headed toward the next room; but before opening the door, she turned. "Did you find something?"

"Excuse me?"

"Did you find something out about the case? Some evidence, or a new lead? That's why you're bringing me in, isn't it? More questions?"

Kusanagi took a sidelong glance at Utsumi before returning his gaze to Ayane. "Something like that, yes."

"What did you find? Or can you not tell me that until we're at the station?" Her tone was as light as if they were discussing the weather.

Kusanagi looked down at the floor for a moment in silence before saying, "We found out where the poison was. We had to run several tests, but it's become very clear that it was inside the water filter in your kitchen."

Utsumi was staring at Ayane's face; barely a ripple passed across the woman's benign expression. Her eyes as she looked toward Kusanagi were calm.

"I see. In the filter," she echoed, no trace of surprise in her voice.

"The problem was figuring out how the poison got into the filter. Based on evidence found at the scene, there was really only one method the killer could have used. And, based on this method, there's only one possible suspect." Kusanagi stared at Ayane. "That's why we need you to come with us."

The faintest blush came to Ayane's cheeks, but the smile remained upon her lips. "Do you have evidence that there was poison in the water filter?"

"Arsenous acid was detected in the filter after thorough testing. However, that was insufficient proof, given that all indications were that the killer put the poison in the filter a whole year earlier. What we needed to prove was that the poison was present in sufficient quantities to be lethal on the day of Mr. Mashiba's death. In other words, we needed to prove that the water filter had not been used, washing out the poison inside, for an entire year."

Utsumi noted that Ayane's long eyelashes twitched at the precise moment Kusanagi said "an entire year."

"And did you prove it?"

"I myself was flabbergasted when I first heard the theory that the killer had put the poison in place an entire year ago," Kusanagi said. "But you don't seem surprised at all, Mrs. Mashiba."

"I'm sorry if I'm not reacting. It's just that everything you're saying is so outlandish, I wouldn't know where to begin."

"I see," Kusanagi said. He shot Utsumi a look. The junior detective reached into her handbag and pulled out a plastic bag.

The smile finally faded from Ayane's face as she saw what was in the bag.

"I'm sure you recognize this," Kusanagi said. "You opened holes in the bottom of this empty can to water your flowers."

"I thought you threw that out . . ."

"I held onto it, actually. Didn't even wash it," Kusanagi said, a hard look returning to his face. "You remember my friend Yukawa, the physicist? I had him examine this can in his lab. To make a long story short, he found arsenous acid. We were also able to determine that the acid had been in water from your filter. I also happen to have been present the last time this can was used—you were watering the flowers on your second-floor balcony. Hiromi Wakayama came and interrupted you halfway through. The can wasn't used after that, because I bought a new watering can, and kept this one in my desk drawer."

Ayane's eyes went wide. "In your desk drawer? Why?"

Kusanagi didn't answer. Instead, he said, in a voice completely devoid of emotion, "We have to conclude that there was arsenous acid in the water filter, enough so that any water from that filter would've contained a lethal amount on the day Mr. Mashiba died. Other evidence shows clearly that the poison was inserted into the filter a year ago. The person who would have been able to carry out this crime was someone who could have prevented *anyone* from using that filter for an entire year—and there's only one person who could have done that."

Utsumi swallowed, still watching Ayane's face. Their beautiful suspect's eyes were downcast, her lips tightly shut. Though a trace of a smile lingered on her face, the aura of elegance around her had begun to fade.

"We'll talk more at the station," Kusanagi said.

Ayane looked up. She breathed a deep sigh, and stared directly at Kusanagi. "All right. I'll just be a bit longer."

"No rush. Take your time getting your things together."

"It's not just that. I also want to water the flowers. I hadn't finished when you arrived."

"By all means."

Ayane nodded and opened the door to the balcony. Hefting the large watering can in both hands, she slowly began to sprinkle the potted flowers.

THIRTY-TWO

Ayane recalled a day about one year earlier when she was watering her flowers, just as she was doing now. *The day she heard the truth from Yoshitaka.* She had listened to him while she stared at the pansies in the planter.

Her friend Junko had loved pansies. The pen name she chose, "Violet Butterfly," was a nickname for the flower.

She had met Junko in a bookshop in London. Ayane was there looking for patchwork designs. She reached out for a book of photos just as another girl reached for the same book. The other girl was Japanese, too, and several years older than Ayane.

The two became close friends in no time at all, exploring London together, and they made an effort to keep in touch once they returned to Japan. Junko moved to Tokyo a short while after Ayane arrived in the city.

Though they were both busy with work, and didn't meet

often, they remained close. Junko was one of the few people with whom Ayane felt she could truly be herself. She knew that Junko valued their friendship as much as she did—maybe even more. Junko was even worse than she was at meeting people.

Then one day Junko told her there was someone she wanted Ayane to meet: the CEO of a company that had used one of her character designs in an online anime.

"We were talking about making some toys to go with the character, and when I told him I knew a patchwork specialist, he said he had to meet you. I know you're busy, but if you have any time at all, it might be worth it."

Junko sounded hesitant to impose, but Ayane was delighted. And that was how she had met Yoshitaka Mashiba.

In a word, Yoshitaka was alluring. His face came alive when he talked about his ideas, and his eyes brimmed with confidence. He was good at getting other people to talk, too, so much so that just chatting with him for a few minutes had made her feel eloquent.

They were walking away from the café after he had left when Ayane smiled and said, "What a great guy."

"Isn't he?" Junko said, happily. One look at her friend's face revealed the extent of Junko's feelings for Yoshitaka.

Even now, Ayane regretted not asking her, not making sure. All she would've had to ask was, "Are you two dating?" But she didn't, and Junko offered nothing.

The plan to include patchwork in one of the character designs was ultimately scrapped. Afterward, Yoshitaka called her directly to apologize for taking up her time. He offered to treat her to dinner in the near future to make up for it.

Ayane assumed he was just being polite, but a few days later he called again with a real invitation. The way he invited her made it clear that he was inviting only her—Junko wasn't involved. *I guess they're not dating,* she told herself.

She met Yoshitaka for dinner, her heart fluttering. Being alone, just the two of them, was even more fun than the last time she had seen him.

Ayane's feelings toward Yoshitaka grew rapidly. At the same time, she could feel herself pulling away from Junko. Knowing her friend's interest in Yoshitaka made it somehow harder to pick up the phone and call her.

When she met Junko again several months later, she was startled at the change in the other woman. Junko had become shockingly thin, and she looked years older. But when Ayane asked if she was feeling okay, her friend insisted she was fine, and that was the end of it.

As they talked about recent events, Junko seemed to perk back up. Then, just when Ayane was contemplating telling her about Yoshitaka, Junko's face went pale.

Ayane asked what was wrong, but Junko didn't answer. She stood abruptly, saying that she had just remembered something she had to do, that she had to go home. Bewildered, Ayane walked outside with her and watched her get into a taxi.

It was the last time she saw her friend.

Five days later, a package arrived at Ayane's apartment. She opened the box to find white powder in a plastic bag. On the bag was written, in permanent marker, "arsenic (poison)." The package had come from Junko.

Immediately suspicious, she tried calling her friend, but Junko didn't answer. Almost in a panic, she went to Junko's apartment. She arrived to see her friend's place cordoned off by the police. The officers were still there. One of the onlookers told her that the woman who lived in the apartment had poisoned herself.

In shock, Ayane wandered the neighborhood, not even sure where she was going. By the time she realized it, she was back at home, staring at the package from Junko.

As she was wondering what the package meant, and why Junko had sent it to her, something tickled her memory. She recalled the moment Junko got up from the table the last time they met. Her friend's eyes had fallen on Ayane's cell phone where she had set it beside her plate. Ayane pulled out her cell phone and looked at it. It had a little decorative souvenir strap attached to it that she had bought with Yoshitaka on one of their dates—the same as the strap on his phone.

Ayane immediately imagined the worst: that Junko had realized she was seeing Yoshitaka and, in a fit of jealousy, had committed suicide. But she couldn't imagine her friend taking her own life over an unrequited crush. Which meant that there had been something more between her and Yoshitaka.

Ayane didn't go to the police. She didn't even go to Junko's funeral. The more she suspected she was responsible for her friend's death, the less she wanted to know the truth.

For the same reason, she lacked the courage to ask Yoshitaka about it, knowing that it could mean the end of her own relationship with him.

Some time later, Yoshitaka made a curious proposal. He wanted them both to go to the same party, but separately, and pretend it was their first time meeting. He didn't want people to think he was seeing someone through work, he explained.

"Idle people with time on their hands are always asking couples how they met, right? Well, I think we should give them a story. And what's simpler than a social mixer?"

Why not just tell people whatever story they wanted? Ayane thought. But Yoshitaka had already prepared his friend, Ikai, to serve as a witness. Knowing him, the thoroughness of the whole charade was unsurprising, but Ayane began to suspect that his real intent was to wipe the shadow of Junko from his own past. Yet she never mentioned her suspicions, instead going to the party as requested and playing her part in their theatrical "first" encounter.

After that, their relationship proceeded smoothly. Half a year later, Yoshitaka proposed.

While her happiness was genuine, the doubts in Ayane's heart grew by the day. Why did Junko commit suicide? What kind of relationship had her friend had with Yoshitaka?

She was torn between a desire to know and the hope that she never found out. Meanwhile, her wedding day drew steadily closer.

And then the day came when Yoshitaka made a startling announcement. *Although,* she thought to herself later, *maybe for him it hadn't been so startling.* He didn't made a big deal of it at all. He simply said, "If we don't have a child after one year, let's split up."

Ayane thought she misheard him. Who would talk about divorce before they even got married?

But when she asked him if he was kidding, he said "It's just a policy of mine. A one-year limit. If no contraception is used, most couples can have a kid in that time. If we can't, it's likely one of us has a problem. And . . . I had a checkup, and I'm fine."

Ayane's skin prickled; she felt her hair standing on end. Staring at him, she asked, "Is that what you told Junko?"

"Huh?" Yoshitaka's eyes were swimming. She had never seen him look so taken aback.

"Please, be honest with me. You were seeing Junko, weren't you?"

Yoshitaka frowned. But he didn't try to hide the truth, even though he clearly wasn't happy about it. "I always thought you'd find out sooner than this. I figured either you or Junko would say something about me."

"You were seeing us at the same time?"

"No. It wasn't like that. By the time I started dating you, I had already broken up with Junko. That's the truth."

"How did you break up with her, exactly?" Ayane asked her future husband. "Did you tell her you could only marry a woman who could bear children? Is that what you said?"

Yoshitaka shrugged. "I didn't use those words, but I guess that's what it meant. I just told her our time was up."

"Excuse me? Your time was 'up'?"

"She was already thirty-four. We weren't using contraception, but she hadn't gotten pregnant. It was time to make a decision."

"So you chose me?"

"Is that so wrong? What's the point in a relationship with no future potential? I made up my mind a long time ago not to waste my life like that."

"Why did you hide this from me until now?"

"Because I didn't think you needed to know. I was prepared if you did find out, though. I figured I would just explain it to you then. Ayane, I haven't betrayed you, and I haven't lied."

Ayane turned away from him, looking down at the flowers on the balcony. The pansies caught her eye; Junko's favorite pansies. She thought about her friend, tears stinging her eyes.

Yoshitaka had cut Junko off, but Junko hadn't been able to let go. Then, when she met with Ayane, she'd seen the strap on her friend's cell phone and realized what was going on. And so she had killed herself—but not before sending a message to Ayane. *The arsenic.*

Finally Ayane understood. The poison wasn't Junko's way of saying she hated her for stealing Yoshitaka. It was a warning:

Someday you'll be the one who needs this.

Junko had been the only person to whom Ayane could open up, the only one Ayane could tell her worries and dreams. Junko was the only person she had ever told about the birth defect that had rendered her infertile.

She knew he would throw me away someday, just like he threw her away.

"Have you heard a single word I've said?"

She turned back to face him. "Yes, everything. How could I not?"

"You might try answering more quickly then."

"I suppose my mind must've wandered."

"Oh? That's not like you."

"What you said was surprising, you know."

"I find that hard to believe. You should be familiar with my life plan by now."

Yoshitaka told her his thoughts on marriage. How a marriage without children was meaningless.

"What are you so upset about, Ayane? You have everything you ever wanted. If there's something I've forgotten, just ask. I intend to do everything I can for you. So let's just stop all this fussing, and start thinking about the future. Unless you see some other way forward?"

He had absolutely no idea how much damage his words were doing. In retrospect, of course, he was right—in a way. His support had enabled many of her dreams to come to fruition over the year they were together. But how could she look forward to their married life back then, when she knew it would all be over a year after it started?

"I know it might seem silly to you, but can I ask one question? What about your love for me?" she asked him. "Whatever happened to that?"

Did you dump Junko just because you thought I looked fertile? Do you love me at all? "My love for you hasn't changed a bit," he told her then. "I can assure you of that. I *do* still love you."

Was it true? She had to know. She felt the love and the hatred in her heart tearing her in two, and realized that she would kill for the truth. And so she decided—she would go through with it. She would become this man's wife, always by his side, holding his fate in her hands, delaying the time of his punishment. She would give him a chance to earn her forgiveness.

She was nervous when she put the arsenous acid into the filtration system, knowing that it meant she could never allow anyone else to be alone in the kitchen. Yet, at the same time, she felt the unmistakable elation of being entirely in control of another's life.

Whenever Yoshitaka was home, she stayed on the sofa. She even carefully timed her trips to the toilet and bath to times when he was least likely to need anything in the kitchen.

He was kind to her after their wedding, and she had no complaints. As long as his affections for her remained the same, Ayane was determined to not let him near the water filter. Though she hadn't forgotten what he did to Junko, as long as he never did the same to her, she intended to let him live. For Ayane, marriage meant offering daily salvation to a man standing on the gallows.

Yet a part of her knew that Yoshitaka wouldn't abandon his

desire for children. When she noticed the way he looked at Hiromi, she knew the time had come.

On the night they invited the Ikais over to their house, Yoshitaka had declared his intention to divorce her, his tone businesslike throughout.

"As I'm sure you realize, we're almost out of time. I'd like you to get ready to leave."

Ayane smiled. "Then, I have a request first."

He asked her what it was, and she looked him in the eye and said, "I'd like to leave the house for two or three days. I hope you'll be all right by yourself."

He shrugged with a smile. "That's not much of a request. Of course I'll be all right."

"Of course," Ayane echoed, nodding. Her days of salvation were over.

THIRTY-THREE

The wine bar was in a basement, at the bottom of a long flight of stairs. Utsumi opened the door to see a bar counter and three tables in the back. Kusanagi and Yukawa were sitting at the table on the left.

"Sorry I'm late," the junior detective said, taking a seat next to Kusanagi.

"What's the word?" Kusanagi asked her.

She nodded. "Good news. They found traces with the exact same composition."

"No kidding," Kusanagi breathed.

They had sent the empty can from Junko Tsukui's mother's house to Spring-8 for testing, and the lab had detected trace amounts of the exact arsenous acid that was used to kill Yoshitaka Mashiba. This backed up Ayane Mashiba's confession that she had put the poison Junko sent her through the mail into the water-filtration system.

"Sounds like the case is closed," Yukawa said.

"That it is," Kusanagi agreed. "Well, since we're all here now, how about a toast?" He called over the waiter and ordered champagne. "I have to admit, you really saved my ass this time, Yukawa. Tonight's on me. Drink all you like."

Yukawa raised an eyebrow. "'This time'? Don't you mean 'again'? And I was under the impression that it was Ms. Utsumi I was helping, not you."

"Details, details. Hey, here's the champagne."

The three brought their glasses together in time with Kusanagi's shout of "Kanpai!"

"What impressed me most was that you held onto that thing," Yukawa said after they had all taken a drink.

"What thing?" Kusanagi asked.

"The empty can Mrs. Mashiba had been using to water her flowers."

"Oh, that," Kusanagi said, a sour look coming over his face. He dropped his gaze to the table.

"I knew you offered to water her plants for her, but I hadn't heard about the big new watering can. Regardless, why did you hold onto the old one? Utsumi tells me you had it in your desk drawer."

Kusanagi glared at the junior detective, but she looked away.

"Well . . . I guess you could call it intuition," he said at last.

"Ah, the famous detective's intuition?"

"That's right. Besides, you never know what might become evidence, so you don't throw away anything until the case is closed. That's standard operating procedure."

"Standard procedure, right," Yukawa said with a shrug, taking another sip of his champagne. "I'd assumed you held onto it as some kind of keepsake."

"What's that supposed to mean?"

"Nothing. Forget about it."

"Actually," Utsumi joined in, "I had a question I wanted to ask you, Professor."

"By all means."

"How did you figure out what trick she used? Did it just come to you at some point?"

Yukawa gave a soft sigh. "Things don't just 'come' to me. The idea occurred after I made several observations, and gave it a great deal of thought. The first thing that tipped me off was the condition of the water filter. I saw it with my own eyes, and it was exceedingly clear that no one had touched it for quite some time."

"Right, which is why we couldn't figure out how she had got the poison in there."

"Yes; except I started to wonder exactly why the outside of the filter was so dusty. From what you told me, Mrs. Mashiba sounded like a fairly fastidious person. Wasn't it her failure to put away her champagne flutes that first made you suspect her, Utsumi? If your assessment was accurate, then I would expect a woman like that to keep things pretty neat and tidy, even under the sink."

Utsumi's eyes widened. It seemed like an obvious observation after the fact.

"It got me thinking. What if she had left it that way, covered with dust, on purpose? And if so, why? That's when my idea occurred to me."

Utsumi stared at the physicist's face, shaking her head. "Well, I'm impressed."

"There's nothing to be impressed with—unless you mean you're impressed with Mrs. Mashiba. Only a woman could come up with a trick so illogical, so full of contradictions, and so perfect."

"Speaking of contradictions, Hiromi Wakayama apparently decided to keep her child."

Yukawa shot Utsumi a suspicious look. "Isn't that straightforward maternal instinct?"

"Yes, but it was Ayane Mashiba who told her she should."

The physicist's expression froze for a moment. Then he slowly shook his head. "That . . . is a contradiction. I don't understand."

"That's a woman for you," Utsumi offered.

"I see. Then I'd have to say that it's nothing less than a miracle we were able to solve this case rationally. Don't you think—" Yukawa turned to Kusanagi, and cut himself off.

Utsumi glanced at the detective beside her. His head was hanging. He was sound asleep.

"No wonder he's exhausted," Yukawa said quietly, with a look at Utsumi. "With the unraveling of the perfect crime came the unraveling of his affection. Let's let him sleep it off."

He raised his glass.

DON'T MISS
the award-winning first novel of the Detective Galileo series

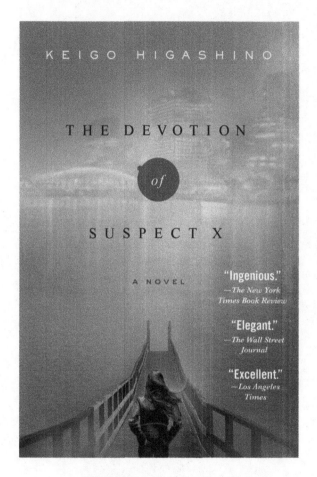

KEIGO HIGASHINO

THE DEVOTION
of
SUSPECT X

A NOVEL

"Ingenious."
—*The New York Times Book Review*

"Elegant."
—*The Wall Street Journal*

"Excellent."
—*Los Angeles Times*

The Devotion of Suspect X
Salvation of a Saint
Malice
A Midsummer's Equation (forthcoming)